SON
OF A
WHORE

SON
OF A
WHORE

MICHAEL JOHNSON

SON OF A WHORE

iUniverse books may be ordered through booksellers or by contacting:

iUniverse
1663 Liberty Drive
Bloomington, IN 47403
www.iuniverse.com
1-800-Authors (1-800-288-4677)

ISBN: 978-1-5320-8973-2 (sc)
ISBN: 978-1-5320-8974-9 (e)

Print information available on the last page.

iUniverse rev. date: 04/28/2020

Mom. I'm writing this letter to tell you what happened up to the time you left. It begins a long time ago.

Somehow, I don't really believe you were a whore, even if it's true. It hurt, though, seeing you almost every night with one of that bunch of guys, the customers. How could I believe *all* of them were my stepfathers?

I think it started when you got a job at Bombo's Club, the striptease joint, just after you quit that cheapskate bank. But you worked in Bombo's gift shop, not in the chorus line. That's where you met them. All of those guys.

Not long after that I found out school is really a drag—I eventually emphasized a different meaning of this word–and it hurts your chances later in life by screwing you up a million different ways, so I didn't go to school beyond junior high, except for a few days. I spent a lot of time watching TV and standing around on street corners. This part you knew about pretty well.

We had a lot of problems. I'm putting the best face on it, but I have to avoid distortion. Except for you and Grandma, everyone in our family was an alcoholic, especially Uncle Robarb. Robarb was your fourth(?) husband and my third stepfather, but I always called him "Uncle Robarb" because he seemed like some character out of a movie like Tobacco Road or Cannery Row.

Uncle Robarb. I was tempted to say that he was a "really great dude", so no one would get offended. I managed to avoid this cornball habit by recalling that he was neither great, nor really, nor even actually, a dude. You always taught me never to lie except when I was sure I could get away with it. This isn't one of those times. Remember how Uncle Robarb used to slouch all day in the armchair drinking those vodka and waters that really did not contain much water? How he used to love the tremendously idiotic entertainment offerings on daytime TV, his "home companion"? That is, until he passed out totally.

You tried, I know. I am wiping tears from my eyes as I remember your constant, but ultimately unsuccessful efforts to make me call old Robarb "daddy". It sounded really off key. Was he "my daddy"? This makes him sound like someone who gave out teddy bears and that sort of thing, which is completely the wrong image. You can't have forgotten the way he ridiculed my first full efforts at cross-dressing (I ought to have found a dress my own size. At twelve, I had to hold those old dresses of yours above my knees just to walk). I rarely suffered for long from his slings and arrows, though. Robarb always moved quickly on to another subject. When you're consuming at that rate, your attention span naturally wanders.

The years passed, but one day I had to ask you, what happened to old Uncle Robarb anyway? Soon he became uncle Robarb, to avoid any possible confusion with loveable Uncle Remus.

Then there was Aunt Revisionista. I'll put her in now, because she hated Robarb like dogs and cats, so they ought to go together. You can't imagine how dear her memory comes back to me. She used to stand in the hallway, just outside of the living room of our apartment and watch TV. She didn't really trust it enough to get close. She claimed it emitted all kinds of x-rays that could cause diseases. (TV came in when she was already nearly forty. She couldn't evolve.) But she was fascinated by it. She turned her face away, but kept an eye glued. The war documentaries really gave her a thrill. They reminded her of the two and a half years she spent stationed in the Aleutians with the Army. The best years of her life. Yes, it was there that she learned to take drugs. Uppers, downers and others and to drink. She never forgot the big thrill it gave you.

I won't say too much about Aunt Revisionista, because she never stayed with us more than a few days at a time. She was the first person to call me Marsha. Marcus was the name you had them put on my birth certificate. It was her slurred speech that turned it into Marsha, you said. Because when you drink and take drugs at the same time it effects your pronunciation. But why did she say, when I was just past twelve, "Marsha, you're wearing too much lipstick"? I wasn't, really. It was too dark a shade, so it appeared too much. You bought the stuff. I was only experimenting. I would have gone for something more pink than red.

Now I have to return to that other path of memory lane, Robarb Alley, not exactly an elegant boulevard.

"Uncle Robarb, I love you." That's what I had to say every time he had a birthday or a Christmas. His birthdays were erratic. They seemed to come every six months for a year or two. Then, it might be a year and a half or two years before he had the next one. You told me he wasn't sure of his exact birth date, so he changed it from time to time. He wasn't sure of the exact date because his parents, just before they split, dumped him for personal reasons when he was about thirteen, or maybe eleven, or even less. I never understood why they did it. Why they felt that they had to do it. After all, when he was young, during the Depression, he certainly couldn't have spent all his time lounging around in a broken armchair, drinking vodka, watching television and smoking a cigar that smelled worse than he did. Television had not yet been created. Prohibition was still in effect. He wouldn't have been able to buy cigars, since he was too poor. "I couldn't afford to work", as he put it. I did not love Uncle Robarb. When I had to utter those five miserable words I felt something go rotten inside me. I was totally embarrassed. Then he started to call me Marsha, just like Aunt. I suppose he thought that since I was queer I had to have a crush on him and he had to fight it off with sarcasm, although I was fourteen at the time and he was almost fifty, and he looked almost sixty, and acted almost eighty. He never looked in the mirror. If he had, he would have realized that his large, grey, heavily maculated face with irregular features arranged around a prominent nose would never qualify him for the centerfold.

I'm sorry. I know you loved Uncle Robarb. Maybe he was some sort of father figure for you, because your own father cashed out early. You must have loved Uncle Robarb. Why else would you have stayed with him for eleven years of drunken unemployable stupor? Love is irrational. You said that you and Robarb would be together forever because he was so easy to get along with. Drink does that to some people. It relaxes them, brings them out of their emotional constipation. Still, that's not exactly love.

It wasn't all bad. Remember that Christmas when Uncle Robarb went down to the liquor store just after midnight because we were almost out of gin? Then we all stayed awake until dawn singing songs about Old Thailand or something? I don't remember the details. You two passed out in the living room. I was able to crawl to my bedroom. I woke up in the dog's bed. When I woke up, a grey noonday sun was coming through the open door. Snauzer, our dog, was still snoring in my bed. At night, there's not that much difference.

Robarb hated Snauzer. He was jealous. For one thing, he knew that I was much fonder of Snauzer than I was of him. Not that he cared. It's just that he hated losing. He always hated losing, it was part of his personality. That's probably why he drank so much. To get over all the hating about losing.

Snauzer ran way. I don't blame him and I don't know if he's still alive. I know that he was in good health and that he always slept a lot. If ever there was a dog with a fascinating personality, it was Snauzie. The way he did tricks, like walking on his two back legs when he wanted to express affection. Or the way he pissed on things he didn't like. He pissed on Uncle Robarb about a hundred times. Most of the time Robarb wasn't aware that he was being pissed on. That can happen when you're almost in an alcoholic coma.

I'm writing this message and I want to emphasize the positive as much as possible, like I said, so enough of that. Another good memory is when Uncle Robarb used to sing German songs in the autumn. If it was singing. If it was autumn. If it was German. Things were always confusing about Robarb. Oh, he was clear enough about memories of his happy days in Oakland in the thirties when he was young, and how he used to buy two donuts for a nickel. Joy. And how the police told the colored people to calm down or else. Things like that. His eyes would fill with tears of happiness. You know those old grey slacks he used to wear? I don't know whether he had ten pairs of the same color and style or just one. They were always dark and wet looking around the crotch. Professional hazard.

I will not go on criticizing your husbands. I know you must have loved some of them anyway. Or, if not loved, at least tolerated, which is just about the same thing, maybe better, as you used to say. Wasn't there one called "Rickshaw"? Or was it Rick Shaw? I don't think he lasted too long. I won't say you could have shown better taste. There's no accounting for it.

Once you said that you loved Robarb more than … something. I don't remember exactly what. That love turned to tolerance, then to endurance, and finally to indifference. I felt ditto, except for the love part.

SON OF A WHORE

I'm not sure if it was in autumn when Robarb's German songs filled the air, or in summer when drink helped us through the heat, or some other time when it helped us through something else, but it was just when I was thirteen that I ran away from home for the first time.

Grandma said that she came here in 1910 because she longed for the unlimited opportunities of the New Land. She too was thirteen years old when she left home, the youngest child of a Carpathian family with a dozen children, and she was eager to get away from a strictly-from-nowhere village and get started somewhere where things could happen. She became an indentured servant for a rich family in Pennsylvania (I think they got their cash selling coal, the stuff they put in your Christmas stocking when you don't deserve anything else). When she was eighteen, she was free. And she had definite goals in life. She told me that stuff herself during those long weekends when I stayed with her because you "had to go away to see the doctor". In Amerika she wanted to have a nice, decent family of her own with a respectable husband and well behaved children. She wanted a house with a front on the street. She wanted her daughters to marry decent men and have proper families. She wanted grandchildren who would be successful in life and religious.

It's cruel to laugh. Of course, she knew something was wrong when you and Aunt Revisionista started acting like you had the devil in you. Things were different in the new land. Different ideals. Freedom. Liberty.

Okay. I'm not going to sing the national anthem. I know grandma felt we let her down. Why did these girls who ought to have been useful and pious daughters and wonderful wives and mothers take to doing all of those things? With a string of boy friends who wore flashy clothes and smoked cigarettes (in Romania old men smoked pipes and rich men smoked cigars) and who showed up late at night drunk asking for Rusalka or Revisionista? That wasn't in the script. Anyway, I think your answer to her would have been that life was different now. Things were modern. People lived modern. They were up to date. You could hear it on the radio, and then, much later, on the TV. You could hear it.

I ran away from home. I had bus fare with the coins I saved from Uncle Robarb's pockets when he passed out. I took the Transbay bus connection to San Francisco. Soon I was on Polk Street. I stood in front of a delicatessen to watch people go by. Uncle Robarb always said that Polk Street was the place for me and I wanted to find out why.

Possibly you are asking yourself why I would ever want to leave a loving home for some disgusting adventures, is that it? First of all, look at the small living room of the loving home. The walls were dead drab, they hadn't been painted in fifty years. The furniture was dilapidated and stained. It stank. In the center of the "living room" was the broken armchair of Uncle Robarb, where he would snore while watching television. You could never tell if his eyes were really closed. They were so small and bunkered by puffy lower lids. I will not complain about the general disorder. It was my job to get rid of the empties and I have to admit that I was negligent. Robarb's resentment at my disrespectful treatment of him manifested itself more intensely because he was surrounded by dead vodka soldiers. They did nothing to maintain the image he had of himself as a suave, handsome, intelligent, professional conversationalist. He growled. He called me names. He threatened, but he was physically unable to rip himself away from the armchair fast enough to carry out his threats. I think I was saved by that physical passivity that defined his nature. The newspapers in those days constantly ran stories about family murders caused by inbreeding and degeneration.

On Polk Street. Jason. Slim, nice features, dark hair, maybe too much hair oil, streetwise, a drop out. He clued me in on ways of making money. You had to stand a certain way, he said. There was no need to smile. It was better to look intense and eager. When men approached you, you didn't bargain for a price. You stated the going rate. It was low enough that few customers were put off. A lot of them weren't too good looking. When you went to work as a young male prostitute, you just closed your eyes, turned over on your stomach, and imagined you were in heaven. It didn't take them too long, usually. Sometimes it took close to forever. Several times I fell asleep while the customer was still working at it. That's human nature.

Grandma never liked Uncle Robarb. Even when he was sober he had that sly, self-satisfied look centering on the thin mustache under his large nose. That grey suit was never impressive, even when it was only a few years old. Grandma wanted to know what he *did*? A hard one. And there was no way of getting around the fact that he was your husband number four and you were only supposed to have one! Unless the first one or two died or something.

And what did grandma think about homosexuality? I hear your question coming from beyond the line.

Answer: she didn't know what it was. It wasn't part of the curriculum for peasant schools "when Franz Josef was Emperor". Even though she might not have known what it was, I admit that she would have disapproved of making money on Polk Street the way I learned to do. Probably something similar went on in Zagreb and places like that, but she would not have heard of it. Not in a tiny village in the Carpathians. News filtered only slowly in those regions, usually when a major world war happened, which was pretty frequent.

Things were different in the new land. They might not have been so different after all. Grandma told us about her father, Laszlo, a horse trader, gadabout, ne'er-do-well alcoholic. He crossed the ocean a half dozen times to work building the railroads in America. When he got back to Carpathia, the wine shop owners wept for joy. He could treat his friends for months on end with the cash he brought home. She said we ought never to talk about Laszlo in front of a priest.

Oh yeah. There was a time when Uncle Robarb actually had a real paid job. He earned good money. Naturally he was a salesman. He sold things to people by pretending that he liked them, that they were all good friends, and that the world was a great place where you could laugh your head off. After years of good earnings there came a time when he couldn't stand it anymore. That is, he could stand the money, but it is eternally to his credit that he could not forever stand the fakeness. He started to drink even more. Instead of going to work he would go to bars in the afternoon. He would come home smiling and thinking about what a wonderful person he was, so loved by friends, wife and step-son (daughter?) It couldn't last. His paychecks began to shrink. Then there was that letter from his boss. "Robarb is in need of professional help. He should receive therapy and counseling for his problem. We cannot employ him at Kruts' Screws any longer at this time". That was the company he worked for, Kruts' Screws. I don't know what Kruts' Screws was about. Maybe some kind of metal product for cars. At least, I hope.

Uncle Robarb had a different story. He claimed that he couldn't work anymore because of a physical injury. He had strained his gluteus muscles during the long hours spent driving from one customer to another. He talked to a lawyer. They filed a lawsuit. Then there was the waiting. These suits could take forever. He took to the armchair. Naturally he started drinking cocktails in the afternoon, while time advanced to the dinner hour. He poured his first one just before eleven a.m. To him, it tasted wonderful. So different from life itself.

The years rolled by. Everyone forgot about the lawsuit. Still, we were doing okay because you landed that job at Bombo's Club, in the gift shop. It was something you enjoyed. The businessmen were good tippers. There were parties after hours in hotel rooms. Robarb was happy that the rent was being paid and the groceries arrived on time. Was he aware that other things were happening? We will never know. There was a bond, a sacred connection between Robarb, the vodka bottle, and television. It prevented outside interference. It was something that lasted.

Children hate school. They always hate school and the best schools are the worst. School is boring with its stupid and phony subjects. What dumb disgusting textbooks! What self-righteous and tyrannical teachers! And the worst thing of all is the other students. They will bully, abuse and attack you. Unless you get the jump on them. The rule is jump or be jumped.

I stayed away from school after eighth grade. I guess I wasn't educated enough to do it earlier. Luckily, I was the one who collected the mail while Uncle Robarb was watching television and laughing through his glass of vodka and you were still sleeping after a late night at Bombo's. I threw away the letters from the school and from the County Board of Education. Eventually, after about four years, they stopped coming. Freedom.

After a certain point, Robarb no longer wondered why I was at home in the afternoons. And he didn't notice that I was pouring my own drinks out of his bottle. Sometimes he would come to life. He would look at me with a blurred but sympathetic expression and say, "Marsha, you should join the navy. You could get out of all this ... mess. Save yourself while you still can!" I thought about it. I could join. I wasn't that far from seventeen years old. They wouldn't necessarily know that I was really a girl, I mean in the personality department. But I knew Robarb only wanted to get rid of me. I think he was subconsciously aware that I was cadging from his bottle. So naturally I refused.

I'll go on with the rest of this part of the story, even though you know it almost as well as I do, mom. Things got worse. Uncle Robarb could not stay sober. After a really bad hangover he would slow down for a few hours. I am only glad that you seemed not to notice the continuing increase of his intake level. You would have been pained more than anything to see what had become of the promising salesman who was your husband number four (?) You were too busy at the Club to see what was happening. Or were you?

One day the ambulance came for Robarb. There was nothing much wrong. Only he seemed to have stopped breathing. He even seemed to have stopped drinking. I was the one who called for help. I used our old dial-a-matic phone to reach 911. They came. Two emergency medical techs brought a gurney into the apartment. They looked around, took in the dozens of vodka empties, shook their heads. They had seen some bad cases before, but nothing like this. I pointed at Uncle Robarb. "It's him. There's something wrong with him."

They hooked something up to his chest. They measured his blood pressure, his heart rate, his breathing. "He'll have to go to the hospital. Do you have his insurance card?"

I had noticed right off that one of the techs was very good looking. He was tall and slim with attractive features and light hair. I wanted to help as much as I could. I ran to the bedroom, to your and Robarb's bedroom. I started to throw things around. To find the card. I tossed everything into the middle of the room. It became a disordered pile of clothes and sheets and blankets and bottles and ashtrays. I couldn't find the card! Where the hell was the card? I ran back to the living room.

"Get some of these bottles out of the way," the other tech ordered. "We can't roll the gurney over that mess." He had a strong, deep voice. It was impressive in a way.

I started to kick bottles away from the exit path. I

tried to make conversation, to show that I was interested. "Is he still alive?"

"Yes." The techs looked serious. This was real. It was like television.

Eventually they got the gurney with him on it to the stairs. They carried it down to the street, where the ambulance was waiting with its flaring lights. I thought I saw Robarb raise his hand and sketch a sign that was probably meant for me. It might have meant "thanks" or "good bye" or "so long, Marsha" or "fuck you, buddy". Then the rescue car was gone. The handsome tech was gone with it. Uncle Robarb was certainly gone. Nothing remained. No, what remained was "the memories of past tomorrows", or something like that. Something emotionally deep and literary. I resolved to tell you what happened as soon as you got back from the club. That wouldn't be until early morning or mid-afternoon tomorrow.

When you got back home I was sitting in the armchair. It was three a.m. and the television was playing some sort of science fiction movie with hideous space aliens murdering everybody. I had drunk about two inches from a former bottle of poor old Robarb's vodka. I was imitating adult behavior. Sociologically, this is normal.

"Robarb's dead," I announced, trying to look sad, but also proud to be the messenger of some important news.

"Don't joke. I'm completely exhausted."

You walked directly into your bedroom and screamed. You came rushing back to the living room. "What the hell happened? Everything is thrown around. It's a mess. I can't accept this behavior after a long night at work!"

"I told you. Robarb's dead. The medical guys came to

help him. They had to throw everything around to find his insurance card."

"Don't play silly games with me, Marcus. I'm too tired. Did you trash my bedroom for some psychotic reason?" You were serious, angry, threatening.

"No. The ambulance techs were here and they had to take Uncle Robarb away. One was really good looking."

"I don't want to hear any more of that nonsense. If this happens again you're going to be sorry!" You disappeared into the bathroom. I think you ultimately concluded that Robarb wasn't home because he had made an emergency trip to the liquor store and forgot to come back. As for the disorder in the bedroom, you might have decided that maybe it wasn't me and that Robarb did it while hunting for some cash to buy another bottle. I ought to put in that you and Robarb almost never argued even after his lazy, hideous alcoholism started. Most likely, I think, because you saw him as a "father figure", a replacement for the one who disappeared. A shrink told me that once.

When you came out of the bathroom you had your make-up off and your hair curlers on and you had that tired-out, somewhat wrinkled, unhappy look that you usually had around three a.m. I was sitting in the armchair. I was giving the vodka a fair go, although I knew that I would never be able to match Uncle Robarb's capacity.

"All right. Now where the hell is Robarb? Tell me the truth right away."

"The ambulance took him. You see, he was sitting here, in this chair, as usual, but he started to cough and to puff and his face turned blue and he couldn't talk. I dialed 911, just like they teach you on TV. The medical guys came upstairs and they took him away on a stretcher. That's all I know."

"I'm too tired to listen to your imaginary tales. I'm going to bed. If I can't find my valium bottle you are going to be in trouble!" You were gone.

God, the space movie on TV was really scary. It was so scary that I couldn't sleep that night. I kept the light on in the medium sized closet that I used for a bedroom. I was afraid that the space monsters were real and that they would creep up on me in the shadows. It was really horrible.

The next morning, to try to butter you up, I had coffee and toast ready at one thirty p.m. when you came into the kitchen dressed in your Chinese bathrobe and with hair curlers and a hair net on your head. You seemed grateful to see that I had gone to all the trouble to make breakfast. You drank some coffee. Then, you looked at the toast and pushed it away. You were suspicious about the hygienic quality of my cooking. I never washed my hands, you used to say, and I suppose it was true.

Ah! You were in a much better mood when you finished your cup of coffee. "But really, where is Robarb?" I was going to tell you again when you put in, "no, don't make up any lies. I know he probably passed out on the way to the liquor store last night. Anyway, I can't wait. I have a lunch appointment in only half an hour and I have to fix my hair and my face and get dressed." You see, even though you really liked Uncle Robarb and considered him your husband, you went out a lot with other men. He didn't mind much because, well, I don't know why he didn't mind much.

What really did happen to him? Shortly after Robarb

went away in the ambulance I ended up in Juvenile Hall for a few days because of a trick I pulled with a rum bottle at the liquor store. I opened the bottle and swigged from it behind a cardboard display, but I got caught by a clerk. Maybe they called about Robarb from the hospital when I was in stir. Even when I got back I never answered the phone, because I was always afraid it might be the probation officer or the school jerks. You always slept in the daytime with those wax plugs in your ears, so you wouldn't have heard the telephone. And of course I always threw away any official looking letters and I didn't answer the door. (You always had to expect the police to show up.) When Robarb didn't return after two weeks you said you didn't care what happened to him. He could be dead for all you cared. You thought he probably picked up some unsavory, pathetic woman who went for severe drunks. Good riddance!

What I liked most about after Uncle Robarb went somewhere was that I could watch whatever I wanted on television. He wasn't there to order me to change channels. We didn't have an automatic command box yet, so that made it even worse a chore to do his tuning for him. I had to get up and switch the TV whenever Robarb felt like it. Mostly he liked old movies from the thirties or forties. They made him feel young again, he said. Black and white films with talky scenes and close-ups of men in slouch hats and raincoats and women with perfect hairdos and well styled dresses. I could almost imagine myself one of them. One of the women, that is.

For some things, Uncle Robarb might have been a role model for me, but I knew that I could not follow in his footsteps. For one thing, there was the stark reality that I could not manage a fraction of the consumption rate that he found normal, if not inadequate. I sat in his old chair and watched TV, but I really couldn't put away forty percent alcohol in any decent quantity. Not at that time. I took a swig every fifteen or twenty minutes, sometimes a very small one. I admit that I was not emotionally convulsed by Uncle Robarb's sudden disappearance. In fact, I felt freer. I no longer had to carry out minor chores or else suffer a bombardment of empty liquor bottles. School was no longer a real threat. Everything looked like clear sailing ahead.

Eventually, though, I couldn't avoid thinking seriously about, you know, "the future". I was past seventeen, almost. I would soon be eighteen. What was I going to do in life? I couldn't hang out with you forever. You had made that plain enough. It would have been the same problem without my transsexual situation. Even if I were a Marine Corp drill sergeant, you would have refused to support me indefinitely.

"You can't stay in this apartment for the rest of your life. I know that you are not going to school. What are you going to do? You'll have to make your own way very soon. You'll have to get a job like a decent man. You'll have to start soon and work hard if you want to be able to marry some day and take care of yourself and your family."

I didn't answer. I looked at my naked feet and tried to appear humble and miserable. That was an attitude that you appreciated. As far as the married man scenario, you had a right to indulge in your occasional fantasies. Go right ahead. I knew I was really a girl.

"Well?" You stood with arms akimbo. "I'm waiting for an answer. You don't have an answer, do you?"

"What is the question?"

SON OF A WHORE

"What are you going to do with your life! I've asked you that question a million times already and you never say anything!"

Suddenly I had a bright idea. "Why can't I work at Bombo's Club like you? I could work in the gift shop just like you and do exactly the same thing."

You had no patience for this. "They don't hire boys at Bombo's, except in the kitchen." You said this with distaste. Kitchen work was repulsive, low class and badly paid. The whole idea at Bombo's was to show attractive women to wealthy men. It was no place for youths, even those who from an early age had shown a predilection for cross dressing, as I had done at my fifth birthday party, to the shock and dismay of all.

"Okay! Just give me some time to think about it. I'll try to come up with something. Maybe I'll join the Foreign Legion."

"You'd better think quick." You were gone.

I did some thinking. There was Polk Street and the street corner customers. But that didn't pay much, hardly more than kitchen work at Bombo's. And the work itself was unappealing. You came back from a gig with your buttocks smeared with Vaseline. You felt those greasy cheeks sliding against each other all night. "Normal jobs" were impossible to get. They never hired you. The Foreign Legion was just a joke, but I did consider joining the army. I soon tossed that aside. In the army you had to get up early in the morning and they had these huge barrel-chested sergeants with lantern jaws and bulging abdomens who shouted orders ten times worse than Robarb. I had seen it on TV and in the movies. So what in hell was I going to do? Well, can't you give me an answer?

I decided to do nothing. It was best to let things take their own course, because I could see no alternative. Maybe this was part of the philosophy of life that I "imbibed" from Uncle Robarb. He always let things take their course. Usually that led to nothing more serious than sitting around all day in front of the TV and swilling vodka. I didn't think you'd actually kick me out. Or, I thought that maybe you would but it wouldn't matter much, because I could just hang out somewhere until something else turned up.

One evening I was drinking coffee in a place on Polk Street, where I had gone after one of our "what are you going to do with your life" arguments. I felt sleepy because I hadn't been able to doze in front of the television after you left. I was too hyped up as a result of the highly emotional level of our interchange. You: "Lazy, unsanitary pansy!" "uneducated little pervert!" Me: "Waaah! You hate me!" On the sticky cafe table in front of me, just beside the stoneware mug of coffee, I had placed all the financial assets that I possessed. Taking inventory. Two dollars in paper and sixty-seven cents in coins. I knew that you were already at work at Bombo's, smiling at wealthy businessmen, trying to seem at first to resist their advances. Then it happened. I got discovered by Harv!

Later, you became almost as familiar with Harv as I was, because I told you all about him, making almost all of it up, since "our relationship" hardly lasted more than a few hours. It was the beginning of a great opportunity, I said, almost like the Army. A career in the making. At least a job. With money. You called him "your Uncle Harv". You were glad that there was someone who might be willing to take me off your hands, someone who at least sounded normal and had decided to fill the role of Santa Claus or Father Flanagan out of the goodness of his heart.

"Hi! I'm Harv." He sat down next to me at the small table. He looked me over at close range and seemed to make a note of the small amount of loose cash lying on the table. He immediately understood the situation. It wasn't like you had to be the new Einstein. "What's your name? Just spending time, right?"

Harv looked like a teacher to me. Of course, I hadn't had a lot of direct contact with that group, but I had seen them at work on TV. Harv was around fifty, I'd say. He was pretty old. He wasn't really fat, but more fat than thin. His hair was an odd color. It wasn't grey or white. It was a funny shade of light orange. It was sparse and teased up to cover most of his scalp. His facial features were nothing to write home about. They were properly rounded and elongated and all there, but nothing else. In that way he resembled a lot of the customers I had met standing on a Polk Street corner. But this was different. I knew it was going to be a definite offer, something more important than your twenty buck one timer, because otherwise he would just have waved the bills and invited me out into the alley. I twigged to this and made up my mind to play it for what I could.

"I'm waiting for my mom," I said, trying to lisp without sounding like a tea kettle.

Harv said something like, "my mom lives in Topeka" or "you must have a very attractive mother." I don't remember exactly what it was. Then he came out with it. "What does your mom do?"

I could see where things were going. Harv probably

got the idea that I wasn't the usual hang-out type of young pansy on Polk Street, most likely because I wasn't outside on the pavement, and he wanted to make things seem respectable by playing the family line.

"She's a prostitute. She's really beautiful and she's my ideal." I didn't see why I shouldn't mention the profession. I knew most people were contemptuous about prostitutes, but that was going to be their attitude about me anyway. I thought it would sound impressively exotic if I admitted my mom was one too.

Harv nodded. His bland and undistinguished face smiled. "Interesting profession."

"I don't mean she just hangs out on a street corner or anything like that. She works at a high class nightclub and she meets men there, men with a lot of money. They're usually staying in hotels and they like to have parties after closing time."

"I see." Suddenly he took my wrist in his hand and brought it close to his face. "You have an interesting wrist. It's small and delicate but I can tell that there's real strength in it."

"Thanks." I drew my arm away. I used it to pick up my coffee cup and drink. "I love this stuff," I said. "It helps me stay awake."

"How old are you?" He was moving right toward the goal. "Sixteen, seventeen?"

"I'm eighteen. Almost eighteen and a half. I already graduated from high school." Complete lie. "I'm just waiting to move on to college so I can become educated as much as my mom. She's a real high class person." I didn't understand why I shouldn't make things up, since he probably wouldn't believe it anyway.

SON OF A WHORE

"Where did she go to college?"

"Mmm. I'm not too sure. I think it was one of those Ivy League places like Bellmore."

The waitress came by to offer more coffee. I smiled at her and tried to look seductive. She was Chinese, really pretty. "Las' cup," she said. "We got too many more customer." She moved off with a fast twisting motion of her hips. I wished I could walk like that.

"Do you plan to go to college at Bellmore?"

"Yeah, if I can. I'm not sure yet. It depends on whether or not they have a course in Computer Economics."

"Computer Economics?"

"That's my major."

"Bellmore's an all girls school. How are you going to get around that?"

I shrugged, smiled. "There are ways," I lisped coyly. I felt I was on the way to something glamorous and exciting. I had to play it just right.

"Are you interested in clothing?" Harv had noticed that I was wearing a pair of your chartreuse pedal pushers and a flowery shirt.

"That's what I usually wear, except in the bathtub."

"Ha! Ha!" Harv appreciated this. He had a sense of humor. If you were Harvey, given his mediocre physical attributes and his rather limp personality, you would have needed a sense of humor, too. "I'm a construction jockey, myself," he told me in a low, gruff, masculine voice. This meant, I found out later, that he hammered and piled things together to make buildings. It could bring in real cash. "I have an interest in art on the side. I'd like to show you my collection. I live just around the corner. How about it?"

Ah. The pitch. It wasn't as crude as it might have been. Naturally, I would be charmed, I told Harv. He probably had a super expensively furnished apartment with an antique collection right in the neighborhood. I knew that was the pattern. But I had already made up my mind that I wouldn't steal anything. It wasn't worth it. The pawnshops and art boutiques got checked all the time by the police, so it was hard to cash in on "art". Of all the habits and virtues that I learned from Uncle Robarb, my sense of honesty was not one of them. Can you believe that he actually stole money from some of the other stepfathers? When he was caught, which was invariably the case, he used to promise to pay them back. It was never a practical possibility.

"It's in here." Harv used his key to unlock a large black door that opened into an apartment on the third floor of an art deco apartment building. I told you it would probably be a pricey place, almost like a movie set, right?

"Wow!" I feigned ingenuousness. "You must have a lot of resources!" I saw a large room furnished with art and antiques and expensive furniture. He went in a good deal for ancient Greek sculpture, mainly anatomically accurate naked ephebes, although mostly just copies. There were a number of statues of women, too, something like that famous one with no arms. Only Harv's women had most of their arms and legs in place.

"I've collected a few things over the years. This one," he touched the arm of a half-scale statue depicting an Olympic discus thrower, "I bought when I just got out of the marine corp."

"God. It's a thrill."

Harv bowed slightly from the shoulders, as if his money meant that he got credit for creating the statue. He appreciated flattery, which obviously could not be about his person. As we stood admiring his statues and paintings and bric-a-brac, I became thoroughly aware that his build was disproportionately developed around the abdomen and buttocks, just as his facial features pulled toward nose and mouth structures. Harv waltzed to a large cabinet. He opened the double cabinet doors. "Would you like a drink?" Inside was a display of dozens of bottles of different colored liqueurs and alcohol.

I picked up a bottle of vodka, pulled the stopper out and drank directly from the bottle. I swallowed two or three ounces. I had good home training for that. I thought Harv would be impressed by this macho feat, which would also show that I was willing to "go the limit".

"Hey! Hold on there! I don't want you passing out in my living room. I'd have to ask your mom to come and get you." I think this last part was a joke.

"I can handle it. My dad showed me how to drink." I took another pull. "The trick is not to pay attention to how much you drink, only to watch how it feels in your head." In fact, I didn't have a "dad", or at least I didn't know who he was, which is about the same thing.

"Oh. So that's how you do it. Makes sense." He nodded, smiled.

The bedroom! Harv led the way to his huge boudoir. The walls were hung with the works of minor painters from the nineteenth century, not impressionist pieces, but realist tableaux that showed interesting people riding on horses through a green countryside or couples walking in quaint streets or high class guys posing for a portrait. There were small antique varnished tables and large commodes and some Louis XIV (XIX?) type armchairs placed against the walls. In the center of the room was a really spectacular bed. It was large, much larger than king size or even imperial. It might have accommodated half a dozen guys at once!

"Cheez! I've never slept in a bed like this before. At home sometimes we just fall asleep on the sofa."

"There's always a first time."

Harv came closer to me. He developed an interest in unbuttoning and unzipping my trousers. When he had my pants and shorts down around my knees he took a closer look. He seemed disappointed. He made me pirouette, so that he could look at me from all angles. Then we were in bed.

It was a feeling I liked. I was familiar with it. It gave me a very feminine sensation that let me imagine that I was anatomically female. He penetrated me without any sort of lubricant, probably to avoid staining his expensive sheets and blankets. He began to move rhythmically. I could not see him of course, since I was face down on the mattress, but he felt much bigger than my first ocular impression.

"Ah. Oh! Ah ah ah. Oooooh!" I was talking.

Harv was concentrating on getting to the goal, on lighting the fireworks. Only he was having some trouble with it. After about ten minutes it seemed that he was about to reach a noisy climax, but he declined into another sustained period of pumping. After twenty minutes it was becoming uncomfortable. He kept flopping out, then putting himself back in. Harv's arm, which was lovingly placed around my hairless chest as I lay on my stomach, was covered with beads of sweat. I looked at the exquisite antique clock on a bedside table. Time was passing.

"Ah ah ah ah oooooooooh!" Suddenly Harv rolled off onto his back and fell asleep. I sat up and looked at his member. It was smeared with some brownish stuff but the tip was as dry as a bone. Was he really sleeping? Did *it* really happen?

I looked at his chest—it was covered with a fairly thick mat of grey hair. He was breathing steadily and deeply now, so maybe he really was asleep. We had not discussed a price. Of course he realized that there would be a price, didn't he? Did he think I did this sort of thing just for the fun of it? I didn't want to wake him, though. He might argue round and round on the proposition that it had been a strictly social affair. That had happened before. I grabbed my shorts. Actually they were a pair of yours, mom, fairly new but discarded for something more fashionable. I put on the chartreuse pedal pushers. Then the flowery shirt. I tiptoed out of the bedroom. I could hear Harv snoring as I quietly closed the bedroom door.

Wow! Again, I marveled at Harv's collection. He had put together an impressive private museum. It must have cost a million! I didn't know you could make that kind of money as a "construction jockey". Not that I would have been tempted by that kind of work, even for ten times the money. It was crude and undistinguished. I preferred what I was doing at the moment. Selling your ass to strange and unattractive men has a flattering dimension, even if it pays little.

I remembered what you always told me about morality and ethics and that sort of thing. We should never steal, because if we do, someone could steal it back from us. This was different, though. It was a matter of rightful pay. I picked up a wonderful looking four inch statue in dark metal. It showed a Greek or Roman soldier in armor confronting some sort of small lion or tiger and about to bash it with a club. The Romans or Greeks probably made it. At least, they probably made the original. I put it in my pocket. Soon I was out in the street.

What happened next was incredible, mom. When I actually told you about it, I had to pretend to swear on a pile of Bibles. To relax and sort of cool down, I went back to Polk Street, which was just around the corner from Harv's Hyde Street apartment. I naturally avoided that smelly little café where I had met old Harv. He might have woken up in the mean time, taken inventory, then set out in hot pursuit. I just walked slowly along the sidewalks of Polk Street, looking into the restaurants, the cafes and the bars, and giving the clientele encouraging looks and a natural sizing up. Then it happened. I was standing in front of this antique store when I saw him. He was almost the most beautiful guy I had ever seen! He was a few inches shorter than me. He seemed to be about nineteen, and I was past seventeen at the time, maybe pushing eighteen and a half. His features were not entirely regular, but they were terrifically handsome. His hair was blond, nearly platinum, and it looked great, even if it might have been dyed. His body was well formed and athletic, but not at all heavy. I just stood on the sidewalk and stared at him. I just gawked. I couldn't think of anything to say. My mouth was hanging open. Fortunately, he opened conversation.

"You're catching flies," he said. He had a sense of

SON OF A WHORE

humor, even if it was deprecatory. He looked me over. At first he didn't seem impressed. In fact, his nearly perfect features registered contempt.

I sized up his crotch area. It looked substantial. I wanted to show him something remarkable in return, which would have to be Harv's little statue and not anything else. "Hello. Hi. Are you living around here? I'm trying to find an antique store where I can get an appraisal for an old family heirloom. You see, it's been in my family for a couple of hundred years or so, but I thought it was time to get rid of it, sort of free up some space at home."

"The antique joints are all closed now, like that one." He pointed to the boutique behind us. "They don't stay open all night. They're not donut shops. Show me the thing." He held out a hand. Even his hand was lovely. It was so pale and so nicely fashioned, not small but certainly not large and fleshy. I proudly took the Roman statuette out of my pocket and handed it to him.

He looked at it closely. "You got this at Harv's," he said with a note of authority in his voice. "I'm pretty familiar with his collection. I lived with the fucker for about six months. You shouldn't have stole it. You didn't kill him, did you?"

"No."

"You sure?" He was skeptical on this point, as if he thought that anyone who had an opportunity to kill Harv would not hesitate to do it.

"Yes." I decided to tell the truth and shame the devil. "He engaged my services as a gigolo. He fell asleep before he had a chance to pay me, so I took it out in goods. I didn't want to wake him, he seemed so peaceful."

"Like at a morgue? No, this thing is worth about a

thousand. He'd never of give you that much." He looked me up and down again. His mouth twisted into an expression of distaste. "Where the hell did you get that outfit?"

"It belongs to my mother," I answered, my voice wavering defensively

"I get it. Yeah." He looked again. "Half the guys hanging out around here want to be just like mommy."

I looked down at my chartreuse pedal pushers. I now realized that they were *not* attractive and that they gave an impression of bizarre effeminacy. "I guess I'll wear jeans next time. You're right. But they looked really great on my mom and we wear almost the same size."

He put out a hand and felt my chest. "At least you don't got on a bra, do you?"

"Oh no. I wouldn't. No reason." I pulled up my shirt. I showed a flat, weakly muscled, hairless, but rather graceful chest.

"Okay. That shows some sense." I could see that I had engaged some sort of interest on his part. "Come on over here." He motioned me into the dark, recessed entrance of the closed boutique. He undid my trousers, pulled them and my shorts down just a few inches, and turned me around. (It was sort of déjà vu from what Harv did. But I guess it was a natural way of *sizing* a partner up). People were passing on street; they ignored us. There wasn't really anything remarkable to see. I think he was only making sure he had exactly the right idea, because, after all, Harv probably paid guys to bugger him sometimes, and they'd have to be pretty well endowed to make an impression on Harv's ass. He had far too much class than to get up to something like that. "Yeah. I see. So he had to do you up brown, right?"

I was ashamed to hear my encounter with the construction jockey described in so crude a manner. "He gave me quite a bit of vodka. Otherwise I might not have done it."

He looked at the Roman hunter again, then put it in his pocket. "I'm gonna give him his statue back. He could call the cops on you and you'd be in bad trouble. It's grand theft."

"But … what do I get for my services? It wasn't exactly Shangri-la in bed with that guy."

He reached into his trouser pockets and searched. "My name's Gavin. What's yours?"

"Marsha. I mean, Marcus. My dad sometimes calls me Marsha when he's mad at me. That's why I said it."

"I get it." Gavin handed me a five dollar bill. "You can buy a couple of joints with this."

"Five bucks! That's all? I would have flipped that guy off in two seconds if I thought I'd only get five bucks. Besides, there was some emotional attachment involved too. What about that?" I readjusted my pushers. I wasn't blaming Gavin, who seemed okay as well as beautiful. I was only invoking the total unfairness of the world.

Gavin took me by the arm and conducted me down the street. "You're not bad looking. I mean, without those girl pants on. I like you because you're sort of, well, all out front, at least as far as you go." Gavin laughed at this. I didn't get the joke at the time. Soon we were in an alley behind Polk Street. He had my pants back down in a second. He turned me so that I was facing away from him. I could turn my head about halfway around. I glimpsed his handsome features as he worked on my rear with genuine enthusiasm. Was it the beginning of love?

SON OF A WHORE

I didn't tell you what happened, mom. Not yet. I didn't know if you'd be mad about it. Although, it's hard to understand why, if you know what I mean. The next day I went back to Polk Street early. I wanted to find Gavin. I was getting a crush on him. He was handsome and masculine, but not, you know, gross, and there was a sort of niceness about him, despite everything. It was about four in the afternoon. I went to the art boutique where we met. I walked up and down the street trying to catch sight of him. Gavin was nowhere. I thought about it. This was natural. He must work late hours. Probably he would still be sleeping somewhere, with somebody. I stood for a long time in front of the art boutique. Just from curiosity I looked at the objects displayed in the store window. I nearly collapsed when I saw the little Roman statue! It was standing in the middle of a display table loaded with old crockery and Japanese paintings. The store was still open. I went inside. While the old bald guy in charge watched me like a hawk, I went over to the statue. It was Harv's statue all right (maybe I should say mine?) I checked the price tag, which was hanging from the soldier's club. Three thousand dollars! I nearly choked. I picked up the statue. I turned, confused, in several directions at once. Then the old bald guy had me by the back of the neck.

"You will put down the object of art!"

I did as commanded. "This was my statue!"

I was soon on the way out, courtesy of the shopkeeper's arm. He was stronger than he looked. "I know your type. You stand in front of my shop all night. It is a disgusting trade." He gave me a good look over. Maybe he was trying to guess how cheap I'd go. Anyway, I was soon outside on the sidewalk. He motioned for me to move off.

I drifted forlorn down the street. I missed Gavin already, even though I hardly knew him. But I was crushed by the fact that he had ripped me off for thousands. And he said he liked me. He even buggered me as a special treat to prove it. I walked.

We were living, you and me, mom, in San Cerrito at that time, not too far from El Pablo, on the other side of the bay from S.F. Cerrito, Pablo, one of those blue collar suburbs, there's not that much difference. A little apartment desperately in need of paint and kitchen/bathroom repairs. It was a cheap place and too near the tracks, even though it was much larger now that Uncle Robarb had flown. Anyway, after the terrible things that had happened since yesterday, I wanted to go back there, back home. I wanted to hop on transportation, cross the bay and end up back in our miserable little apartment. Now I wanted to tell you all of the awful things that I stumbled into, even though you'd just say it was my own fault for doing disgusting, perverted things. Tears were dropping from my cheeks. And Gavin, the person I would have liked most in the whole world for a boyfriend, had caused it!

Without even knowing it, I was standing in front of Tramp's, a bar with large plate glass windows that gave its customers a full view of the street traffic. I was crying openly. I could not believe the cruelty, the rottenness of the world!

Suddenly I was being cradled in loving arms. She was wearing some sort of kimono. I could smell the liquor on her breath. "Honey, what the hell happen to you? Did someone beat you up? Did some man mistreat you? You can tell me. This is your momma talking."

She was a drag queen. I could tell immediately. Drag queens are always, almost always, or very often, really very, very nice people. They care. That's one of the things they do. She had seen me through the plate glass windows of the bar and come out to give me emotional support.

"Took my money," I sniveled, wiping oceans of tears away from my once pretty features.

"Oh, darling, that is really terrible! You must call the police right away! They will catch the robber and return your money. Don't you worry at all!"

She gave me a full examination, like she was a bone doctor or something, even though we were standing on the sidewalk in front of the bar. She felt my arms, my shoulders, my back, my legs. She was probably trying to ascertain if I had been injured and where. "He didn't kick you, did he? I mean here." She felt between my legs.

"No-o. It was more on the other side."

She felt my buttocks. "Ah. That makes more sense. You do feel sore back there, honey. We'll fix you up!" Trilla (that was her name) pulled me into the bar and made me sit at a table.

"I can't be in here," I said. "I'm not old enough."

"Don't worry. You look about eighteen, and that'll pass. Here, just you drink some of this." Trilla pushed a large glass of whiskey in my direction.

I took a big swallow. It wasn't bad. It was a lot better than old Uncle Robarb's vodka. I mean, that stuff made you feel like a Volga boatman after you swallowed a gulp or two. I snuffled back some snotty tears through my nose.

"Honey, just you tell me all about what happened and what some people did to you." Trilla put her arm around my shoulders. I think she appreciated the fact that I could never have been a football player.

"This man gave me a little statue."

"A man gave you a little statue," Trilla repeated. She was puzzled. Probably she wasn't sure if I was using the expression literally or figuratively.

"Something from the ancient Romans and Greeks. It showed a hunter fighting a lion. It was worth a lot of money."

"Hm." Trilla was still confused. "Why would anyone want to make a statue out of a hunter fighting a lion? That's not really a very pretty subject."

I took another drink of whiskey. I drained the glass. This was the moment of truth. "They liked that stuff back in ancient Athens. I don't know why. Later that same night I met a guy on the street. He seemed real nice and he said he'd be my friend. He was just so handsome." I raised my hands and held them in the configuration of a picture frame.

She nodded and stared at me in an attempt to guess the sort of person I might find "so handsome". She could only be a mother figure to someone like me, not a lover. "I know you're the kind of boy who likes other boys." Trilla signaled the waiter for another drink. "Make it two quadruples this time," she told him, meaning a glass with four shots of whiskey for each of us. "And you lost your statue?"

I nodded. "Gavin took it. He said he'd give it back to the rightful owner, because he thought I stole it. Then, today, I was passing an antique store and I saw it in the window. It was on sale for three thousand dollars!"

"Gavin took your statue? I know that little creep, that whore."

I broke again into tears. The waiter brought the quadruples and I grabbed one and drank at least a third of it at a swallow.

"Slow down, honey. At this rate, you ain't gonna last."

"I was going to use the money I got from the statue to buy something for my mother."

"What does your mother do?"

"We live San Cerrito. She's a prostitute."

Trilla had no answer to this for several minutes. She took a pull off her drink. Only about half was left. "Well, you do what you gotta do sometimes, that's all."

"She works in a club called Bombo's," I explained to broaden the original information. "They get all these business guys for parties."

Trilla nodded. She understood the scene right off. Then she switched gears. "I'd help you get your money back from Gavin, only I know he's halfway to Hollywood by now."

I took a slow swallow from my drink while this information sank in. I looked for a moment at the passersby who were crossing constantly in front of the bar window. Everything was over. Gavin had disappeared. I was alone facing nothing.

"And you thought he was going to be your friend. Well, that ought to show you a lesson if nothing else. Never trust a low down, two bit whore like Gavin. He'll take you for your last nickel."

"He seemed so nice at first." This wasn't exactly true. I embellished to make the experience appear more reasonable, to show that I had not grossly misjudged.

Gavin was great looking and had a strong personality, but he usually wasn't all that nice.

"Mm-hm. That's how he does it. I seen him at work. He likes to fool young kids, and older men too, just to get their money." Trilla checked out a fingernail. Two pieces of glitter were missing. "See, he got this idea, he think he gonna be a big movie star, all he got to do is get to Hollywood. Mm-hm. I know he ain't bad lookin' at all, even kinda sexy in a way, but he ain't no Marlon Brando. Only just you try tellin' that to him."

"He said he liked me." I knew I was repeating. There didn't seem to be anything else to say.

"What we gonna do with you now?" Trilla looked me over again. She added me up with an air of professional seriousness. "You ain't bad. You really sorta cute. The thing, you look like a little boy." She reached a hand out and rubbed my cheek, then my upper lip. "No beard. That's what give you that little boy look in the face."

"I can't grow one yet. My mom gives me a lot of flack about it. She says it makes me look like a sissy. But it could sprout up any time."

"That's right, but if it does, all you got to do is shave it off. Use a razor. Give you a smooth look."

I took a little mirror out of my pocket and looked at my reflection. I laid a finger across my upper lip, just to see what I might look like with a mustache. It wasn't encouraging.

"So honey, what you lookin' at right now, that's your market share. You gotta go for the men that likes young boys, even if you shootin' eighteen." Trilla opened her purse and took out a small vial filled with a cream colored liquid. Make-up. She opened the little bottle, tapped out a small amount of the contents onto a fingertip, then dotted it on my face. She used her hands to smooth it on my cheeks, around my eyes, on my forehead, on my chin. When she had finished, she leaned back and took in the effect. "Damn," she said. "If you don't look just like Bambi!"

I checked myself out in the bar mirror. I had used cosmetics before, in fact, I almost lived on them, but Trilla knew how to apply the stuff, the professional touch. I still found it hard to understand the comparison with a beloved cartoon character, but now there was a difference in my looks. I had regressed a few years in age. I didn't look like army material at all.

"So far, you doin' pretty good. There's a lot more to do, though. Stand up."

I dragged myself up. I was at least three glasses of whiskey down.

"Just what I thought. You need some work on the lower zone." She grabbed me by the hand and led me to the ladies room. She brought her purse in tow.

She pulled me in front of the large mirror on the ladies room wall. She showed me my reflection again. "See, that's what you look like. It ain't bad at all in the face area, but you need some more fixins. I know you been workin' on your own already on the street. I can tell. I got experience. But you gotta move up to the professional level if you wanna make real cash." Trilla unzipped my trousers and pulled them down with a yank. "See, we gotta bulk you up in a certain zone, otherwise, it don't work." She stretched the elastic of my shorts in front, took a large pad of cotton from her purse, put it in the strategic place, then pulled my pants up again. "Yeah. Uh-huh.

Better. Now you gonna bring in some good customers. See, most don't like to see that tiny look in front. When you already hooked up they gonna forget all about it bein' mostly cotton."

We were back in the barroom. We celebrated with double whiskies. But I wasn't completely comfortable with the ingénue role that I was playing now. I hadn't just rolled off the cabbage truck. "Yeah, I've turned tricks before, and usually it didn't end up too bad. All I had to do was stand on the corner and that brought them in."

"Yeah, but see, honey, that sort of thing is a real risk. You never know when someone like them street customers is gonna try to cut you into little pieces. That's that psycho element you read about in the newspapers. I guess you read the newspapers?"

"Yes." I lied.

"Then you know that one of them, one day, is gonna try unauthorized transgender surgery on you. I'm gonna give you a chance with a high class clientele, guaranteed safe and a lot more money."

I was going somewhere. I could see a career opening up for me. Trilla was protective, motherly. You never did the street sort of thing, mom. So it made me happy to feel that, now, as far as the profession, I was following in your footsteps.

In the next few days I started working in the really professional career that Trilla had opened for me. She gave me the leads every night. She had a little notebook with client numbers and addresses. She just called them and set up a "date". Naturally I already knew what to do when I got there. You had to smile at the customers, look pretty, then roll over. Sometimes I went to hotel rooms, although usually I visited some high price apartments and houses. Most of the time the physical part of it wasn't difficult. From my position face down on a mattress, or lying on my side turned away from the clients, I couldn't see the mediocre, if not plainly unappetizing physical aspect that most of them presented. I enjoyed playing the passive role, at the same time appreciating the fact that I was pretty enough to be paid for my favors. As always, I felt a strong feminine sensation as the other party worked away at me from behind me. I felt almost like a girl, or at least what I imagined a girl would feel. It was more than just a thrill: I thought it made me into my real self.

A few times I was away from our apartment in San Cerrito for a whole week. Sometimes I would stay with one john until my next appointment with another. Often I stayed overnight at Trilla's place. It could be wild. She had these large, aggressive boyfriends with heavy intakes of alcohol and drugs. They liked to listen to loud soul/rock music on the player. The party never seemed to end. I slept in the unoccupied bedroom, when it was unoccupied. I don't know if her boyfriends knew that she was not really a woman. In fact, I'm not sure that she wasn't really a woman. Does it matter, as long as you're making it?

Later you told me that you didn't notice that I was gone for a week at a time once or twice. After all, you usually came home around three a.m. or even past noon, then rested up for the next night. You said you thought I was hanging out on San Pablo Avenue, just watching the cars go by, or having parties with friends. What friends? I never really had a friend before Gavin. But that started later.

SON OF A WHORE

The gigs arranged through Trilla were not as bad as you might think. The guys were just homely or socially inadequate older males who were looking for an erotic moment and willing to pay for it. After a while, it started to wear. It was a stressful schedule, since you were always wondering about what (who?) might turn up. I was starting to develop dark rings under my eyes, which I covered over with eye make-up, but with decreasing success. Also, I began to suffer from an irritation in the anal/rectal area. Trilla showed me how to use a cream to treat this, but the clients noticed and they were alarmed and dissatisfied by the messy appearance.

I was making money, but not as much as promised. In theory I got a hundred dollars a gig, but Trilla subtracted a fifty percent commission, which she had to split with somebody else, and I was paying a certain amount for food and board when I hung out at her place. So sometimes I was only pocketing about forty dollars per gig, and I had alcohol and drug expenses to meet out of this reduced sum. It wasn't an easy job. I decided that I had to go back to San Cerrito for a much longer period of R and R. That's what the troops in Vietnam called it at that time. Rest and Recuperation.

I went back home. It was evening. I went inside and turned on the television. I had never seen it turned off before. I opened a beer and sat back in poor old Uncle Robarb's chair. Then I heard some noises coming from the large bedroom, your bedroom. I took a long sip, tried to concentrate on the TV (something intellectual was showing, like the daily news), but the noises got louder. They were regular, a sort of alternate gasping and rough breathing. I was afraid that some wild animal had broken

41

into our apartment and set up its nest in the bedroom. Eventually I garnered the courage to get up and to take a peek. It was a shock! I saw you in bed, mom, with a guy that I didn't recognize from before, a big guy, heavy, brutally concentrated.

He didn't leave for about three hours. At first he was going to try to throw me out of the apartment as a burglar or unexplained interloper, but you introduced us.

"That's my son, Marsha. He really doesn't do anything at all, since I could never force him to go to school."

"Hi, boy." Mr. X shook my hand. His palm was sticky. He squeezed my hand with the same brute force he used for other things, just to show who was boss.

"Ow!"

"Sorry, son. I guess I forget I'm a fuckin' strong guy sometimes."

When X was in the kitchen, probably drinking vodka straight from the bottle, I asked you, "how much did you get?"

You didn't answer. I'm sure it was a couple of hundred bucks, not a measly thirty.

Later X and me were sitting in front of the TV while you got dressed and rearranged. "So why they call you Marsha?" he asked. Just curious, not confused or even contemptuous.

"I don't know," I lied.

I would have to start buying my own panties. All of the ones that I borrowed from you, mom, got soiled. You just couldn't wash them clean after the gigs. There was always a brown or grey stain at the bottom or front. You gave me hell for that.

Buying girls undergarments was not an embarrassment for me. I had got used to the looks, the smirks, the amused stares from clerks and customers. Also, I discovered that if I wore enough make-up, well applied, as Trilla had taught me to do, most people weren't sure if I was a girl or an underdeveloped boy. I wasn't completely decided on the question myself, although I tended more and more to favor the former option.

I had no desire to wear skirts. They felt loose, floppy and uncomfortable and, again, for some reason, I actually looked less feminine in a skirt than in trousers. It was common for women to wear trousers, so there was no difficulty on that score as far as my psychological needs.

Now I was resting. While you were at Bombo's, slaving away in the gift shop and waiting to meet rich businessmen, I relaxed in front of the television, or lay down on your bed in the big bedroom and just dreamed. I dreamed about what it would be like when I was fully an adult and operating on my own. Would I be able to attract big paying customers like Mr. X (he gave me a twenty dollar bill before he left, just for a tip, and I hadn't even done anything, or, more accurately, he hadn't even done anything to me)? Or was I condemned to be a thirty buck a blow worker under Trilla's direction until my youth years gave out?

Suddenly I was feeling sad, nostalgic, and lonely. Everything seemed so indefinite at this point. I decided to go back to Polk Street, just on my own account, without contacting Trilla. I wouldn't even stand on the street corner and wait for the chances. I would just look around, check out the street, the stores, the bars, the cafes. There was always a possibility that you could meet someone real, not necessarily a customer.

It was Saturday night. There was a big crowd on Polk Street. A lot of straight couples passed by, probably on their way to Chinese restaurants or Italian cafes. Most of the men were middle aged, sometimes dressed in suits, and accompanied by women wearing fashion dresses and high heel shoes. I looked at the men with some curiosity. I wasn't attracted to them physically, that was for sure. Most were more or less bloated around the middle, often balding, and not too well favored. Their shoulders carried too much bulk for what appeared to be smallish legs. I looked at them and I remembered that I didn't know who my father was. You didn't know either, mom. You said it could have been any of a bunch of guys. What was the difference, anyway? I thought it was probably some tall guy with light hair, but even that wasn't certain. I could have inherited recessive traits. Actually, I think on the whole that I lucked out by missing the whole fatherdom business. From what I gathered from television programs and movies, the father/son relationship is often a pain in the ass and sometimes ends in an angry divorce. Some sons killed their fathers. And vice versa. Suddenly it got real clear to me that what I was looking for on Polk Street was not the father/son routine, but Gavin.

I had several hundred dollars saved up. I knew that I would give it all to Gavin if he needed it, if he wanted it, if I ever saw him again. But Gavin was in Hollywood and might never come back. When his money ran out he would obviously become a hooker on Sunset Boulevard or one of the other places that you heard about in movies. I walked up and down Polk Street. The bars, restaurants and cafes were packed with boisterous fun seekers. I looked in at Tramp's, the place where Trilla had once brought me in an effusion of maternal feeling and where she taught me some tricks of the trade. She was there, as big as life. She was laughing, drinking, joking with a whole crowd of enthusiasts, cross-dressers, gigolos and curious hangers-on. I stayed out of sight. I headed down the alley that ran off Polk just by the side of Tramp's. I had to piss. I certainly didn't want to go into the bar to use the restroom since I hadn't reported for work to Trilla for several days.

Down the alley. It was dark, but you could see that several trashy sex gigs were taking place in various area ways. I really had to go. I shouldn't have drunk an extra large beer at that Chinese restaurant near the train station, but it was so cheap! I turned to the wall and let go a stream that would someday join the Amazon and increase it to ultimate flood stage, when I became aware of a pile of clothes behind the large dented cans. It was a pile of clothes that was capable of moving! It even spoke, or rather mumbled. Ah. Just a drunk, I thought, which I might be one day if I didn't keep a watch on my intake, especially at home, where you always kept a good supply of whiskey and other stuff for the customers' convenience. (You didn't care too much if I helped myself to the supply, and even if I took quite a bit. I think this was your way of making it up to me for certain things.) Men, especially, are prone to heavy, hard stuff alcoholism, although some of the greatest boozers in world history have been women. Not to mention transsexuals, and I think I caucused with that group. (The psychological part of gender is crucial, like I explained to you, mom, out of that Dr. Spock psychology book.)

The pile of dirty old clothes lying behind the alley way trash cans moved again. It emitted groans. I can sympathize with poor people and I don't mind helping them when I can, but I'm no Mother Theresa. I think charity starts at home. Anyway, if you give a drunk some charity, he will just use it to buy more drinks and you're worse off than before. I looked closer. In the poor light of the alley it looked like some old guy who was finishing off a busted up life by drinking himself or herself to—I was going to say "death", but that's too harsh, don't you think? Like some old guy who was drinking herself into oblivion. I turned around and headed back to Polk. Then I heard it. A faint word, barely perceptible, ill-pronounced. It sounded like "Marsha".

I rushed back to the pile of old clothes. I bent over it, brought my face as close as I dared to its face. Not possible! But it was. It was Gavin, looking fifty years older and even worse for the wear! I nearly passed out cold from the shock.

"Gavin! What happened? They said you went to Hollywood!"

Gavin was in such a miserable state that he could only whisper, "bad trip, man."

"You mean, they kicked you out of Hollywood? What the hell did you do?"

"I never went anywhere. I took the money I got from selling off that statue you stole from Harv and I went on a drug binge. Wow!" Gavin rubbed his head, which was probably where the main pain was, but he smiled a little anyway. "I didn't think it was possible to do up that much dope in a few weeks. Must be a record." He started to groan again at the thought. He clutched his head with one hand and his stomach with the other. "I wish I'd never seen that fuckin' statue of yours! Why the hell didn't you steal something cheaper?"

"That was the smallest thing I could find. I needed something I could carry in my pocket."

"Yeah. I twig." Gavin smelled quite a bit. Probably he had stopped bathing at the start of his drug binge. It's fairly common. Drugs can alter your sense of smell.

"What are you going to do now?" I asked. "You can't stay next to all these garbage cans for the rest of your life." I still liked Gavin a lot, even after the crap he pulled on me. I even felt that I could never not like him a lot, whatever happened.

"I don't fuckin' know!" He grabbed his chest with both hands. He started a coughing spree. It must have been one of those upper respiratory things. Excessive drug use can provoke them, unfortunately.

"You have to come home with me." I gave this out firmly. There was no Plan B. "I'll get you well again. Then maybe you can move in with your mother. You can stay out of trouble that way."

"I don't know where my fucking mother is. I think she moved to some other country."

"Which one?"

"How the hell do I know?" He started coughing again. The coughing lasted several minutes, while I tried to pat him on the back in a petty attempt at nursing care. Then he spat a large gob of blood and mucus on the alley pavement. "Or fucking care!"

"You're really sick. I am taking you home. Me and mom will get you fixed up again as good as new." I looked at Gavin again. He was still good looking in a rough sort of way, although I doubted he would ever again be as handsome as before. But I was Mother Theresa, remember? Besides, he once said he liked me. Maybe that really meant something after all. Problem: he was in bad shape from a bad trip, more probably a bunch of bad trips in a row with a lot of booze thrown in for good measure. He couldn't stand or walk without help.

I helped Gavin up. He was really filthy. He had been incontinent for some time, judging by appearances. I strained to get him to his feet. He was heavier than someone with his graceful build appeared.

"Thanks, Marsh. You're really okay. I liked you from the start. You're pretty, too. And you look almost like a girl. I mean, in the face."

I had to cart Gavin to regional transport. We had to get to San Cerrito. The station was ten blocks away. I liked the cozy feeling, with Gav's arm around my neck, although I had to supply most of the muscle power to move us both. I think it was at that time that I started to get hernia symptoms. I bought two one-way tickets at the station. They weren't cheap. Three-fifty each for a ride to a dumpy town filled with bums and prostitutes.

"Thanks, man. It's neat for you to do this stuff. Best boyfriend—or even girlfriend–I ever had." We were on the train. It went into a tunnel and rumbled under the bay for what seemed like forever. What if the tunnel collapsed and we were drowned together? It seemed to me that might be great, a beautiful romantic ending. I now realized that all the time since Trilla told me Gavin had hit the road for Hollywood, and while I was starting a more professional career, I was thinking about Gavin, somewhere deep inside, because I knew that he was someone who counted for me.

From San Cerrito station it was still about a mile to our apartment, a heavy trek. Arm over shoulder, we went ahead. I think Gavin was asleep most of the time, but he talked anyway. He gave out short phrases like "oh baby, do it, do it." "Man, you got a cock like horse. Go, go!" We stopped at a pedestrian red light and Gavin suddenly woke up completely. He took a bottle out of his pocket and drank. It was sloe gin. He said it was the best stuff there was for getting off a bum trip. Best medicine in the world.

Then we were home. Pulling Gavin up the stairs to our apartment was the final ordeal. There was a hand rail and I could use it to hold Gavin up and drag both of us along. Inside, we toppled together onto the floor.

"Oh man, what a work out. I'll just sleep here." Gavin rolled over onto his side and seemed to lose consciousness again.

"You can't, Gav'. My mom will be home in a few hours. If she sees you blocking the doorway she'll get pissed as hell and kick you out."

"Oh. Then where the hell can I crash?"

"First, you'll have to take a bath. Mom would insist on that. Then I'll get you settled real nice in a large bed." I winked.

"Cool. 'Sreally great a you." Gavin finished the bottle of gin. "I feel better already."

I turned the water on in the tub, then I helped Gavin get out of his filthy rags. His body was slim and muscular, well-formed and graceful. But it was filthy in the most strategic places. He relaxed in the hot water. "This is way cool, dude. Maybe I'll just crash right here."

I started to soap Gavin's chest, then his arms and legs. He seemed to enjoy it. I certainly did.

His crotch was a main problem area. I could see that even under the soapy bath water. I began to run the bar of soap over his genitals, then to work up some suds.

"Stop it, pervert!"

"You're the one who buggered me in the alley behind Polk!"

"That was you?"

I could think of no adequate response to this. Anyway, it looked like Gavin was out of service at least temporarily, as far as his ability to produce an erection. His rear took some cleaning. His buttocks were nicely molded and they were hairless, unlike his athletic legs. I had to drain the bath water and refill the tub three times to complete the cleaning process. Adequately scrubbed, his face was as handsome as before.

He was drowsing in the warm water when I finished. "I'll get you to bed," I told him. "Can you try to stand up?" I didn't want to get any more strain. I could imagine the ugly scar a hernia operation might leave.

"Yeah. No problem." He fumbled about quite a bit, and finally I had to raise him with an arm around his chest. It was a nice experience, in that sense.

"It's just in the other room." Soon I had him sprawled out on your bed, in the large bedroom. He was lying on his back. His pubic hair was an attractive reddish blond color.

He lolled back comfortably. "Hey, can you get me a little drink? The gin's finished."

"Sure. Wine or vodka?"

"Um. How about both?"

I covered him with the blanket and headed to the kitchen. I poured a moderate but significant amount of vodka into a glass. I wasn't going to let him have the bottle. It was the last one we had in the apartment.

When I got back to the master bedroom, Gavin was asleep. His head was resting on a pillow and his mouth was hanging open. He was snoring. I downed the vodka. I needed a physical pain reliever. I had this tense feeling near the left side of my groin.

The thing now was to let Gavin recover. When he woke up I'd give him some soup or some toast, assuming we had any of the stuff. When you came home, mom, I planned to butter you up with some sort of nonsense to explain why Gavin was in your bed. It probably wouldn't work, but what else could I do?

I sipped from a glass of vodka as I sat in Uncle Robarb's old chair and watched television. I really would have preferred whiskey, like I drank with Trilla, but it was what we had, so what the hell? I usually watched television a lot, since there wasn't much else to do when I wasn't working for Trilla, or even before I started working for her. Only morons watched television. That was clear. I told myself that I was only laughing at the parts that weren't supposed to be funny.

I was asleep when you got home. I heard the turn of a key in the lock, then I saw you come in dressed in your full fur-coated glory. It was too late to head you off. You walked directly to the big bedroom, in your high heels, with that quick, directed gait you had. I finished my glass of vodka at a gulp. No sense letting it go to waste, whatever happened.

Then I heard the scream. Your scream. You came

rushing back to the TV room. "Who have you got in my bed? I have been working long hours and it has been more difficult than you could ever imagine. Then I come home to find a young deviate in my bedroom, in my own bed. This time you've gone too far, Marsha!"

"Um. It's. No … it's not what you think. It's …"

"I don't care what it is! Do you understand me? Get your pervert friend out of my bed and out of this apartment. Then change the sheets! This is disgusting!"

"But, see, mom, Gavin is really sick. I helped him all the way from San Francisco. I told him that my mom and me would help him get well again. He's an old friend."

"I don't give a shit!" You rarely used profanity. You said the customers didn't like it. This didn't fit the case. "You could have put him in your bed, in your bedroom."

"My bed's too small. There's hardly enough room for one and there's no window to let in fresh air. And he's sick, so I have to give him soup and stuff like a nurse."

"Little Miss Nursie. All right, do Florence Nightingale, but get him out of my bedroom now!" You strode back to the master bedroom.

Gavin was sitting up. The blanket was covering him from the waist down. You softened when you saw that he was a very attractive youth.

The arguing had woken him up. "Hi m'am. My name's Gavin."

"Well you'll have to leave. I don't let Marsha bring home just anyone he finds in the street."

Gavin coughed. He lay back on the pillow. He breathed roughly.

You looked at him, bent your head and took more of him in. Something clicked. "I'm sorry, Gavin, but it's impossible. I have to work long hours and it's necessary for me to rest in a large bed."

"Mom. Gavin can't even stand by himself!"

"I won't hurt anything m'am. I'll just stay on one side of the bed and just sleep."

You raised the blanket and had a full view of Gavin. A revelation. "At least you're clean. All right. But you'll have to leave as soon as you are physically able."

"Thank you, m'am. You're a real nice, beautiful lady. I hardly ever met anyone so good looking."

The problem was almost solved! I was overjoyed. You went to the bathroom to take your make-up off and to change your clothes.

"My mom's really nice most of the time, once you get to know her," I told Gavin. "I can make you some soup if you like."

Gavin thought about this. He wasn't hungry. "You got any more vodka?"

"It's all gone," I lied.

I went back to the kitchen and poured myself a glass of vodka that would have to be carefully hoarded. Then I took Robarb's place in the living room. I thought I could hear Gavin snoring.

You emerged from the bathroom wearing your bathrobe and slippers. You stopped in the living room. "Normally I wouldn't even consider anything like this, but I know that a friend of yours couldn't have any interest in women. And he's very young."

"Gavin'll only sleep. I'm sure he'll be a good patient. I'll give him some soup when he wakes up."

"I may need some of it myself." You went to the bedroom.

SON OF A WHORE

Later, it must have been around one in the afternoon, since you usually came home around three in the morning after working all through the night and then slept for about ten hours, I heard some moaning that seemed to come from the bedroom. It wasn't coming from the television in the living room, where I had fallen asleep last night. The screen was showing some sort of used car commercial. You know, the kind where a man in a suit bangs the car on the hood and says, "take 'er away". I was certain that Gavin must be suffering and that he was expressing his pain, possibly while still asleep. I tip-toed to the bedroom, since I didn't want to wake you, mom, while you were still sleeping (you know how you could get), and peeked inside. There I saw something that not even the professional training that I received from Trilla had prepared me for. You and Gavin were entwined in an amatory embrace and you were both trembling in the last phase of passion! I couldn't believe what I was seeing. Gavin was my boyfriend, after all. And you were supposed to act like my mother. Imagine the negative role model education that I was receiving! But I couldn't just barge into the bedroom and break up your amours, illicit as they were. That would have demonstrated jealousy and lack of filial feeling. I rushed to the kitchen, opened a can of soup, then set it on the stove top, with the burner turned up high. I had to hurry if I wanted to break in on the bedroom scene while there was still something left. When the soup was boiling, still in the can, (since we had no clean pots to cook in), I managed with the help of some old newspaper pages to tip the contents into a passably clean bowl and rush it to the bedroom.

"Here we are," I announced. "Nice fresh nourishing soup!"

Gavin was now leaning against the bolster, his naked chest displayed wide. Beyond any doubt, he was a good looking guy, much better looking than I was. At least, as a guy. "Ah, thanks Marsh." Gavin took the bowl from my hands. The main event was obviously already over. You were resting with the blanket pulled up to your chin, mom. Your eyes were closed, although you had to be awake.

He sipped from the bowl. "Damn! It's fuckin' hot! Don't you got no spoons or anything?"

"I couldn't find any. I think one of the customers probably took all that stuff for a souvenir."

Soon Gavin was drinking directly from the bowl, at first in tiny sips. "'Snot bad. You make it yourself?"

"From scratch," I boasted.

You gave me a knowing smirk. "He's lying. It came from a can."

Mom, you just had to ruin my attempt to demonstrate maternal care and capacity!

"It's real good, anyway." Gavin drank the soup in full swallows now, then reached the bowl in your direction. "You want any of this stuff, Rusalka?" Grandma gave you that name. She was from Romania or someplace like that, remember, mom?

"No thank you. I'll sleep for another half an hour now." I could see that you were naked, because your shoulders, which now stuck up in their thin and graceful form above the edge of the blanket, showed it. What had happened to your beautiful silk nightgown?

You turned on your side and pulled the blanket over

you. Gavin belched and gave the empty bowl back to me. "Thanks, man. You're really great. I don't know anyone who would have done stuff like this for me." I was fully prepared to believe it. Gavin's friends were not, in general, the maternal type. And, as far as I know, they didn't park boyfriends in their mothers' beds.

I went back to the living room. I collapsed into the armchair and drank from a glass of vodka that wasn't even there. I couldn't believe it! My own mom fucking my own queer boyfriend! I was blown away. I felt really totally pissed, too, but I couldn't say or do anything in front of you. I'd probably get slapped for it. That's what usually happened. No whining and no complaining! You taught me that early on.

I started to cry alone in front of the TV. Now they were selling washing machines. We could have used one. I began to drink my second imaginary drink. This time I had changed out for whiskey. It was almost half an hour before I managed to get myself together enough emotionally to go to the kitchen and pour a real drink. Gavin, so well formed …

Later, after you left for work, I fell asleep again in front of the TV. I could have gone to my bedroom. This was actually a medium sized closet where there was a mattress on the floor. Our apartment was really only a one-bedroom unit. But, emotionally, I refused to withdraw, to signal in this way my isolation and defeat in the struggle for love.

Back in the bedroom, Gavin slept for the rest of the day. I don't know about the following night.

You were the first one up the day after. You had to be

at Bombo's Club by three o'clock p.m. That was opening time. While you were busy in the bathroom I went to check on Gavin. He was asleep. The blankets had been thrown off the bed and he was lying on his stomach. His nicely muscled shoulders and hairless buttocks were the main points of interest; his legs were athletic and furry, and his abdomen flat and smaller in circumference than his chest.

I gave Gavin a push. "How about some toast? It's morning. You must feel a lot better." I tried to cover up my jealous feelings. That seemed the best tactic at the moment.

"Ah, hi." Gavin turned his head to see who was talking. He turned over suddenly onto his back. I could see that his penis, understandably, was smeared with a dry stain. "Yeah, sure. Thanks, man. I feel sorta hungry."

"I'll cook you something as soon as mom leaves. I can't get in her way while she's getting ready to go to work. She'd cut my nuts off." Not that it would make that much difference. I mean, they're not really necessary for the transsexual thing.

"Mom's still here?" Gavin folded the top sheet in quarters and wrapped it around his waist. He hit out for the living room.

You were coming out of the bathroom. You were fully dressed. "Hello, Gavin." You kissed him on the cheek. He returned one to your chest. Then you turned to me. "Marsha, why can't you keep the bathroom clean? I have to work very hard to pay the rent for this apartment and to buy food for the two of us. It is your job at least to keep the place neat. You don't do anything else. You refuse to work or to go to school."

That stuff again. I'd heard it a million times. I didn't answer. I could have said, "I whore my ass around." But anything I said would have been held against me. I half-turned my head to Gavin and winked, as if to say, "You see how she gets?"

Gavin looked from one of us to the other. He scratched his naked chest. "Rusalka? How come you call your son Marsha?"

You exhaled your breath in noticeable exasperation. "Because since he was very young he has tried to look and to act like a girl. I've even caught him using my make-up." Fortunately you didn't say anything about the panties.

Gavin looked at me. It wasn't a look of disapproval, only curiosity. "Why don't you buy your own make-up, Marsh? It's cheap. I know you're makin' money."

I *was* buying my own cosmetics, but I didn't want to admit it while you were standing there accusing me, accurately, of practically being a transsexual. A lot of people don't approve of that sort of thing.

"I have to leave for the club, now." You turned and took a few steps toward the kitchen. "I suppose you haven't made any coffee, Marcus."

"Um, no. I don't know if there's any left."

"Did you look?"

"I was looking for more soup. Gavin likes soup."

You pointed a long, well shaped finger at me. "I want you to start doing things to help around this place or you are going to be out on your own!" You looked at Gavin. "Try to get some more rest, Gavin. I don't think you're fully recovered from your illness. I'll try to be home early tonight."

You were out the door.

"Wow," Gavin gawked. "Your mom was pissed as hell at you on account of all that stuff."

"She always does it." I started to cry. "She hates me. She's always criticizing everything I do!" A flood of tears turned my face into a wet, red battleground of emotions. What I was really upset about, though, was that Gavin seemed to take your part on everything.

Gavin patted me on the back. "Oh man, don't take it too hard. If you knew my old lady, you'd know how lucky you are. She tried to cut my fuckin' balls off once. I ain't kiddin'."

The shock of this admission shut off my crying jag. "Why did she do that?" Now I was curious.

"Well, as far as I can make out, it was because I sort of reminded her of my father, and that's bad enough. That and the fact that I lifted a bunch of money and some drugs out of her purse. And I was putting the make on one of her customers."

"Oh." The anecdote was becoming more comprehensible. "Well, I don't think my mother would ever go that far."

"See? You got it pretty good. So stop crying. And you know what? You're a lot better screw than your old lady."

I didn't believe this. I knew he was just saying it to make me feel better. When Gavin did it to me in the alley behind Polk, it was just an ordinary run, probably the kind of thing he did all the time to release the pressure on his huge libido. With you, mom, I could tell it had been four stars. Still, I was happy that Gavin was at least trying to please me. That meant something. And after all, I had dragged him, filthy as he was, out of an alley and practically carried him all the way to Cerrito, so I think he appreciated it. Gavin, so handsome and sexy.

"Hey, where'd you go with my clothes?" Gavin looked around the living room.

"They were so messed up I had to throw them away. They would have clogged up the washing machine. You can borrow some of mine."

Gavin wasn't sure about this. "Show me what you got. I don't want no purple pushers."

We went back to the bedroom. I opened a drawer of the large dresser. Your clothes, mom, and mine were mixed together in the drawer. "Hey, half this stuff is girls' clothes. I'm not gonna wear anything like that."

"Some of my mom's clothes got put in the same drawer as mine. It was an accident." This was not exactly true. I often borrowed your underwear, and some of your pants and blouses, so they got put back in "my" drawer. We wore the same size.

"Oh. Okay man. I'll try to find something." He was standing naked in front of the dresser. I had my eyes on the areas of interest. Gavin picked out some jockey shorts, a t-shirt, a pair of jeans and a light jacket. "This ought to do." He started to get dressed. These were clothes that you bought me, mom, to try to head off the trans thing.

"What are you doing? You can't get dressed. You have to stay in bed and rest. Mom just said so."

"Naw, I'm okay. Your mom's real nice, but I gotta get back to Polk. I gotta check on some deals."

I saw my chance for sexual and romantic fulfillment vanishing in the direction of Polk Street. "You can't be well yet. I had to carry you all the way here just yesterday. You couldn't even walk."

"Aw, I just overdosed a little. I'm over it now. That stuff happens."

"Wait. I'll make you some more soup. How about 'vegetable potato'? That's my favorite flavor. Just try it."

"No, man. I'm in a hurry. Thanks for everything."

"At least wait till my mom gets back home. She likes you." These phrases were the sign of my desperation. "She likes you more than she likes me." The way I saw it, this wasn't really saying much.

"I got it on a little last night with your old lady, but that happens all the time. It didn't mean anything special." Gavin put his arm around my shoulder and gave me a hug. I almost melted. "And I'm sure your mom loves you. Why else would she let you stay here with her paying all the rent and shit?" Then he gave me another good look-over. He wasn't too impressed. Probably he didn't really go for transsexual guys that much. It happens a lot. He put his legs through the shorts. It was when he pulled the jockey shorts full up that I was most impressed. He was porno star quality. Immediately I did something that Trilla had taught me to do with the better customers. I dropped to my knees in front of him, pulled his shorts back down, and started to suck him.

"Stop it, man. I'm not in the mood."

I kept on. He relaxed. He began to emit little sounds of intense satisfaction. "Ah. Oh. All right. Ah. Oh."

He started moving. He pushed his thing into and out of my mouth. "Oh baby. Oh." In a few minutes my mouth was filled with a sticky, salty substance. That was okay. I was used to it. I even liked it.

Gavin pulled away. He patted me on my head, since I was still on my knees in front of him. "Not bad. You're as good as your old lady." He sat on the bed. "Like mother, like daughter." We both laughed. He put his arm around my shoulders and kissed me. I dissolved into happiness.

After a few minutes, Gavin began to collect the borrowed jeans and t-shirt that had fallen to the floor just before our romantic incident. Suddenly he had doubts. "Hey wait. Rusalka didn't teach you how to do it, did she? I don't think that's right."

"No. I've been hanging around Polk Street for a long time. Trilla taught me most of the tricks."

"That fuckin' fat whore? I wouldn't screw her with a lamp pole."

"I didn't. I mean, she didn't. She just gave me some pointers, orally." I realized at once that this was the wrong word.

"I wouldn't hang around with that bitch. She's not pimping for you, is she? She tried that out on me."

"No. Absolutely not. My mom would kill me if I started working for a pimp. She said you lose half your money that way." Two lies.

Gavin put his shorts back on. He was starting to pull the jeans up from his feet.

"Don't leave now, Gav'. Rusalka will be really pissed if she gets home and finds out I let you leave when you weren't completely well yet. Besides, when she gets back late at night, she usually has a lot of tips from her customers. She could lend you some cash so you wouldn't be on the street without a dime." I called you Rusalka sometimes, mom. I picked it up from the customers.

"That's okay. I know a bunch of guys where I can move in for a few days." He was dressed. He walked toward the apartment door.

"I thought you would stay and we could get to know

each other real good," I whined. "And now mom's gonna take everything out on me. She likes you."

"I gotta get back. I told you, man. I got deals." He was at the door. I grabbed hold of his (my) jacket.

"If you stay, I know you'll be happier here. You could sleep in my mom's bed again."

Gavin didn't seem to notice the tears that were overflowing my eyelids. "Thanks, but so long."

He was gone. A jacket button had dropped to the landing floor. I stood in shock. I wanted to run after him. I would have run after him, but it was clear it wouldn't have mattered. There was one thing, though. He forgot that he didn't even have train fare back to the city. After a few minutes there was a knock at the door. I opened it and silently handed Gavin a five dollar bill. He was gone.

I sat down in front of the TV. I felt like Juliet would have felt if Romeo had landed her a big kick in the ass right at the start of Act One. Something was playing on the screen. People were talking. They were happy. Probably talking made them happy. It took more than that for me. Mom, you always taught me that boyfriends end and you shouldn't put too much feeling into it (them). This time I had, even though I tried to sublimate it into, like, cooking school. (You can see that later I learned to talk more educated, more like you did, since you went to college, and not in that slang dialect that you used to say was the only way I could talk. I read a lot of books later. I had time for it, in jail.)

I retrieved the vodka bottle from the kitchen. I felt a lump in my throat when I saw an unopened soup can, meant for Gavin, set next to the sink.

There wasn't a whole lot of vodka left. I watched the screen and drank for as long as it lasted. Fifty-five minutes? Gavin was gone, and it seemed like the end, but he had to come back some time, didn't he? It stood to reason that he would probably need help again sooner or later.

I wiped away the last of my tears and decided that there was work to be done, after all. I hadn't reported to work with Trilla for a long time. She was not going to be happy. First, I had to dress for the job. I went to your bedroom and opened the drawer where my stuff and yours were mixed together. I chose a pair of panties (the bulge around the crotch would be acceptably small), a yellow sleeveless undershirt and a pair of flowery trousers that tapered downwards and ended above my ankles. I couldn't kick the pedal pusher habit. Then I went to the bathroom and helped myself to your cosmetics, a lot better than the cheap stuff I bought, although I knew you'd notice it and all hell would break out when I got back from Polk. I smeared a lot of moisturizing cream on my face, smoothed it in, then put on some basic, and finally some cover make-up in the strategic places. I looked at myself in the full length mirror that hung on the bathroom door. Wow! Did I look like a pansy! This was exactly the effect that Trilla advised me to try for. It brought in a certain type of customer.

When I walked into Tramp's on Polk Street, she was there, as she almost always was. "Well look who finally show up. Where you been, Marsha? Been using your cash up on drugs?"

"Uh-uh. I had to stay home to take care of my mother. She almost developed into pneumonia."

Trilla broke into one of her long, deep horse laughs. "Ha! Ha ha ha! That's a good one. I don't know nobody dumb enough to use that one for a long time. Anyway, you feel like doin' a little work now?"

"Yes. I have to pay the doctor bills for mom."

Trilla laughed again. "You know, that's kinda real sweet, although I know it's a lie."

I sat down at the table next to her. "It was a lie. The truth is that Gavin came to stay with us for a few days in our apartment. I found him overdosed in the alley behind here and I practically carried him home to Cerrito. Then, when he was supposed to be recovering, he screwed my mom. Then he refused to screw me." Not entirely accurate.

"Now that sounds just like honest gospel. That's just the sort of crap Gavin gonna pull on you. Done it a million times to everybody. Why don't you leave that no-good freeloader alone? Oh, I know. You think he's real cute. That's the only thing he got going for him. Otherwise he's a complete asshole."

We had whiskies now. That's the way Trilla always started the assignments. It relaxed you and put you in a friendly mood for the customers. "And you got make-up on, don't you? You look just like Bambi all over again. Hold on." Trilla stood up and went to the passage to the rest rooms, where there was a pay phone on the wall. She put a quarter in the slot and dialed. She spoke for what seemed twenty minutes. Nervous, I drank all of my whiskey and a large part of hers while I was waiting for her conversation to end. Then she was back.

"Okay, my little man. We got a date on for you tonight." She gave me an address. "Collect a hundred from the customer. Tell him if he don't pay he gonna have trouble with his head."

Fortunately, I was able to play the passive role with the guys Trilla sent me to see, like I mentioned previous (?). I don't think I could have done anything else with them (too plain). Anyway, it was what I preferred. It gave me that very feminine feeling that I liked. It made me feel like I was a girl.

It was about one a.m. when I finally limped back to Tramp's. Trilla was sitting alone at a table. The usual crowd had left early. I eased myself into the chair opposite. She picked up immediately on the expression of pain on my face. There wasn't much Trilla didn't notice.

"What happened? He didn't rough you up, did he? Come on, you can tell everything to your momma."

Whiskies were served. Trilla always ordered triples, unless it was quadruples. That was her habit. I can understand it, with the tiny amount they put into a single shot. "No, it wasn't that. It's …"

"Yeah, honey, come on, you can tell. Spell it out. Nobody gonna hurt you here."

It wasn't embarrassing for me to say it. I was just trying to find the right words. "It's, well, he had a really big cock. I mean, it must've been two feet long and three inches thick." I rubbed myself behind, where it was really sore. There had been some bleeding. "He didn't do anything to try to hurt me, but it was just because of that huge dick."

"That happens. Well, the fucker oughta have told me, I would have sent two of you to see him." Trilla looked at me. She did an ocular diagnosis of my general condition. "Um."

I slipped a hand under my pants in back. There was still some blood.

"Come on, honey, I'll fix you up." She grabbed my hand and led me to the ladies' room. "In here. Don't be shy, it's where you belong anyway." Soon she had my pants and shorts down. She turned me around and examined the affected area with an experienced eye. "Um. Yeah. He give it to you, all right. Uh. That guy musta had to really push to make it go in."

I was sniffling and whimpering. I was well aware that I would receive only thirty for the whole miserable exercise, plus the twenty dollar tip the customer already gave me.

"I know just what to do. Stay here. If somebody else come in, she'll think you just normal in here." She meant the ladies' room.

Trilla was gone for almost ten minutes. I looked at myself in the mirror. My make-up was oily and grey looking. Usually you can't leave it on for more than five or six hours or you get that cheap whore look. Anyway, the pain from the stressful forcing made me look like a poor candidate for a hundred dollar gig. There was a Kotex dispensing machine on the wall. I wondered if those things would help in my current condition. I had used them before. Then she was back.

"This gonna fix you up so you can get back to work in no time." Trilla had a tube of some sort of cream in her hand. It had an applicator that she introduced into my butt. She squeezed the tube and a cool, relieving substance filled me up.

"Ah."

"Better, huh? You oughta be back to work in a few

days at most." She handed me the tube. "Just give yourself a dose every four or five hours. Maybe your momma could help you out with it."

"No. I better not tell her. She doesn't approve of that kind of thing."

"What kind of thing?" Trilla's voice had an edge of indignation.

"I don't know. She just gets mad when you talk about certain things."

"Okay. Use the medicine in front of a mirror. It gonna work real fast."

After the bar closed it was too late for the last train, so I had to wait around the transport station until the first morning train to San Cerrito left at 5.30 a.m. Even though I was pretty exhausted by that time, I stood up during most of the return trip to get relief for my rear end from the bumps and jiggling as the cars went over rough track. The whole time, as we went into the bay tunnel and came out again on the Oakland side, I worried. I was afraid that I might never again be able to experience that very feminine sensation I got when guys did it to me. I might never get it from Gavin again! Also, I might never work again. Sure I could do a plain oral gig, but that paid much less.

Mom, you wouldn't believe how glad I was when I finally got home—it was around seven a.m.—and found that you had restocked our liquor supply! You always said that the customers liked a "little" drink now and again. And you didn't mind if I helped myself more than a little. I guess this was some sort of compensation you were doing for me because of, well, the whole thing.

SON OF A WHORE

I eased myself very carefully into the armchair. Soon I would have to give myself a reapplication of that marvelous ointment that Trilla had supplied me with. I had a glass of vodka in one hand. I used the remote control to turn the volume very low, because some sort of discussion program was going on. Heads were wagging and twisting. I could not understand what they were talking about, but it was comforting just to listen: normal life.

I assumed that you were in the bedroom sleeping and I did everything possible not to awaken you. I knew how you could get. After several sips from my glass, I became curious. Were you alone or not? I got up and tiptoed to the master bedroom. The door was partly ajar. I peeped in. You were there, sleeping soundly and healthily. There was some other dude next to you. This one was a heavy kind of guy too, not my type at all.

Back in front of the TV I watched the heads. I was more than halfway down on my second (third?) glass of vodka. Now it seemed to me that you had a much easier time of it, as far as "the profession", than I did. They treated you nice, just like a lady. No one tried to bust your ass with a giant dick. But then, after all, I was a boy, so I ought to be tougher. Or was I a boy? Since I could remember I always thought of myself as sort of a girl, at the same time not really understanding what the difference was anyway, in a psychological sense. I guess it all depends on definitions.

I fell asleep in the chair. It must have been hours later when I was woken up by the booming voice and heavy footsteps of the large man I had seen in the bedroom. I twigged immediately to the situation. Customer leaving, sale closing. I smiled at him. I was wearing twelve hour old makeup and fancy dress.

"Hey! Who's the dumb little twerp in the chair? He ain't some kind of street pervert, is he?"

You laughed. Once again you had to explain. "That's my son, Marsha. He's not in perfect mental health. He's confused on sexual subjects and it makes him dress up that way. His father was something of a brute and it made him turn out unsure of his sexual identify."

Big Boy gave me a close look. "That right? Yeah, he looks kinda like he wouldn't know what gym class to go to." He laughed in his enormous voice. NDLR: at this period of history there were separate high school gym classes for the *two* sexes.

"Just ignore him. He's really harmless." I thought it best not to add anything. This was about the most favorable description you ever gave of me.

I pretended to have fallen back asleep. My fingers clutched the nearly empty vodka glass in a comfort seeking reflex.

After a few days I was feeling much better. I had used up all of the tube of medical ointment that Trilla had given me. To apply the stuff, I had to face away from the bathroom mirror and drop my pants. Then I turned my head around to try to aim the applicator to the right place. Usually this method worked. At the same time, I could see why the customers that Trilla sent me to became sexually excited to the point where they cared only about getting to the target. My buttocks looked smooth and creamy in the mirror reflection, with a nice gentle roundness to them.

I was almost back to normal. Meanwhile, you started complaining about the amount of time I was spending in front of the television, although you admitted that I had scrubbed the kitchen sink and run the vacuum cleaner over the living room rug.

It was time to get back and check out the scene on Polk. One afternoon after you had already left for Bombo's Club, where the nude floor show had just been rearranged to be "even more thrilling and extravagant than ever", according to the new hand bills you brought home, I left for Polk Street.

I just looked around the street. I wasn't going to drop in at Tramp's, not yet. I thought I could use maybe another half tube of ointment before I was ready for that. I passed a café and looked inside. I saw this old creep at a table who looked like Harv's twin brother. He looked angry as he peered into a cup of coffee. Probably he was still pissed about his Greek and Roman statue. I walked by fast. Some of these guys could get real violent over a few thousand dollars, especially when they couldn't call the police about it, since the whole thing involved prostitution.

Judging from the reactions of people I passed on the sidewalk, I guessed that I had probably put on too much make-up once again. Their faces registered first confusion, then revulsion. But, after all, they were mainly straights, not at all the same breed of cat. I stopped to look at my reflection in the glass window of a shop. I could see the same generally good features as always, nose, mouth, eyes, all harmoniously arranged, even if not up to Hollywood standards. There was an added, almost unnatural paleness, though. In my rush to get out of the apartment, I had just slapped it on. This is always the wrong method. I was using my hands to smooth out the excessive cosmetic and rub some of it off when I heard the voice.

"Marsha!" I turned, a bit scared, shocked at being recognized, maybe by some former customer. It was Gavin! He gave me a hug. He almost crushed me in his affectionate excitement. I was going to add, "like a bunch of flowers", but it wasn't really like that at all. "Where the hell you been up to? I thought for sure I'd see you around here before now."

I was glad I was under Gavin's control again. I say under his control because I knew that I would do anything that he told me to do. He was back! Everything didn't matter. I forgot about the miserable way he left, the depressed period I went through after his walkout. I didn't even think about the money that you later discovered he took from your purse, mom. Probably you'd never bring it up either (it was forty dollars or so, not bad, but a lot less than what you made in a single night. You never kept more than forty in your purse. You said with the customers you never knew what they'd try.) I was so overjoyed to find Gavin again that I didn't even wonder about finding him sober and *not* lying in an alley. It was Gavin! His handsome features were more rugged than I remembered, but this made him look even more sexy. He was the person I wanted to belong to. "I had to take care of my mother for a few days. She had a bad experience." I used this lie a lot. It seemed sort of believable.

"Bummer." Gavin didn't ask questions. He could be discreet. "Man, you look great." He looked at me, hugged me again, gave me a kiss on the cheek. "But, say, you're not using a little too much of that Lady Whoever-it-is make-up, are you? Your mom said something about that."

"This time, yes, maybe I overdid it. It was all the worry about my mom's condition. I got distracted. Do I look really bad?" I looked again at the shop window, at my reflection. It did seem sort of strange.

"No, man. You look really pretty. Almost like you were really a girl, with that one main exception."

I laughed. Gavin was not only fantastic in the looks department, he was smart, too. (Wait. I think I'll say "also" here instead of "too", just for the variety.)

"But, see, I was just thinking about you and your old lady. C'mon. Let's get us a cup of coffee and I'll tell you about it." He took my arm and directed me toward the nearest café. It happened to be the one where Harv's duplicate sat brooding.

"Not here!" I stage whispered. "That's Harv in there. You know, the one with the little statue. I think he's still in the grudge stage."

Gavin looked at the seated figure. "Damn. You're right. He always was a prick. Let's beat it. I mean, let's go." I laughed again at the pun. "There's no short supply on cafes around here."

Finally we were both sitting around a table with cups of coffee in front of us. This was La Crunchola, a snack shop very popular with the transsexual crowd. Nobody here would care if a customer had overdosed on Lady Something's complexion enhancer. Gavin sat stirring his coffee with a spoon while he seemed to collect his thoughts. He hadn't shaved in a few days. It was attractive, but I suspected it meant some sort of experience. He picked up on this suspicion right away.

"I was in jail for a few days," he said, serious and sad. "A deal went bad and I got busted. I didn't have anything on me at the time, so they won't file charges. Damn lucky I had a fake id with me at the time that was a pretty close fit. Otherwise, I'd be in the joint for the next seven Christmases." Gavin drank from the cup. A twisted look on his mouth showed that he was dissatisfied with the taste, like it brought back something of the prison savor. Probably he would have preferred to have it sweetened with vodka, but I hadn't brought the bottle with me.

"While I was there, in the shit house, I had time to do some thinking. I thought a lot about you and your mom. In a way she's my mom, too," Gavin smiled at the thought and the memory. "She really treated me like I was her own son."

She never treated me like that, I thought. Fortunately, because otherwise it would have been incest. But I knew that Gavin was not talking about that part of his stay with us. He had been impressed by our overall warm loving protective family environment.

"You and Rusalka are real nice people, see. That's what I finally decided when I was passing all this stuff through my head when I was in there. Only you got yourself into a kind of bad situation. What I mean is, with both of you on the make. There's nothing really wrong with it, but it always turns out bad in the end for one reason or another. For the whore. What the customers get, I think they fuckin' deserve it."

I nodded. I knew that this was true. I always thought, mom, that you and me were just in it till something better turned up, and that eventually we'd get out of the game, only it seemed to string out with no end in sight.

"And I'm not preaching at you, hell no! You know I sold my ass more times than you could shake a dick at."

I laughed again. Gavin was a great comedian as well as a terrific human person. I drank some coffee. I always put three or four sugars in my coffee. It gave me a pretty good high.

Gavin bent over the table in my direction. His tone became confidential. "I came to the idea that you and Rusalka need me to help you if you're ever going to get back on the straight and narrow. I can help you get your lives together." He sat back. He smiled. Gavin was so sexy and so convincing. He was like a cross between a porn star and a psycho-therapist. I know you were generally impressed by him too, mom.

"Okay." I was buying, even if I wasn't sure exactly what the product was.

"Your mom works for that nude floor show, right? That's where she meets those guys?"

"No. They have nude shows at Bombo's, but she works in the gift shop. That's where she meets them."

"Okay. My project is going to be to get both of you away from that stuff. Otherwise you'll just end up a couple of wrecks. I've seen it a million time. My mom, for instance."

I nodded. He had told me about his mother. She seemed like Castrasta in the ancient Greek play.

"You don't go into the whore trade because of the money you can make," Gavin explained. "It never comes out to all that much anyway, after you subtract the drugs and the medical expenses. You go into it because you're insecure. Because you got all these emotional problems. I figured all that out. You and Rusalka need someone who can keep you from thinking you gotta sell your ass all the time to feel good about yourself. That's gotta be me."

I nodded. I was very happy with the idea so far. At least it looked like Gavin would be coming home with me.

"Yeah, so that's the plan. The thing is you're both real nice people, but you're both insecure as hell, too. That's why you do it. What I'm going to do is help you feel automatically that you're worth it, so you don't have to whore it around anymore."

Now I understood. I was one hundred percent in agreement. I knew Gavin would save us. He was a guy who was emotionally strong and he loved both of us. He had made love to both of us, you and me, mom, but also he liked us a lot. He felt responsible for us. "Okay."

"See, I learned a lot of psychological stuff when I was in the Juvenile Facility. They had me talk to this therapist lady twice a week and she taught me a lot about myself and about other people. I know I can help you." Gavin smiled to himself. "The psych really liked me. Once, in her office, she made me sit in her chair at the desk while she got under the desk and sucked me off! It was way cool, dude."

Again, I nodded. "Maybe I should tell Trilla that I won't be working for her anymore."

"Hell! Don't tell that bitch nothing. She'll only try to make trouble for you if you pull out. I mean, figuratively speaking."

Gavin was probably right on that account. Trilla was very nice to me at the start, but before long I got the idea that she was in it mainly for the cash. She and her partners got the biggest part of the take while I took it in the ass.

"Okay?" Gavin had laid out the program. "How's that sound to you? It's not going to be easy. It's gonna take time and hard work. In the end, though, I think the three of us are going to make it. We're going to pull out of the shit and live like real people, like decent human beings."

Tears were flooding my eyes. I could hardly speak because of the love I felt for Gavin and the gratitude I felt for his plan to help us, to drag us into the world of ordinary, real people. "Yeah," I finally managed to say in a weak, high voice. "You're right. If only you could do it, if you could help us, we'd love you more than you can imagine."

Gavin considered this. Probably he could imagine it. "Let's get going. You got train fare, right? The deputies stole every cent I had when I was in the slammer." I knew this could happen. It was a specialty of the Juvenile Hall screws, where I had been a lot of times.

Then a sort of second thought came into my head. "Yes. But see, the only problem is, I don't know how my mom is going to take the idea of you helping her get out of the business and all, at least at first, before she understands the whole plan. She likes you a lot, but she's real proud. She's very beautiful and men have always loved her. She likes being admired that way. And she's got a lot of education from when she went to college for a couple of years, so she might not like being saved by someone …" I was going to say, "younger than her son", but I left that off.

"I know what you mean." Gavin took it in right away. "Okay. What we gotta do is spring it on her slow. When we get to your place we'll say that I'm going to be, like, your tutor. I'm going to teach you all the stuff you never learned in high school, so you can take the high school equivalent test and get a regular job, or maybe get to be a doctor or something. We'll say I gotta move in with you because it's going to be a long haul, seeing how you only went to high school for three days."

"Four days," I corrected. "I went to King High for four days. I couldn't stand those bastard lousy teachers always bossing me around. And the other kids called me names. They're the ones who started calling me Marsha." It actually had been Revisionista. "Well, I guess they'd never seen a fourteen year old boy in full make-up before. I won't even tell you what happened in P.E. after they found out I wasn't wearing jockey shorts like everybody else."

"I can imagine it. Anyway, let's try to get this tutor thing to work. You said before that your mom wanted the best for you, like maybe to see you get to be a doctor or a lawyer, so she ought to be hot about the plan."

"She once wanted me go to psychotherapy. That was the big first step, according to her, so I'd be more normal. I wouldn't go, though. I always managed to miss the appointments. It seemed like being back in school again, where they led you by the nose all the time."

"Ha ha! That's good. Yeah, that about explains that sort of thing. I've had a lot of it."

We agreed that we'd tell you Gavin was going to be my tutor and he was going to take me up at least to high school graduation level so I could take the test. In fact, I soon learned that Gavin hadn't gone to high school, not even for four days like I did. He never went to school at all! He could barely read and he couldn't write. He was good at physical therapy, though.

You got home about two o'clock the next morning. Early shift. Gavin and me were watching television. We had finished the whiskey off a few hours earlier. Gavin could really put it away, although he wasn't actually seventeen years old yet. He never seemed to get drunk. We kissed a few times and he admired my lace underwear. I told him they were yours. I sat on the floor with my head leaning against his thigh as he sat back in the armchair. We were watching some sort of police adventure flick on the screen.

"Hello Gavin," you said right away when you came in, and with almost no expression in your voice. You went immediately to the bathroom, to clean off your make-up and change your clothes. Gavin and me went right into action. I pulled my trousers back up and carried the whiskey empties to the kitchen. (Vodka was our family heritage, but Gavin liked whiskey. That's why we made the big switch). He sat in front of the TV, but not really watching. He was waiting for his cue.

You came out of bathroom looking tired and serious.

"Hi mom." I caught you in the hallway on the way to the bedroom. Gavin was still in the living room, waiting for the right moment. "I have to talk to you about something really important."

"I don't have time for your nonsense right now, Marsha. I had a bad experience at work. I'm going right to bed. Tell your friend he's welcome here tonight but he'll have to leave tomorrow."

"Um, that's what I wanted to talk about, mom. You see, Gavin got kicked out of his apartment in the city by a bunch of dope dealing crooks. He can't go back because they'd try to kill him. I just wondered if he could stay with us for a few nights. He could share my bedroom."

"No. Absolutely not. You know I have guests all

the time. They'd be turned off if they saw a couple of overgrown high school boys who did nothing but drink and watch TV." And bugger each other. I could tell you were thinking that but you didn't say it.

"That's just what it's about. Gavin has a plan to change all of us to a regular life style. He wants to get us both out of that paid boyfriend business. He told me all about it. He knows a whole lot about therapy and he's sure he can help us turn into a normal family, like on TV." I didn't intend to put in the whole explanation yet, but it seemed the right step at the moment.

"Absolutely fucking not! I'm doing what I have to do in order to survive after your lousy fucking two-bit father left me! Tell him he has to go. I let him stay before, but this is going too far." You went into the bedroom. After two minutes the light went off in your room.

"She says no," I told Gavin. I was devastated. Hope had gone down the toilet.

"Don't worry about that a bit." Gavin was standing up. He was adjusting his crotch. "I can bring her around. I did it when I was here before, right? I could always do it with my mom, until she went off to Bolivia. Or was it Italy? Anyway, I know it's going to work."

"I think you better sleep in my room for now. That way mom won't flip out in the morning if she sees you in the living room."

Gavin had seen my "bedroom": a mattress on the floor in a medium size closet. Inside, there was a bare light bulb hanging from the ceiling. The mattress had quite a few stains and lumps after years of nocturnal activity, even though puberty had come late, if you'll excuse the expression.

"No. It's your bedroom, man. I couldn't take it from you. I'll crash here in the living room. Just get me a blanket. I'll be all right. Your mom won't get up till past noon, probably, and then she'll be in a better mood and I can talk to her."

"I'd love to share my bedroom. I feel real lonely sleeping alone," I suggested with a thrill of happiness.

"Uh. No, man. Your old lady'd think we were fucking around or something. That's not the way to start. I got it all planned. Don't worry."

I felt emotionally robbed, but I knew I couldn't argue with Gavin. He was in command. I went back to my bedroom, to the closet. I said a few prayers for Gavin, like grandma taught me to do in case of need. Reaching upward with a thin but graceful arm, I pulled the string for the ceiling bulb.

I fell asleep after a few minutes. This is hardly a surprise. Gavin had drunk most of the whiskey, but the part I put away would make your average wino dizzy. At about six o'clock in the morning (daylight was starting to come in from the hallway, since I always kept the closet door open to avoid claustrophobia) I got up to piss a half quart of former whiskey. I was crossing the living room on my way to the bathroom when I heard these strange but familiar sounds from your bedroom. There was a lot of "oh baby" and "I love you, Rusalka", plus a good deal of heavy breathing. Of course I knew right away what was going on. I even regretted that Gavin had come up with the idea of "therapy/tutoring". It wasn't turning out like I thought. You were getting the main part of the therapy. And Gavin was supposed to be my boyfriend, wasn't he?

You liked Gavin because he was so handsome, but I'm sure you didn't love him like I did.

I knew that I should ignore the bedroom scene that was going full blast. Couldn't Gavin love both of us? In any case, I had seen that stuff before. Still, there was a sort of jealous curiosity that drove me to be a witness. I walked slowly and quietly to the bedroom door and peeked in. What I saw I have to tell you I will never forget. I had seen quite a few things, even at eighteen, and I had been in business myself, but I never imagined that two people could take physical positions like *that* during sex! Really, mom. We weren't puritans, obviously, but weren't there *some* limits?

I went to the bathroom, then back to my closet. I pulled the blanket over my head. I thought I could still hear myself crying when I dozed off.

When I woke up it was well into the afternoon, as I could tell from the little travel alarm clock that you gave me one Christmas and that I still kept in a corner of my room. I stumbled out into the living room. Gavin was sitting in the armchair. He was watching some sort of comedy show on the screen. He was laughing. You had obviously already left for work at the club, otherwise there'd be like water running in the bathroom or a lot of ruckus going on in the kitchen.

"Hey! Morning, Marsh! Don't worry about a thing, like I said. I got it all fixed up with your mom."

I had noticed. Glum, I went to the kitchen. I was looking for a can of soup. I was good at heating up soup and I wanted to show that to Gavin, even though for now I felt I hated his guts. The traitor.

I brought back a hot bowl of soup. "Drink this."

"Wow, thanks man." Gavin took the bowl. He is a person who can drink a full bowl of soup without a spoon and not spill even a drop on his chin. He put the empty bowl on the floor. "Okay man. I know you're pissed because I got it on with your old lady. But that was the only fucking way, don't you see? Rusalka is a really great lady, and you fuckin' lucked out to get her for a mom. You said you didn't believe it, but she really loves you. She loves you more than you can believe. She told me. She's had a hell of a hard time with life, though. That makes her suspicious about people and she doesn't like to show she cares about them, even though she really does."

I sat on the floor. I did not rest my head against Gavin's thigh. "You never fucked me like that," I said quietly and sadly.

"No, man! You're a guy. It'd be physically impossible. Don't you see that? That doesn't mean I don't love you and that I wouldn't like to bugger your ass till the cows come home."

I started to cry. I did that a lot. I'm still not sure whether it was the transsexual thing working on me or whether it was because I knew it was a good way to manipulate some people.

Gavin had my pants down in two seconds. He put me in a position on all fours. Then he was inside me, moving back and forth. Without a doubt, he seemed to enjoy it at least as much as I did, judging by the moans of pleasure. He could really do it, an athlete, an expert, and a long runner. It took him about ten minutes to shoot at the target. Then he fell back against the armchair. "Ahhh."

My doubts were relieved. And penetration hadn't hurt

a bit, despite the fact that I wasn't completely recovered from my experience with the last customer Trilla had sent me to.

After a few minutes Gavin was focusing again on the TV. "Marsh, sweetheart, here's the deal. I gave it my best try, hinting about stopping the prostitution gig for both of you, but all I could work out with your mom is I'm going to be your tutor. I'm going to get you ready to take that high school test thing. You missed the whole shitload of classes, but I'm going to clue you in on biology, algebra, history, physics and the rest of the crap. Your mom's totally on board for it. She thinks it's the greatest thing since sex hit the streets. And that's because she loves you."

"Great!" Things were going much better than I imagined last night when I saw *that*. Gavin was going to be my very own personal tutor! "How *are* we going to work on her about the therapy angle, though? The way you said you could get her out of the whore business too."

"That's gonna be a lot harder, sort of a long term effort. Anyway, so far, so good. She even gave me some cash to pay for your first lessons." Gavin dragged two twenties out of his pants pocket. "By the way, how about going down to the liquor store and getting us something to celebrate with?"

The man at the liquor store knew that I was underage, but he also knew I belonged to Rusalka and he usually sold me a bottle when I showed up with a note from you. Sometimes they were forgeries. I came back to the apartment with several bottles, a large bag of the tortado chips Gavin ordered, and six cans of soup. It was amazing how domestic you could get in a short time.

Gavin opened the whiskey bottle first. All that sex made him thirsty.

He took a big pull. "Stuff's great!" he said before he started coughing. He had choked on the extra-large swallow. "Don't you got no glasses, though? Half of it went down the wrong fucking way!" He coughed a couple dozen more times.

I brought a glass from the kitchen. It was one of those engraved crystal drinking glasses that a customer gave you, with the name *Bombo's Club* on it. One of the guys you met at the Club. Gavin poured only half a glass. "This is still morning, sort of." It was about four-thirty p.m. "I gotta go at it slow or I'll be totally plowed by the time your old lady comes home."

We watched television. Daytime TV has a bad reputation for entertainment quality, but it's not entirely deserved. I drank out of a smaller glass, one with a little stem. I thought it was sort of more elegant. We laughed at some programs and went through traumatic empathy with others. I marveled at the way Gavin could put it away without showing the slightest sign of intoxication. He once told me that his mother and father had both been big drinkers. It was a family tradition, like with us. There was something genetic going on there probably.

It was starting to get dark out. Before too long I'd have to warm up some more soup. "I guess we better get started soon on the tutoring business," I told Gavin. I looked around the room. "We don't have any books, though." There was nothing, not a dictionary, not a Bible. "I suppose I could go down to the library and borrow some. I'd have to take out a library card, but I think it's free."

"Yeah. Great. Good idea. We'll do the first lesson like tomorrow." Gavin swallowed a moderate dose of whiskey. "Just don't forget the tutoring's mainly a cover, so I can stay here with you. If I go back to S.F., they got a million police warrants out on me for all kinds of shit, most of it fake. But what I'm really going to do is give you and Rusalka some deep therapy."

"Yeah. I think I'm already getting the benefit of it. But we'd all be a million times happier if you could get her to stop bringing those ape-like bozos home." By an association of ideas, I rubbed my rear end, which was starting to hurt a bit now, but not too bad. Gavin was not like Trilla's Mr. Horse Cock, but he was pretty well endowed. That was another of his good points, if you'll excuse the expression.

"Hey, don't get me wrong, man. I think education is okay. I don't see why I couldn't give you a hand up on that end, too. We'll get a bunch of books together and have a whack at 'em. That way Rusalka won't get suspicious before the therapy stuff starts working on her."

"Okay, great." I was impressed by the way Gavin had everything figured out in advance. He really was a genius. That was another reason I loved him. It wasn't entirely the physical business. Also, I think Gavin's way of not worrying too much about things and just taking them as they came reminded me a little of my father, whoever he was.

It was inevitable. Gavin moved into your bedroom. He shared the big bed with you. I accepted this without much whining and complaining, especially since he was alone with me for most of the day and all of the evening.

Anyway, his libido, like his prick, was big enough for two. And there wasn't anything that I could do about his move into your room. It was the logic of the thing. Gavin had convinced me that it had to be that way in order to bring you around to the therapy goal—getting both of us out of prostitution. He had to establish a really close relationship with you. That's how the psycho-thing works. The shrinks call it "transference". Now he started calling you "mom" when I was the only other person there.

Gavin and me worked up a routine. You usually left for work at Bombo's Club just before 3 p.m., then you came back to the apartment a few hours after midnight. During this time Gavin was supposed to be giving me lessons so I could take the high school test and get a job where I could use my brain, not my ass. That's the way Gavin put it and he was right.

I went to the San Cerrito Public Library and I brought back four books. That's all they let you check out at one time. I tried to get a selection of different types, not all just geography, for instance. Back at the apartment, I showed the books to Gavin.

He was going at it slow that afternoon, just sipping a bit from his whiskey glass occasionally, mainly out of boredom. He took up one of the books (they were all worn and old and covered with dirty plastic covers). He turned it around a few times in his hands, then read out loud slowly, phonetically from the cover. "Meet a Horseman." He shuffled through a few pages. "What the hell is this? I ain't no cowboy Bob, dude."

I took the book and looked closely at it. I read the back cover. "It's just some kind of story where a boy meets a girl. It's a romance novel." I had grabbed the books without looking them over a lot. I'd never really been into books all that much.

"'A boy meets a girl'. That's out for you, Marsha. You wouldn't have any practical need for it."

I couldn't answer this. If I read a story like that I'd probably think of myself as the girl, or maybe as the boy and the girl. It would have been confusing.

Gavin opened another book. "A History of the Trans-Danubian Ukraine." He read it out a syllable at a time. "I guess we could run with this one. What the hell is a 'Trans-Danubian Ukraine'? Not that I suppose it matters."

"Must be some place in South America, maybe just east of Mexico."

"Sounds about right. Okay, we'll start on that one." He didn't even look at the other books. One was called, "Know Your Arithmetic" and another was, "The Human Body for Beginners". Gavin wasn't exactly a beginner on that line, so he'd probably be able to teach me a lot even without the book.

Gavin slumped back in the armchair. He exhaled in relief from the effort of study. Then he swallowed a huge draught from his engraved crystal glass. "This being a professor stuff is a hard row of shit. Why don't we do the first lesson tomorrow? Meanwhile I'll check out the books and see what kind of angle they're taking."

Soon it was time to think about dinner. I offered to heat up more soup for Gavin.

"Naw, man. I'm getting kinda tired of that stuff. Don't you have nothin' else?"

"I'll go look in the kitchen." I went to the kitchen and searched through the cupboards and drawers. I brought back what I found: three bottles of liquor, a bottle of hot sauce, a plastic sack containing some very stale bread, and a raw vegetable of some sort, maybe a rutabaga. "This is all there was, except for the soup."

"Yuck. Can't you go down to the avenue and bring me back a hamburger or something?" He handed me a five dollar bill. "Get some fries, too, and maybe like a milkshake."

"What flavor?"

Gavin considered this question for at least five minutes. "Strawberry, I guess."

I was back from San Pablo Avenue in half an hour. I had Gavin's hamburger, fries and strawberry milkshake in a paper bag. I had bought a fishburger for myself and gulped it on the return trip. If I got hungry later I could warm up the rutabaga, or whatever it was.

Gavin was asleep in front of the TV when I came in. I shook him awake. "I got your food." I handed him the paper bag.

"Hey, thanks man. This being a teacher stuff really takes a lot out of you. I could eat a hog." He took the burger out of the bag and started to eat. With his mouth stuffed, he said, "you know, man, you make a damn good fucking housewife."

I was very pleased with this evaluation. "Thank you. Remember, I can always heat up some soup if you get hungry later, and maybe make some rutabaga salad or something like that."

He made what sounded like an affirmative noise but it was muffled by his full mouth.

You came home from the Club early that night. It was hardly past two a.m. when you walked in and found Gavin and me watching the television. We both had drinks.

It must have been Gavin's fifteenth for the day and my eighth. Our zippers were open. Gavin was playing with both of us. You expressed your exasperation by a word that sounded like "ughh!" and went into the kitchen. I guessed the problem right away. Besides the "decency" angle, you could hardly bring customers here with two "overgrown teenagers" crowding up the apartment and doing amateur queer porno tryouts in the living room. It only added to your disgust to see perversion up close. Gavin twigged just as fast. He sprung into action. "Zip it up, man!" He ran into the kitchen. He must have been hugging you and trying to kiss you, to judge from the sounds I could make out. I went as near to the kitchen door as I dared and tried to eavesdrop. First I heard your voice.

"It's revolting, but you two can abuse yourselves as much as you want, for all I care. It's not my business. Just don't make a mess on my expensive rug!"

"What it is, Rusalka, honey," I heard Gavin's voice say, "we're a family, you, me and Marsha. So we all love each other. Maybe we could even go to church once in awhile. Nothing else matters."

Grandma had taken me to a Catholic church when I was little and I knew there were lots of them, but I didn't know where any of them were.

Gavin went on explaining in an effort to distract your attention from the little scene. "The big problem is that poor boy of yours, Marsha, is sort of confused. It's not his fault, it must be something his old man did or didn't do, some psychological deal, but he's not sure if he's a boy or a girl."

"He's sure," you answered. "He knows he's a girl, at least as far as his personality. He's said it a million times."

I heard Gavin laugh. "You're right. What I was thinking, though, is that confusion he's got is making him sell his ass around Polk Street. He even got mixed up with this lady pimp called Trilla and she sent him to some bad customers. He's still really sore in the butt. He can hardly sit down for long. That's why I have to watch him real close."

"There is nothing more that I can do to control Marcus. You don't know what a problem I've had with him over the years. He started wearing girls' underclothes when he was eight years old. I had to watch him every minute or he'd leave for elementary school with lipstick on."

"I know. But, see, Marsha really loves you as his mom. He thinks everything of you. He told me. Only he's afraid that no one loves him, because of his bastard old man. That's causing all his insecurity and making him act that way. I mean, selling his ass on Polk Street and going drag whenever he can. It's not the money. He's reaching out for human contact. So that's what I was doing in the living room when you walked in, I was trying to angle him toward something else."

I listened to this and I thought that there was something to it, but that wasn't all of it.

Gavin went on. "And that's why I got together a plan to get him out of that shitty stuff. We have to make him feel loved and accepted, like my mom did for me."

"You make him feel loved. I'll work on the acceptance." You said this in a definite tone, mom. I think you interpreted the word "love" in a physical sense. That was always a big problem.

"It's a deal!" Gavin shouted.

"I'll try to increase his self-confidence," you said.

Gavin had convinced you. He had a gift for interrelations. "Maybe I could do something with his hair. And I'll even raise his allowance so he'll have more spending money without having to engage in those repulsive escapades you mentioned."

"I'm sure that'll help, Rusalka, honey. Only, like I said, I don't think he does it for the money."

You and Gavin came out of the kitchen. You hugged me around the shoulders. "I don't see how you could ever get the idea that I'm not extremely fond of you, Marsha. Haven't I always done everything possible to take good care of you, in spite of everything?"

I thought about this. The only answer I could give without asking for a long lecture was "yes".

Gavin smiled and nodded. "This is going real good. It's like one of those TV shows, 'The Hour of Truth', or something like that, where couples finally get to like each other after they've been fighting like shit for donkey's years."

I went to the kitchen and brought back a glass of whiskey for you, mom.

"Thank you, Marsha. You can be really sweet."

By the way, mom, I have to say that I admire the fact that you didn't drink a lot, not compared to me and Gavin, anyway. That's on your plus side.

The next day, Gavin felt an urge to go to the city. He had some business affairs to settle, he said, and he couldn't put it off or get out of it.

"Don't get involved dealing drugs or go on some trip again, or stay away overnight," I warned him. "You shouldn't go at all, anyway. Mom and me don't have the money to go bail for you if they catch you on one of those warrants." I was worried that I might have to scrape him off an alley floor, like the first time. Worse, I might never see him again, if he overdosed too much.

"I'm not going for that. Don't worry about that shit. This is something else. Some guys owe me money and I gotta get it so I can contribute to our little family here."

I straightened Gavin's t-shirt, smoothing the fabric over his chest so that his muscles were well outlined. "Okay. Don't do it like last time, though. Come back as soon as you can. They're showing an old war movie on TV late this afternoon, *Dive Deep* or something like that about submarines."

"I'll be back before mom gets home." He kissed me before heading out. "We have to take good care of her to get her away from that hustler shit."

Gavin got back just after midnight. He looked tired but happy. "Fuck! What a trip! I met up with some friends and we really partied, dude."

"Mom's gonna be home soon," I cautioned. I was mad at Gavin. It was fine that he had a good time, but naturally I was jealous about what he might have been up to. Wasn't he supposed to be *my* boyfriend? I was afraid he'd been trawling the bars in SF. I already had one rival for his affection in you, mom. "Don't let her know you spent the day pissing around San Francisco with a lot of dopers and drunks."

"Got ya." Gavin went to the kitchen and returned with a full glass of whiskey. He drank a third of it before he sat down in the living room armchair. "I'll be real mellow when she gets here. Therapy, that's what she needs." He slunk back in the chair. "Man, I'm fucking wearing myself out being a head doctor for both of you. Anyway, I don't mind if it helps you get out of the shit."

You weren't happy when you got home, mom. Tips were getting slim, since Gavin asked you to lay off the extra-activities with the business guys. I could tell this was the case because the only groceries we had left were two quarts of liquor, two cans of soup, and a loaf of "Genuine Mexican Sourdough Bread".

We all went to bed early. I had been drinking more than usual because of worrying about Gavin's trip out. Three times I made myself up totally using your cosmetics, mom. I was always dissatisfied with the result when I looked in the mirror. I washed the last attempt off just before Gavin got back.

Probably it was the drink, but I fell asleep as soon as I lay down on my mattress. I think Gavin was feeling the same experience because I could hear his snoring from the big bedroom before I turned my light out. About four o'clock I got up to use the bathroom. I was crossing the living room, dressed only in panties, when I heard it. A crude scream came from the master bedroom. "You've got shit on your dick!"

Gavin came galloping in the nude across the living room. He looked at me as I stood wondering at it all in my panties. "Gotta take a shower, man!"

Clean and dried off, Gavin went back to the big bedroom. Soon after that sounds of hitting and shoving reached me as I stood at the door to my bedroom-closet. Probably Gavin was taking some hits from you, mom. It sounded like all the times I got it, only a lot worse. I lay down on the mattress. At this point I felt unable to influence events any further. Things were getting too raunchy.

A few minute later Gavin crawled into the closet and stretched out beside me. He was whimpering. "Damn your old lady, man. She's one hell of a strong son of a bitch!"

Shortly after, Gavin made a good faith effort to bugger me, but he couldn't manage it—too tired out. He had to make me suck it, which took less effort on his part. It tasted like … shit.

We both slept late the next day, not daring to get up until we were sure that you had left for work. Then I went to the kitchen to heat up some soup for Gavin. There is nothing like good nourishing food when you've been kicked out of bed and beat up by your adoptive mom.

We ate in the living room, Gavin typically occupying the armchair. After he had finished, he put the bowl down on the rug. He looked calmer, but sadder. He sat thinking about things for quite a while.

"You see," Gavin finally said, "this is the thing. You and me are queers, man, and everybody looks down on us and hates us for it. Even if some of us like women too. They still got it in for us. It's like total discrimination, man." He had put some clothes on over his black and blue body.

I'm not a queer, I thought. I'm a girl who looks kind of like a guy, at least in the waist area.

"I don't really blame mom for getting pissed off at me last night, even if she got carried away with it. I guess I shoulda remembered about washing off what she got so pissed about."

"She'll get over it. I can't even tell you some of the stuff I pulled that really got her goat. She got over all of that."

"Like what?" Gavin was curious.

"I can't tell you. It's way too embarrassing."

Gavin considered this and seemed to understand. He had a sense of discretion. "Yeah. Okay."

I was pleased that Gavin was so sympathetic to my sub-standard past. I decided to treat him to one anecdote. "Here's just one thing that happened. I was on San Pablo one night and I met this guy, just a few years older than me, and we went back to the apartment. I don't know why, but I asked him to spank me. We were in the living room and I was lying nude across his lap getting my butt whipped when mom came in the front door with a customer. She was so mad she took over where that guy left off and I couldn't sit down for a week!"

"Wow! You're kinda kinky." He seemed to make a mental note of this.

Since I couldn't find any spoons, I was using a fork to eat my soup, scrapping it down the sides of the bowl into my mouth. Gavin watched me with a look of surprise. "Just tilt the bowl and it'll run down," he advised.

We spent the rest of the afternoon watching television. Gavin fell asleep right in the middle of one of our favorite soap operas. I could understand. He had had a really hard night of it. Mom, you never gave me a whacking that was quite that bad and I pulled some crazy shit that I didn't even want to tell Gavin about. Like the time three years before when I came back from the charity clothing store dressed in a mini-skirt and a flowery blouse with the shirt tails tied in front that left my graceful abdomen nude.

You gave me a double smack across the face. Then you pulled my skirt up and gave me a super serious paddling. (I think you had twigged that that sort of thing got my attention.) "Never dress like that in front of me again!" I started crying and shrieking in a high voice. It wasn't the slaps against my face, and my ass, although they were pretty hard, and it wasn't the humiliation of being treated that way at my age, already fifteen. I thought it meant you didn't like me!

Gavin woke up after a good thirty minute snooze. "Hey Marsh. Could you go and get me a bit of whiskey? I'm still fucked up in the head after all that crap last night with mom."

I brought a beaker of whiskey back from the kitchen and handed it to Gavin. "Ummph." He took a good swallow out of the glass. "S'great! Sometimes you just need the right medicine."

Three loud commercials came on the screen in a row. Gavin was mellow enough now to offer a considered judgment of recent events. "But what the hell does mom expect? I mean, she knew I was your boyfriend, so that meant that I had to do you up brown sometimes, and maybe some other guys too. So that kind of thing was bound to happen. Guys are guys."

I nodded. "Don't worry about it too much. She doesn't think too clearly about a lot of stuff when she gets pissed off. She used to tell me sometimes when she was mad at me that she ought to have had me castrated by a doctor when I was younger. That way I wouldn't want to do dirty things with other guys. I didn't dare, but I wanted to tell her that, yes I would. In my case it wouldn't have made much difference."

Gavin laughed. He had a good sense of humor. And he understood everything almost by instinct.

The rest of the day and all of the evening we just took it easy. That's what we seemed to do best. I made sure Gavin went slow on the liquor. I limited him to about ten glasses. I had about six. Just after about one a.m. I ran the bathwater for Gavin. Even after only ten drinks he probably wouldn't have thought of it himself. He had to be super clean before you got home. We couldn't risk a repeat of last night's disaster. And if things went okay tonight, we'd be back on an even keel.

I soaped him all over. Wow! Mom, you wouldn't believe the great body he had. Yes you would. You had seen it as often as I had. He was slender but muscular. You could see the outline of every muscle, as if he was an anatomy model.

I started stroking his soapy and fully erect dick. He stopped me after a few minutes. "Not now. I got to save it for the big event, or everything will be fucked." Of course he meant for you.

Gavin went to your bedroom and lay down on the big bed. He covered himself with the sheet. "Wish me luck," he said, laughing.

You came home at about two-thirty a.m. I was watching TV. I had a very small drink in my hand. I wanted to show you that I wasn't overdoing it. I was taking it easy, behaving myself. To show I'd never be a real lush.

You looked around the room. "Where's your friend?" You were not happy.

"Gavin went to bed early tonight. He wasn't feeling well. He stepped off a curb the wrong way on Polk Street this afternoon and fell. He hurt his leg but he's too much of a man to complain or go to a doctor about it." I think I used this one before, but you didn't seem to notice.

"I hope he's in your bedroom, because I'm not going to tolerate any more of his revolting antics."

"Mom, there's not enough room in my little closet for him to stretch his leg out and get the rest he needs." In fact, there was at least seven feet lengthwise, but I knew you weren't going to get out a tape measure to check it out.

"Is that so?" You went to the bathroom to start the nightly ceremony of removing your make-up and putting on your night creams.

I continued to watch TV. They were showing some sort of antique movie again. I think it took place in Casablanca or somewhere, but I wasn't really paying attention. I was too nervous about what would happen. Gavin had promised to help us both get out of the miserable lifestyle that we were living, selling ourselves just like we were prostitutes, but he had to stay in our apartment, and particularly in your bedroom, in order to have a chance to do it. He was going to give us therapy, if you let him.

You left the bathroom, then went into the kitchen. Soon you came back to the living room. "Take it easy on the liquor, Marsha. It's bad enough having a confirmed pansy for a son; I don't want an alcoholic one too."

"I will, mom. I mean, I won't." I was too nervous to think clearly. Naturally I didn't tell you that most of it had gone down Gavin's throat.

You went to the big bedroom. I shut the TV down and beat a retreat to my closet. I turned the light off and tried to listen. What I heard sounded like this:

"Gavin, this is really absurd. I don't mind the fact that my son has homosexual friends. He is a homosexual, or something very close to it. But I think you'll understand that it is out of the question for you to sleep in my bed! I won't put up with any more of it and I don't care if you are sick."

I guess it was pretty bizarre for a transsexual's lover to sleep naked with his mom. I mean, most people wouldn't believe that it had actually already happened a lot of times before.

You shouted something. It sounded like, "police … underage delinquent", or something like that. Then I heard Gavin say, "honey, I love you. I love you. You're so beautiful." Then I heard nothing more. Soon I fell asleep. Operation therapy AOK.

"Mom gave me twenty dollars for your tutoring." Gavin was bringing me up to date on events after you left for work around mid-afternoon. "It was a lot less than last time, so I explained that we had to spend some money on books. She threw in another ten, sort of like a tip."

"Good. Now we won't have to use up her liquor supply so much. We can buy our own. She's been bitching about it."

The day and the evening passed in the usual way. I can't say it's in our favor, but Gavin and me were really getting off on TV. I guess it helped that we were putting it away at a pretty good rate. We were sort of celebrating.

Just after midnight we were still glued to the entertainment machine. I notice that Gavin was getting horny. He kept rubbing his crotch and looking away from the screen. Suddenly he said, "take your pants off, dude. I gotta do it!"

Gavin hadn't noticed that I wasn't wearing any pants. I had taken them off an hour ago to attract his attention. He was already on drink thirteen for the day, and large ones at that, so maybe that explains it. Usually a drink is a one ounce shot of liquor plain or over ice or mixed with water. I poured Gavin a full beaker of the pure stuff every time. That's what he liked.

Then he was lying on top of me while I was spread face down on the floor. I like it that way better than any of the other positions. I enjoyed having him inside me while I faced the floor and just felt it. In feelings, in emotions, I was totally passive and feminine.

Things go wrong, even when you think they're all fixed up. Anyone who has followed this story so far is well acquainted with this fact. So how the hell was I, much less crashed-out Gavin, supposed to know that you would walk into the apartment just after midnight, just when me and Gavin were doing the Liz and Dick routine? That was like the middle of the afternoon for you.

You threw your purse—an expensive one, too, it cost maybe five hundred dollars cash—at Gavin's head, then you fled to your bedroom. I could hear you raging and crying from where I lay on the living room floor. It had happened before, with just the zippers, but that was nothing compared to *this*.

We stopped our terrific erotic activity. Gavin pulled out, ejaculating at the same time on my bare buttocks. It was coitus interruptus. He looked at me with a confusion born of drink and post-intercourse disorientation.

"What the hell can we do now?" Gavin whispered

like a yell. "Mom looked like she was super-pissed! That's gonna fuck everything up."

I picked up your purse. I had admired it from the first day you brought it home from the department store. I tried it on my shoulder. I looked inside for loose cash or drugs. "You have to tell her you're really sorry, Gav'. Tell her it was only because you were under the influence. That would be a lesser offense."

"Sorry? What the hell for?"

"For fucking me when she thinks you should be fucking her."

Gavin rubbed his chin. He was letting his beard grow, mainly because it took too much effort to shave every day. It looked really handsome and sexy. "Oh yeah. That's right. It was just normal stuff, but women can get jealous. I remember some things with my mom. Why the hell did she have to come home so damn early anyway?"

"I don't know. Maybe they had a fire at Bombo's."

"I'll go talk to her …" Gavin's face translated fear and shame. He pulled his pants on. "I know she won't believe me. She won't forgive me. Not right away, anyway."

There was a good probability that Gavin's analysis was right. But it could turn out the other way, too. "She could forgive you now. Once she forgave me for flashing my ass at a man she brought home from the gift shop. She got in a good mood because he was a big tipper."

For a moment, Gavin's face registered jealousy. "You oughta leave her boyfriends alone."

"I know. He only gave me a kick, anyway. Mom got a real good laugh out of it."

"Get me a drink," Gavin ordered. "I'm way too confused to think about anything right now."

SON OF A WHORE

When he had the beaker in his hands, he quaffed deep. "Okay," he said. "I'll give it a try, even if mom tries to cut my fucking balls off. With you it wouldn't make any difference, but that's another subject." When he had finished his large glass of whiskey—it took him about four and a half minutes—Gavin got shakily to his feet. "Wish me luck, dude, I'm going into the dragon."

"Tell her you got desperate for sex because she wasn't there, and you had too much to drink, so you took a try on me. I look a lot like her, according to some people."

"Yeah. I'll try that." Gavin waited, trying to think. "You got the ambulance number, just in case?"

"Yeah. It's 911. I learned it from a stepfather I once had."

"Okay." He was gone. I saw his athletic form disappear into the large bedroom. I turned the TV off. There was like a huge silence going on without the screen, like you were living near the ocean and listening to the waves all your life and suddenly you went inland.

Then I heard it, at high decibel level. "Get out of my room! You nasty pansy! You're worse than Marsha!" Then there were the sounds of heavy things being thrown, of buffetings and kicks and shoves. It wasn't working out for Gavin.

"Rusalka, honey. It's only you I love. I was desperate with you not there so I had to try to get off on Marsha, that's all." Then something shattered. It must have been the Chinatown vase that you kept on the table next to your bed. The one with beautiful blue pictures of ancient wise philosophers and lovely ladies and warriors in chariots.

Gavin came out running. "Shit! Your old lady's pissered than hell! What an arm! She oughta play for

103

the White Socks or something." Gavin wasn't really into baseball. I watched it sometimes on TV, but just to look at the men.

We both fled to my bedroom. Gavin threw his pants off and lay down on the mattress. "Get me another drink, dude," he said in a voice of desperation. I was about to exit to the kitchen when I noticed that he had fallen asleep. No surprise, all that booze and *another* big time brawl.

The next afternoon you looked into my closet before you left for work. You were fully dressed and made-up. Gavin was still asleep. Fortunately, he wasn't on top of me this time. He had been so worn out from the night before that he hadn't even tried to do it again. But he had thrown off the blanket. He always slept naked. There was a small pool of half-dried viscous fluid on his abdomen near where his penis was resting. Probably he had self-abused during the night, maybe unconsciously. You didn't pick up on this, or maybe you thought it was just normal.

"I'm bringing a friend home tonight, so tell your little buddy there that he'll have to sleep in your room again, if he's still here. And you can tell him he's not welcome much longer."

You were gone. I shook Gavin awake. It was three p.m. My little travel clock showed the time on its luminescent dial. "Gav', wake up! Mom's still pissed as hell."

Gavin shot up to a crouching position. His body was so attractive in this pose, with his flat abdomen and well defined but not massive chest muscles, and his large genitals dangling heroically between his legs. I thought that maybe I was prettier in a girl-like way, but Gavin had such a fantastic body and he was so handsome. He mumbled, still only half awake. "Baby, Rusalka, wait. I got real love for you, like nothing I ever felt before …" Then he noticed that you weren't there. He stood up and peeked out of the closet. "Where the hell is she?"

"She just left."

"Um. This is one bad trip, dude." Still naked, he walked out of the closet and went to the living room. He sat down in the armchair and turned the set on with the automatic control box. He put one leg over an arm of the chair. His large member and testicles dangled against his other thigh. "Hey, can't you get us some of that soup? I don't feel too great after last night. The therapy gig isn't working too good with your old lady. I guess I'll have to try another plan."

"She said she's bringing someone home tonight. That's what she does, you know. It's only professional, though." I knew you had to do it, mom. You only made the minimum at the gift shop. They expected you to make it up with tips.

I went into the kitchen. Minutes later I came back with the soup. I was getting to be quite the good little homemaker, I thought, happy for an instant even in the midst of the general ruin.

Gavin drank quite neatly from the bowl, as always. His mother had taught him some good manners. He was not in a good mood though. "I don't like mom calling me a pansy," he said. "I'm not a pansy like you." He saw that I was hurt by this formulation, even though I knew that it was true. "Don't get me wrong, Marsh. I love you and I think you're pretty like a girl and there's nothing wrong with that. I like getting it on with you. I like pretty guys. What grabs my ass is her calling me a pansy when I like took her to the moon three or four times."

"She was jealous, because she saw you getting it on with me. When she gets jealous she gets pissed. I've seen it about a million times."

"Yeah. They're all gonna do that. I got it on with Trilla a couple of times. That pimp woman who used to manage you. And the one time I got out of line she practically knocked me out of the ballpark. I mean with her fucking fist. I had to go to the Polk Street Clinic and they put a bandage on my face. I couldn't work for two weeks."

"Wow! I knew she was strong."

"She's okay with you, because she knows you couldn't do anything with her anyway, and she can't see why she should run a dildo up your ass."

I laughed. This was all true, as far as it went. "I'll go fix up mom's room. It's my job to make her bed and clean up when she's bringing someone home. Only usually I don't do it. That's one reason she's mad at me all the time."

I went into your bedroom. I pulled the sheets—I couldn't see any stains–smooth, tucked them under the mattress and put the blankets and the pillows in place. I covered it all with the flowery bedspread you bought at Macy's, eighty-seven dollars cash. When I came back to the living room I heard Gavin's voice shout from the kitchen. "Where the fucking hell did you hide the whiskey, dude?"

We watched TV for the rest of the afternoon and on into the evening. Gavin was getting bored. Even I was getting bored. He didn't feel like getting it on. Our problem home life was draining his libido.

Then, before I knew it, midnight was getting close. I went to the kitchen and warmed up some more soup. I knew we had to be out of the way before you came back with the customer. I handed Gavin his bowl. I wanted to give him some extra nutrition to fortify him for what I was sure would be a disagreeable experience.

"Oh, man. Same old shit every time. I'm not hungry." He drank the soup anyway.

"Don't eat it if you don't like it. You can blame the soup company. I only warmed it up."

Gavin had put his clothes on several hours earlier. He did have a certain sense of modesty.

When it was getting late, I announced the inevitable. "We'll have to move into my bedroom."

"Okay. I'm probably gonna be movin' out of this dump pretty soon anyway."

When we were in the closet I handed Gavin a glass beaker and a bottle of whiskey. He rejected the beaker. "Naw. I don't need that." He drank deep, directly from the bottle. Soon he started to sing. "Ninety-nine bottles of beer on the wall/ Ninety-nine bottles of beer …"

We were both drowsing or meditating when we heard you come in. It sounded like there were two of you. A deeper voice talked most of the time and you laughed.

Suddenly Gavin sat up on the mattress. He listened. He was upset. I propped myself up on an elbow. "We might as well relax and try to sleep. This goes on all the time. Mom only stopped bringing these guys home for a while when you moved into the bedroom." I twigged right away that this was the wrong thing to say. Gavin went red.

"I know! I had a plan to get both you suckers out of the ass trade, but you blew it! How much fucking therapy can one guy give? Didn't I show both of you how much I loved you?"

We heard more laughter from the bedroom, then the sound of two heavy objects tumbling onto a creaky mattress.

"She got jealous when she saw you buggering me in the living room. She wanted it to be with her instead. That's why she did it. I mean bring the customer home."

"Why'd she want me to bugger her?"

"She wouldn't. I'll explain it a different way. She felt like I was, you know, another woman making it with you."

"Makes sense." Gavin nodded. "You are another woman."

There was little I could say in response. He had it sort of right. Maybe not completely. Then we heard giggling, oohing and ahhing and moans of contentment.

"What the fuck! Don't your old lady have no sense of decency? Doin' that shit when her own son's in the next room?"

"It's her job. It doesn't mean anything personal. Relax, Gavin. We can work on her with more therapy tomorrow." I handed him the bottle of whiskey.

Gavin took a hard slug of drink. "Fuck it. I gotta do something now."

He stood up. He was completely naked. Again, I saw the graceful lines of his body and his well developed muscles. They were even more attractive than I remembered. He charged out of the closet.

I stopped at the closet door. I didn't dare follow, not even to see what happened. I knew how you could get, mom. I had to respect your space. The fact that you brought home some heavy lout just seemed normal to me. Anyway, I'd been living with it about a million times since Robarb left and even before.

Now there were battle sounds from the bedroom. I could hear shouts, banging, fighting.

Gavin's voice. "You get the fuck out of here, you fat old slob! This is a decent, respectable home and this here is my mother-in-law!"

Voice of fat old slob. "What the hell is going on, Rusalka? Who the fuck is this nude boy?"

Slaps, hits, kicks. Probably. I heard your voice say "Gavin!" What else could you say? I mean, you could hardly say, "don't interfere with my trick". You were a respectable person.

"Get the fuck out, you slob!" Gavin.

"You nude little turd!" Slob.

Hits, slaps, kicks, falling, hits, slaps, kicks.

Then I heard a two hundred and fifty pound sack of cement tromp across the living room. I peeked around the corner of the hallway just in time to see the last of a guy with a head the size of a coconut and a stomach the size of a cow. He slammed the apartment door. From outside the apartment came something that sounded like "lousy thieving hooker!"

You and Gavin came out of the bedroom. You were wearing the silk bathrobe (you always kept your basic sense of decency). Gavin had taken several hits in the face, but he didn't seem to be in bad shape. He was still naked. You put your head on his shoulder, but said nothing. You started to cry.

I had had the decency to pull on a pair of panties. I walked up to you. "It turned out bad on this one, mom," I said, "but that's the breaks." You slapped me. Then *I* started to cry.

After that, you turned on the tear ducts again and

began making little sounds of violent distress. You put your face on Gavin's naked chest. He patted you on the back. What you wanted to say but never got around to saying was probably something like, "I admire what you did, Gavin, and why you did it, but it was wrong because I invited him here. He was a guest."

A paying guest. "Well," I said after the crying started to dry up for both of us, "I guess we all better go back to bed now. Tomorrow's another day." I grabbed Gavin's arm and tried to lead him back to the closet.

"Sorry, Marsh, I gotta stay with Rusalka tonight. You can see how she's all worked up."

Gavin spent the night in your bedroom, mom. I didn't even try to listen to find out what was going on.

I woke up around noon the next day. I didn't get out of bed. I seemed to be on the outside of everything now, even though, the way I looked at it, I brought Gavin to our house to be my lover and I tried to help him with his plan to get us both out of the trade. It hadn't worked out that way at all, so far. About three o'clock (I could tell the hour from my travel clock), Gavin peeked into my closet.

"What's up, dude? You gonna sleep your life away?"

"I didn't feel like it." That is, getting up.

"Your mom gave me some more money for your tutor lessons." Gavin rustled two twenty dollar bills between his fingers. "Party time!"

"Great." I felt miserable. If you want to know the truth, I think me, and especially you, mom, were dragging *him* into the whore business and I wasn't sure whether I had a lover or not. I was still wearing the same panties from last night. I fished around in a pile of clothes in a corner of the closet and came up with a pink skirt. I added my yellow shirt and tied the tails in front of my stomach. Like when I was about fifteen.

"Okay! You ain't so bad at all that way," Gavin commented optimistically. He was wearing jeans and a t-shirt, really dressed up for him.

I followed him into the living room. The television was already on, naturally. I sat on the living room floor and we watched some program about teaching mentally retarded adults. Gavin slumped back in the armchair and tuned in. He nodded at the screen, at the narrative. "That shit sorta makes sense."

Announcer: "Mentally retarded adults are quite capable of learning. They can assimilate enormous amounts of knowledge. Their ways of learning are different."

"That dude last night didn't take long to learn." Gavin.

"I guess mom didn't get a chance to collect from him before he left," I said maliciously.

"Yeah she did. Where the hell do you think this come from?" Gavin took the two twenties out again and waved them in the air.

I glumly watched the educational program about the retarded people. They still used the expression then. The truth is that I was jealous, hurt, resentful and pissed at Gavin. Finally, I came out with it. "Which one of us is the better fuck, me or mom?" I said this, which sounded gross even to me, most of all to get even with Gavin for leaving me alone.

He laughed. He slapped his thigh. "You're a real comic, man." Then he thought about the question seriously, which he had answered before in a different way. "You're both damn good, just at different ends."

I was satisfied with this, even though I knew it was mainly flattery. I smoothed my pink skirt down to my knees.

"But hey, Marsha, can't you get us anything for breakfast?"

I got up and I went to the kitchen. I found a bottle of whiskey. I went back to the doorway to the living room. "Catch!" I tossed the bottle to Gavin.

He caught it right on. Gavin had fast reflexes and good coordination. Probably he would have been really good at basketball as well as baseball. He took a drink, not a large one, right out of the bottle. "That's not exactly what I meant. Man does not live by booze alone. You got any more soup?"

Gavin could be philosophic. He might have made a good tutor, if he hadn't been illiterate.

Ten minutes later I came back with the soup. "Hey, thanks man. Fighting with fat slobs all night really makes you hungry." He drank from the bowl even though I had provided a small spoon that I found under the kitchen sink. It was sort of rusty. I mean the spoon. Gavin burped enormously without inhibition, then put the bowl down on the rug, as usual. It was at this point that I learned that Gavin had a libido that would have astonished Freud himself and sent him off packing to work on new theories. Even after everything that must have happened last night, Gav unzipped his jeans and took out his thing. It hung in a long, semi-erect condition. "Go for it, man."

It didn't bother me that Gavin often called me "man" or "dude". These were just speech tags, I knew. In any case, people our age called girls by these terms all the time. I don't know if Gavin thought I was a transvestite or a transsexual or a transgender person. I wasn't sure myself what the difference was. Probably it didn't matter a lot to him. Gavin just took life as it came, if you'll excuse the expression.

Gavin moved back into the big bedroom. The next morning, or rather afternoon, I brought him his soup as he lounged in your bed. You had already left for work at Bombo's Club.

"You know, man," he said as he lay back against a pillow after finishing the soup, "it'd help pass the time if we brought the TV in here. It's a hell of a lot more comfortable here than in that broken down old armchair. Who the hell used to sit there? He must've weighed a ton."

I didn't want to waste time explaining about old Robarb. He was a guy who, if he had enough water, could easily sink to the bottom. "Okay. I guess we could bring the TV in here. We can take it back to the living room before mom gets home. She might not like us cluttering up her boudoir with that box."

"Well, can you go get it? I strained my back out when I beat up that slob the other night." Gavin pulled the top sheet and blanket away from the bed. He was naked, of course. There was a large wet spot in the middle of the lower sheet. "You got any more sheets? This one had a workout, mother."

I carried the TV into the bedroom. It was heavy, but I found that I could handle it. I was stronger than I thought. I propped it on a chair near the foot of the bed, then adjusted it so that Gavin got the view he wanted. He had to get up from the bed while I changed the sheets. This resulted in a number of loud groans while he twisted his body in some exercises to loosen cramped muscles. At one point he stood on one leg while he used both of his hands to pull the other knee up to his abdomen. I could see how marvelously constructed his sex was. His member seemed to point at me while he pulled his knee upward. It might have been saying, "you're next, dude."

The day passed in a whiz. Gavin gave me a few thrills and we both sucked entertainment from the screen. When midnight was coming on, I thought I had better give him some good advice. I knew you were very particular about the way people acted in your house (a small apartment, but home sweet home), and especially in your bedroom. "Gav', you ought to get dressed. Mom might surprise us with an early visit, you know, like that time before."

"So what? She knows what the fuck I look like. She thinks it's cool."

"Yeah, but she can be real tricky about things like that. She's usually pretty tired when she comes back from Bombo's or from somewhere else after work, so she can get mad easy."

"Fuck. Okay." Gavin pulled on his jockey shorts. "That make you happy?"

"Something more. At least the jeans."

Gavin put on his jeans, then his t-shirt. "I feel dressed up like I been invited to some fucking royal wedding or something."

I loaded the TV back to the living room. We had to get ready. You'd be home soon.

"Ah man. Right in the middle of a good program. Shit." But Gavin had the sense to follow the TV into the living room, where he eased himself down into the

SON OF A WHORE

armchair. He was on his fifth glass of whiskey for the night. He was taking it slow.

It was just after three a.m. when you walked in the door. It was clear you hadn't had a great night of it. Your face showed those fearsome stress lines that I had learned to recognize. Your clothes weren't arranged in the usual elegant manner. Something had happened. I could make a lot of guesses, but I never found out what.

"You two little wastrels have had a fine day of it, I suppose." You tossed your purse on the floor and went into the bathroom. When you came out, half an hour later, Gavin had a request. He was not really attuned to the exact situation, being naturally a very easy going person.

"Mom," he began, "can you leave us with a bit of cash for tomorrow? We're almost all out of whiskey. It's the only thing that helps ease the pain in my broke leg."

I gasped in horror. I knew this was exactly what no one should ever say to you, even before you picked up your purse and threw it, again, at Gavin.

"Get off your fucking little ass and earn some money if you want whiskey! I'm not going to kill myself to keep you in food and shelter and alcoholic splendor!"

"Sorry, mom." Gavin shriveled back into the depths of the armchair.

"Don't call me mom! I'm not your mother, even though I feel sorry for her, whoever she is."

You went into the kitchen and we heard objects being tossed around. At least two glass items must have broken against the wall. You came out, you collected your purse and left for the bedroom. I knew you had to have your purse because that's where you kept your tranquilizers and sleeping pills. Dr. Shitaka kept you well supplied. He knew you needed the treatment.

Gavin got up and shot toward the bedroom. "Rusalka, honey, you know the way I love you. That's the real thing. Forget the rest of the shit. Nothing else matters."

I heard you shout, "You are a delinquent little boy!" Then there was the sound of hand meeting cheek. Gavin came back out looking shocked and red.

He sat down in the armchair. He whispered to me. "Your old lady's going through a mad bitch mood. I mean for real." He rubbed his cheek. "Why don't you go talk to her? Get her calmed down. Tell her I'm her boy friend too. She oughta figured that much out by now."

I had to explain to Gavin that it was pointless, even counter-productive, for anyone, especially me, to talk to you now. When you were angry, the world had better just stop and wait. "It would make things worse. Mom gets like that sometimes. We just gotta cool it till she forgets about it."

Gavin groaned. He knew he would have to spend the night in the closet, instead of the much more comfortable bedroom. "Shit! I guess I better pull out of this dump and go back to the city tomorrow. I got some deals goin' there anyway."

Soon we were both stretched out on the mattress in my closet. Gavin took his clothes off *after* he lay down. It was a bit awkward but he said it took less effort. I stripped to my panties and lay down on my side, facing away from him.

About an hour after the light was switched off, Gavin recovered his habitual libido. In the dark, he touched me around the waist. He pulled my shorts down and soon he was making good steam. Just before the crescendo he gasped, "'Salka, 'Salka!"

When I woke up Gavin was missing from the other side of the mattress. I looked at the travel clock. It was three thirty p.m. I got up and took a peek outside the closet. I went to the living room, then checked the bedroom. You had gone already, mom. Gavin wasn't in the apartment either. I went back to the closet to get dressed. I noticed that the empty coffee can I used to save coins and small bills was lying on its side. It was empty except for a few pennies. Naturally, because Gavin would have needed the money for train fare to San Francisco! All the money he got from you for my tutoring had already gone for booze and snacks like those barbecue taco chips he loved so much.

Gavin was gone. I sat in the armchair, where I imagined I could still feel a bit of his warmth. He was gone, but he had to come back. Probably he just went to see about those "business deals"—drugs, no doubt. He had to come back, like last time, didn't he? I didn't see how he could avoid it. Even if he did deal a bit in drugs from time to time, I don't think he was making much money. If he was making a lot of money, he wouldn't have to borrow my underwear, right? Unless he spent all of it on partying. I sat in the armchair. The television was off. It seemed like a power outage or something that almost never happened. Off. Practically the last time the TV had been cut off during waking hours was when a dissatisfied customer of yours threw a lamp through the screen. (He wasn't disappointed with you. He was one of those guys who can never get it up, probably because of some spanking he got from his mother eons ago.)

SON OF A WHORE

Gavin, gone. But he had to come back. Or else it was the end. I was hooked on Gavin. To me it seemed great that he kept you happy and made an effort on me as well, even if I thought the shares weren't equal. It wasn't only that he was so handsome and sexy. He had a personality. He had no education, but his personality made a dozen Ph.D's look like a bunch of dried figs. He was a presence. When he was in the room, you looked at him before anything else, you listened to what he said, no matter how trivial and unimportant. The fact that Gavin said it made anything important. He had his faults, I knew it. He put away more booze than one of those wino conventions they have in SF. He was lazy. He was a flatterer. But the fact that it might be a lie or an exaggeration didn't make any difference if it came from Gavin. He had a kind of force that made up for everything.

When I was having sex with Gavin I usually didn't come (have an orgasm. I just found that word in the dictionary). That didn't bother me. It didn't seem to matter. He always did it in a way that gave me a special feminine feeling, sort of forcing it in, but gently. But the sex part was not the main thing about Gavin. You got more of the sex than I did, mom, but you didn't seem to feel the personality part so much. At least you didn't show it. Maybe that was the trick.

I was sitting in the armchair when you came home a few hours after midnight. You looked around the living room. "Where's Gavin?" You sounded desperate, like you were saying, "Where's my bottle of valium?"

"Gavin took off early before I woke up. He told me last night that he had to visit his mother, to see if she was okay and that sort of thing."

"You're lying." You went to check the closet, then the bedroom, then you came back to the living room. You even looked behind the armchair. I turned my head around just out of curiosity. All there was behind the chair were those books I borrowed from the library for the tutoring, now long overdue, and a pile of liquor empties. "Okay. Why did he leave?"

"He just got bored staying around Cerrito and watching TV all the time. He said he had to get back to the city for a day or two."

"You're a liar, Marsha. You've always been a liar. What else could I expect from you?" You were pissed. Maybe you didn't miss Gavin all that much, but I think it really got to you that he ran out on you after you slapped him.

"He had to look after some drug deals. That's what he told me. Only he didn't say drugs."

"All right. That makes sense." You dropped your purse and went into the bathroom. While you were gone, I fished around in your purse and took out a bit of cash and a few valiums.

You were back after the usual half hour. Your make-up was gone and moisturizing cream was in its place. You were calmer, but more dissatisfied. "What are you ever going to do with your life, Marcus? You're eighteen now and you have no job and no education and all you do is watch television and drink."

"I don't drink half as much as Gavin," I answered. "And I do have a job. Just ask Trilla at Tramp's on Polk Street."

"That black woman who encourages you to engage in dangerous and revolting activities."

"They're not that dangerous."

"I don't care, but I'm not going to put up with your antics much longer. If you don't change, you're going to be out on the street, and then you'll be faced with making your way in life by hard work, like all the rest of us."

You went to the bedroom. I wasn't worried. I had heard this before. You were just punching on me because you couldn't get at Gavin.

That night I slept on Gavin's side of the closet mattress.

Gavin wasn't back by four p.m. the next day. I decided to go to Polk Street, not exactly to look for Gavin, or so I told myself, but just in case. I put on jeans and a rose colored shirt. I only had the six dollars I pulled out of your purse the night before. Fortunately, I had an account at a bank on San Pablo Avenue, not far from the liquor store. I was saving for a rainy day. There was like a whole run of rainy days lately. I only had about a hundred bucks left.

The phone rang. It might be Gavin! I rushed to the receiver. "Hello? Hello?"

It was Mrs. Suesseter from the county school attendance office. "I'm eighteen now. I don't have to go to any stupid school. Fuck you!"

With the twenty I took out of my bank account, I had a total of twenty-six dollars in cash, far more than train fare. It seemed like a lot of money. I didn't know what I was going to do with it all. Maybe I could buy Gavin a welcome gift if I found him and convinced him to come back home with me. A bottle of whiskey and a bag of barbecue taco chips would be perfect.

I was back on Polk Street. I was standing on Polk Street, thinking about what happened on Polk Street. I was across the street from Tramp's. It was no problem seeing inside the bar through the big glass windows. Trilla wasn't there, unless she was masquerading as a short, bald white guy. I didn't want to go into Tramp's. Maybe Trilla was just in the ladies room, or making a call from the payphone in the restroom hallway. I felt guilty that I hadn't reported for work in a long time. But I had to follow Gavin's orders about the prostitution business, didn't I? In a sense, although it wasn't true in the ordinary, anatomical way, I was his girl friend.

I stood watching from across the street. I checked out the foot traffic on the sidewalks. There was no one even vaguely like Gavin. After half an hour I was ready to give up. About five blocks down Polk, towards Market Street, there was another bar I had been to a lot. This was Frankie's In-Scene. Transvestites and transsexuals hung out there, so did drug dealers. It was worth a try. I started down Polk when I saw a familiar figure. In the deep doorway to a closed boutique that sold clothing in extravagant styles, a young blond of medium height was in close conversation with some other guys who looked older and like they came from the Fillmore district (I mean they were black guys). I rushed in. The group was gathered in a circle. It was pretty clear they were dealing and exchanging cash and substances.

"Gavin!" I was soon hanging onto his arm. "You left so fast and we didn't even know where you went to!"

He turned from the others, who were saying things to each other like "shit, fuck you, bastard mother fucker", and took me in with a look that included sympathy, but also a good deal of exasperation.

"Mom got really upset when she found out you weren't there. She's not feeling well at all. She didn't even go to work today. She asked me to try to find you." Not literally true.

"Not now, man. I'm doin' some business. Cool it for later, okay?"

"It's really serious, Gav'. See, if mom gets too upset, she can have like these psychotic things, where she starts shouting and wrecking junk. She even hurt herself once with a razor blade." Mostly lies, but worth a try.

"Look man, this is business. I'll contact you real soon later. Don't mess things up." Gavin to me.

Someone in the group said, "hey, Gav', who's the bitch? Tell him to shove off."

"Yeah," another voice added. "Get rid of that punk ass sissy."

I was wearing too much make-up, as usual. This could draw negative comments from a large range of individuals.

"You gotta help me save mom, Gav'." I clung to his arm and looked into his handsome, serious, distracted face.

"Later, dude! I can't help you right now." Gavin gave me a shove that almost sent me toppling onto the sidewalk.

I started to cry. I stood four feet from the group and set up a huge caterwauling.

Now Gavin was really mad. He came forward, turned me toward the street, and administered a greater than moderate blow with his foot.

It was the end. I wandered along Polk Street, indifferent to the looks of shock and disgust from the crowd. A grown boy, almost a man, looking like a girl, and crying fit to shake the walls of Troy. Later I thought I'd change this to Jericho. Grandma would have been happier.

SON OF A WHORE

I had been home for several hours when you got back from Bombo's, mom. I was drinking a little whiskey, but without Gavin I wasn't very thirsty. Hours before I had stopped crying. After that I started going into the bathroom to look at myself in the mirror from time to time. I looked glum, haunted, disturbed. Nothing I could do by slapping on and changing around your make-up on my face made any difference. I was sitting quietly in front of the TV when you came in.

When you came out of the bathroom and went to the living room you stood and stared at me. "Well?"

"A friend of Gavin's told me he got busted by the police, something about drugs. I went to Polk Street today." I gave a genuine sniffle, even though I knew he wasn't in jail, not yet anyway.

"I'm not surprised." You were upset and embarrassed, as if you had been stood up for a date. "Your friends are a pretty low life crowd. Don't drink too much of that whiskey. It's expensive." You went to the bedroom and closed the door.

I could have told you what really happened, but I didn't, just as a normal precaution. You might even have been happy to hear that I had been rejected and kicked. I did not feel humiliated by what happened on Polk. I don't think I've ever felt humiliated—it should be obvious why. What I felt was heartbreak, as they said on the daytime soap operas Gavin and me loved so much.

I watched television for an hour or so. I had a few more drinks. It was time to go to bed, but I couldn't stand the thought of sleeping alone in the closet where Gavin and me had slept together. I took my jeans and shirt off. I went into your bedroom.

SON OF A WHORE

It was dark and you were stretched out on the bed, turned on your side. You seemed to be sleeping. I touched your shoulder. "Mom? Mo-om?" You stirred. Your head shifted ever so slightly on the pillow. "Can I sleep with you tonight? It feels really strange and scary sleeping alone. It's spooky and lonely in the dark."

You made another little shift against the pillow, which I interpreted as "yes". I climbed into the other side of the bed. Soon I was asleep, but I remember thinking that this felt better than anything that happened since I met Gavin.

A few days later I was faced with a real ultimatum. When you were dressed and ready to leave for work I was still dozing in your bed, but you pulled the covers back to check something. "Marcus! I told you not to wear my underwear! You can buy your own panties if that's what you want to do. In any case, you have two weeks to find a real job, or you're out. You refused to go to school all through high school, but you're not getting out of working!" You were gone.

I got up after another hour. Now I was worried. Of course, you tried out all that 'you're not getting out of working' crap a million times before, but this time it seemed real. Something in your super-serious expression, tone gave me the creeps. Your maternal ultimatum about work stuck in my mind. I had to do something and quick. I considered that my paid whoring ought to count as work. After all, you thought of it that way for yourself. But I had to follow a different rule, apparently since I was a guy (or was I?)

I put on my orange trousers and a shirt with a bright

print pattern. I put on your make-up, the whole show, moisturizer, basic, cover-up, eye make-up, eyebrow liner, lipstick. Then, because I knew I tended to overdo it, I rubbed my face with a towel to soak up the excess cosmetics. I checked myself out again in the mirror. Yeah! This ought to do. I felt a lot better. Once again, I looked like a cheap eighteen year old transgender hooker. Essentially, that's what I was.

It was about five-thirty when I walked into Tramp's. Trilla was there. I knew she would be. She's a permanent monument.

"Donchu even talk to me!" She pointed a long, thick finger in my direction. "Where the hell you been all this time?"

"My mom was real sick," I whimpered. "They had to take her to the hospital."

"Fuck that! You the sick one, dude. You already use that one on me three times."

I bowed my head. "Sorry. The truth is, I was sick. I got VD from a customer and it took two weeks for the antibiotics to work. Old Dr. Shitaka almost flipped out when the test came back positive for anal gonorrhea."

"Uh." Trilla nodded. "That shit can happen. Well, it's part of the trade. Anyway, that's the first time it ever happen to you, right? I mean, from one of my customers."

"Third time." This was a lie, like the first part, but it was the sort of thing that Trilla would likely believe. It was actually eight times for me before, total. I mean, the lab couldn't tell Trilla's customers' gonorrhea from the others.

Trilla motioned me to her table. Two triples. She was sympathetic about my occupational injury. "You all right now, aren't you?" She gave me a suspicious look and backed just slightly.

"Oh yes. Dr Shitaka had two tests made after I finished the medicine, and they both came back negative." What a liar! I probably would have made a good novelist.

"Glad to hear that. You look like you could use earnin' a few bucks." She looked me up and down. Probably she thought my clothes looked old. She was right, but it's hard to find orange pants my size in the stores, so anyway I had to stick with my old ones.

"You ready to work?"

I nodded. I looked at my reflection in the broad mirror behind the bar, where the bartender kept giving me funny looks with grimaces and a twisted mouth. I saw that I was still wearing too much make-up. About half as much would have been enough.

"Marsha, you do go heavy on the face paint, you know that?"

Again, I nodded.

"Okay. I'm gonna fix you up, like before." Trilla grabbed me by the arm and led me to the ladies' room. She turned on the water in the washbasin and bent my head toward the facet. For about ten minutes, or so it seemed, she rubbed my face with water and a little of the hand soap from a push container. Then she raised me up again and wiped my face with paper towels. We both looked at my image in the mirror. "Yeah. That's what you really look like."

In the mirror there was a rather ordinary looking eighteen year old boy, but without any hint of beard and with a pronounced girlish look, probably due to the soft expression.

"I'm gonna fix you up. Don't you worry." She started in like the first time she discovered me, the night Gavin stole my statue, only more thorough this time. Trilla opened her purse and took out a small bottle of makeup. She must have had about a dozen shades on hand just in case of need. She dabbed little points of cosmetic on my cheeks, my chin, my forehead, my nose. Then she smoothed it into the skin with her large motherly hands. It felt nice. My own mom had never done that for me. Now the eyebrow liner. She used more than what would have been optimal, just to give the customers the right impression. Lipstick. She applied just a tiny but noticeable amount. "Now don't lick too much, or it'll all go away. I mean, don't lick nothin' till you get it on with the customer." She laughed. I smiled. I liked the way I looked.

When we were back in the barroom and sitting at the table, Trilla had a question. She asked it with the whiskey glass still in her mouth. "How is your mom, anyway? She still workin' at Bombo's Club?"

"Yeah. She's not doing too bad." Then I had to blab it without thinking, just to have something to say. "Gavin stayed with us for a couple of weeks and he kicked a customer out of the house. He was trying to protect us."

"You let that phony little bitch stay with you at your house?" Trilla sounded pissed. "You really lookin' for trouble."

"He left after mom got mad at him for something. Then, yesterday, when I saw him on Polk Street and went to say hello, he shoved me and kicked me!" I started tearing up again when I reported this part.

Even Trilla was shocked. "If that don't beat all!

Anyway, you mess around with that dude, that's what you gonna get."

I drank about half of what was left of my whiskey. I still wished I was with Gavin. It was worth a hundred kicks.

Trilla looked at me straight on. "I'm gonna get you a payin' date, not one that sucks all your money like that two-bit operator."

I could see her at the pay phone in the passage. She tried one number, then another. She was using up quarters again. I looked out the window at the foot traffic on Polk. The obvious straight types stared at me through the big windows. They seemed to be thinking, "so that's what they look like."

Trilla came back to the table. "I got you a good one. This one got money and he treat the boys real nice." She gave me a piece of paper with a street address and apartment number on California Street. "It ain't even that far away. You don't gotta take no bus, you can just walk a few blocks. That make you look fine when you get there, sorta athletic and all." She checked me out again, then hummed a bit. "Anyway, it make you look awake and ready to go."

Trilla was right. This customer was not the problem type at all. He didn't want to beat me or tie me up or shave my nuts. I think he was some kind of professor or teacher. His apartment was full of books about psycho-sociology or something like that. All he wanted to do was to bugger me. He used a pharmacy lubricant, so I hardly felt anything. This was aided by the fact that he was not very well developed. In fact, it was something of a disappointment. He paid the standard fee and a good tip. Twenty bucks!

It was close to midnight and I was heading back to San Cerrito. I couldn't leave you alone, mom. You were depressed, and not just about Gavin. A lot of male partners had left you over the years. Maybe that's why sometimes you didn't seem to care how many you dated.

I was coming up to the train station entrance, where the escalator takes you down to the level of the rails, when I saw a forlorn figure leaning against a wall, a cigarette in his mouth, a visor cap pulled over his head. He was hunched over like he was wounded or sick and he mainly looked down at his own feet, except for a glance at the street from time to time. He caught sight of me and came right over.

"You gotta help me, man. You gotta get me outa this!" It was Gavin. He grabbed me by the arm and held it tight.

It was Gavin! I was happy. I hadn't been so happy since you gave me my first makeup kit when I was twelve years old. I had been making your life miserable by constant begging and whining for weeks. I looked at him at close range. His face was unshaven, unwashed, a bit bruised; his hair, the part not covered by the cap, looked almost flattened against his head by oil and dirt. His clothes were torn and stained. "What happened?" I was frightened at the thought of the mistreatment he must have received. I took one of his hands between mine and brought it to my face. I kissed it.

"You wouldn't believe how those guys fucked me up!"

"The ones you were with a few days ago on Polk?"

"Yeah. Those guys. They ripped me off for my cash, took my stash, then went to work on me, three of them in the alley."

"Oh!" I put my fingers on Gavin's face. I tried to smooth out the blood stains and swelling. He winced and pulled my hand off.

"Ouch! Fuckin' hurts! They didn't stop at that, man. They had to finger me to the cops as a big dealer, when all I was doin' was buying a little from them, like for my own use! So now I gotta hide out big time."

I looked around. I wanted to make sure the police or the gang members weren't watching us. "Let's go. They'll never find you in San Cerrito. Nobody ever goes there." We went down the escalator.

"Thanks man. You saved my life. You got train fare, right?"

I nodded.

"I saw you around six o'clock in Tramp's, but I didn't go in because I didn't want to meet up with Trilla. I knew you'd be heading back to Cerrito sooner or later, so I camped out here."

"Yeah. So we have to go home now. Mom'll be overjoyed to see you! She thinks you're so wonderful."

Gavin took this in. He seemed to understand the effect he had on you. You had to be pretty thick not to twig to you being sex hyped on Gavin. And more than that, mom, how many mothers get a lover less than half their age delivered to the door by a son interested in the same services?

In the train, while we passed through the tunnel under the bay, Gav' took out a little cigarette and lit up. It wasn't tobacco. He offered me a toke. I sucked in the acrid smoke. It seemed to be hash, but maybe laced with cocaine. Gavin took the little cigarette from me and leaned back in his seat. "Man, you saved me just in time. Two minutes more and I coulda been headin' to the slammer or the sick tank." "Sick tank" was Gavin's word for the hospital.

The train went on with its clatter, clatter over the uneven rails. Then we were in Oakland. The cars stopped at half a dozen stations. Gavin had dozed off, but he looked up when a crowd of well dressed people got on at Downtown. He looked at them, taking in the adult couples, their clothes, their high class prestige. He was impressed. Then he seemed to focus on me.

"You been doin' okay?" He looked me over in the light of the train car. "Yeah, you look okay. I guess you did some work tonight, right?"

"It didn't take long. This guy was some kind of teacher, not too physical."

"Then you sort of lucked out. I mean, thinking about it that way." Of course Gavin meant that it was lucky it didn't turn out to be a big pain in the ass, like with some customers.

When the train left the last Oakland station I knew we'd be home in a few minutes. I grabbed Gavin's hand and held it. "I'm really glad you're coming back, Gav'." A station later I still had his hand. I didn't want to let go. We were getting funny looks from the other passengers. This didn't bother me, since I was used to unfriendly stares and even liked it, for the attention, and Gavin wasn't exactly bashful. "Me and mom were both miserable when you left. You were helping us. I think that plan you had to get us out of the trade was working, but when you disappeared everything just went back to normal."

"Sorry, man. I didn't want to be away more than a few hours, but I met up with those guys and things got complicated." He rubbed his chin. "It had to be the one with hands like a ham who turned out to be the real bastard."

I nodded. I expressed sympathy by a tearful look. I wiped my eyes with a shirt sleeve. A large make-up stain came off with the tears. Probably Trilla used that cheap kid stuff this time.

Soon we were climbing the stairs to home. Then we were inside the apartment. "You ought to hug mom and kiss her when she gets back." I looked at my fake diamond Princess Watch. "But that won't be for a few more hours."

"Man, it's good to be home. I'm gonna take a bath, sort of wash the crap off. You got any food lying around?"

"I'll warm up some of your favorite soup. I think we got tomato vegetable." I busied around in the kitchen, overjoyed to be cooking for Gavin again! I set the pot on the stove, turned the gas to a low setting, then went to the bathroom to check on him.

He was in the tub, lying back against the end opposite the tap. "Hey! Come on in, the water's fine." He splashed about.

I wanted to. I looked at his body and was impressed as much as before. It was hardly at all worse for the wear. Then I noticed with a shock that his pubic hair had been entirely shaved off. He took in my surprise, then laughed.

"That. I had to do a gig with some weird nut. Just to get money to finance a deal. All he liked to do was to play barber with other guys' balls. I made him use a safety razor, just in case he decided to get carried away."

I nodded. I knew that stuff happened. I started to take my clothes off. I was down to my panties when I remembered that I had soup on the stove. "I got to check on what I got cooking." I rushed off.

"Hey," Gavin called to my back. "Get me a whiskey while you're there, okay?"

The soup was just starting to boil over when I got back to the kitchen. I took the pot off the stove. Then I filled Gavin's habitual whiskey glass to the brim and carried it to the bathroom.

"All right!" Gavin took the glass.

I was so excited by the prospect of a "swim" with Gavin, that I tore my panties off and threw them behind me. They landed on the medicine cabinet and hung there covering the upper part of the mirror. I had a full erection already, although I could tell by Gavin's look that he wasn't impressed by its extension. What was the difference? I didn't do anything with it except stroke it around a little from time to time.

We were both in the tub. Talk about a fast worker: Gavin's glass was already empty. I would get him a refill later.

Gavin was a really strong guy. He was a year or so younger than me, but in physical development he was a young man. He bent forward, grabbed me around the waist with both hands, turned me around and sat me down, facing his feet, on top of his thing. It was pre-soaped for easy entry and eight inches long. "Ah!" It felt wonderful. It was that feminine feeling, but more than ever as he used his hands to move me up and down on himself. I worked my front with a hand when I could tell he was nearing orgasm. We were both over the point when, sensing something, I turned around and saw it. Mom! You were standing in the bathroom doorway. You saw everything! And you were more pissed than hell! Shit! History repeats itself and history's bunk.

"You sick little queer!" You threw your purse at *my* head this time. It glanced off and landed in the water. You stomped out of the bathroom. You weren't mad, you were incensed (I found this word in the dictionary, although it can also mean something that smells), and I could understand why. There was some kind of understanding, not talked about, that we would share Gavin, and here I was hogging him all for myself right off the bat, just after he returned!

Gavin sprang into action. He jumped out of the bathtub, still sporting half an erection, and ran after you. I followed close enough to wrap a towel around his waist. Don't say I never gave a thought about decency!

"Rusalka, mom, honey." Gavin tried to hug you but you landed a good one on the side of his head. "You leave this house right now! I don't want you debauching my son any more than he already is!"

"'Salka." Gavin grabbed you with both arms and kissed you repeatedly. Soon everyone was calmer. You and Gavin were doing the Liz and Dick routine. You both seemed to like it. I mean romantic kissing and that sort of thing. You weren't really that mad now. Maybe Gavin's long absence had put (this is called the pluperfect tense. It's sort of dumb) you in a state of severe deprivation and you were finally getting relief.

"Hi, mom," I put in rather stupidly. "There's a lot of soup if you want some."

Soon you and Gav' were waltzing off to the bedroom. Gavin turned at the bedroom door. "Get me some re-hydration, won't you, Marsh?"

He wanted a refill on his whiskey. I could understand this. He must've lost a lot of fluid in the last few days, not to mention the last few minutes. I brought the glass of whiskey to the bedroom. There was a more serious mood now. Probably you didn't think charging right into sex was too cool as far as dignity and stuff, so now you wanted to wait off a little. You and Gavin were lying on top of the blankets, on opposite sides of the bed. I put the glass down on the bedside table next to Gavin, who was still wearing the towel around his waist. I stood watching you both.

"Gavin and I have to discuss things alone, Marsha."

I slowly retreated, looking back at Gav', then at you. When I reached the living room I heard the bedroom door slam. It was like Tutankhamen's tomb closing. I was locked out for eternity.

Of course this time I sneaked back to the door to listen. I could hear talking for a long time, but I couldn't make much of it out. I thought I heard something like, "he's a very disturbed boy". That would be you describing me. Then, "trying to help him". That was probably Gavin giving his version. After about half an hour the talking died down, then stopped. Soon there were a lot of sounds like bedroom gymnastics. I went back to the living room. A really old movie was running on the TV (that's about all they played on those cheap UHF channels), with guys in slouch hats who talked slow and women in really neat dresses but not too much make-up. I went to the kitchen. The whiskey bottle had suffered enormously in the short time since Gavin's return. I poured a glass from what was left. (I have to explain that we had stopped buying our traditional family vodka and changed out for whiskey. Gavin said "that vodka crap's all right, but it don't have no taste.") The soup was getting cold as hell. I went back to watch the hats and dresses.

Afternoon, the next day, Gavin was sitting in the living room armchair, eating his breakfast soup. He had already twigged to how I felt about him spending the night with you again. Managing both of us at once was a real problem for him, and it was clear he wanted to make me feel better. "You know, Marsh, your mom's really serious about helping you, getting you into school and all that stuff. She wants you to be educated in college and that kind of shit. She told me all that again. That shows how much she loves you and all. She even gave me some cash to start tutoring you again. And she asked how you were doing on that junk. I said you weren't doing too bad, but you were sort of bogging down on prepositions. I suppose we oughta look up prepositions in one of those books, just in case she wants to know what the hell it is."

"I took them back to the library. They were three weeks overdue."

"Bummer." Gavin was not visibly disappointed.

I was not in a good mood. How would you feel if your lover had just spent the night with your mother, again, after you rescued him from all sorts of hell? I wanted to talk about it with Gavin, but I didn't know how to start. I was jealous, and that wasn't very pretty, but I had a right to some sort of resentment. "Gav," I began.

"Ha ha ha ha!" Gavin broke into laughter. There was a cartoon show playing on TV. Two mice had just crushed a mean cat under a huge rock.

I waited for a commercial to occupy the screen. "Gav'," I started again. "Are you sure you're supposed to be screwing my mom? I mean, she's probably older than your old lady. That's not, like, really ethical."

"Why not? She's good looking as hell." Gavin saw my reaction to this remark. I must have looked like a guy who found his wife sleeping with some bum. "Aw, Marsh. You're my girl friend. Didn't I give it to you twelve inches up last night in the tub?" Twelve inches was an exaggeration, but it hardly matters if you're facing the other way.

I looked down at my bare feet and sniffled.

"Yeah. I mean, your mom's okay, but you're my real sexology interest, like they say on TV."

I sighed in relief when I got this message. I looked up from the floor where I was sitting. I stared at Gavin in appreciation. He was so handsome in his tough, young, masculine way. Maybe he was a bum and a flatterer. That didn't seem to make any difference. He was Gavin, and everything else was just cold soup.

An hour later Gavin sent me to the store on San Pablo Avenue to buy a couple of bottles of whiskey and some taco chips. That used up most of the cash he got from you for tutoring me. Even though the truth is that he was tutoring you as much as he was tutoring me.

We were watching TV and drinking whiskey. Things were really getting mellow around seven o'clock. That's when Gavin decided he could use some head. As I mentioned before, he had a fantastic sex drive and even Dr. Freud would probably freak out about it. He undid his zipper, took it out, and gestured to me with the hand not holding the whiskey glass. I got the message.

It took about fifteen minutes. I was moving my head

in slow, steady, repetitive in and out motions, just like in the porn movies. From the corner of one eye I could just barely see the TV screen. Usually Gavin stood up when I did him orally, but it was just as good with him sitting down. Then he shot to the point. "Ah uh ah ooh oooh!" It tasted good in my mouth. It was salty this time. Maybe that was because of all the soup.

The telephone rang. The phone was on a little table next to the armchair. "Uh ... uh ... hullow?" Still out of breath, Gavin answered. "'Salka, mom, hi! Nice of you to call. Naw, we're not doing anything much. Just sort of hitting at the old geometry. Yeah. Yeah. Triangles and squares. That stuff. Important for school. Yeah. Yeah. Come home early and we'll all just sit around and watch TV and maybe have a drink or two. Yeah. Yeah. Love you." He made kissing noises into the speaker. "That was mom," he told me after he hung up. "She said to clean up the kitchen before she gets home because it's getting to be a fucking mess with all those soup stains. I noticed it too."

"Okay. She's always saying stuff like that. I usually didn't clean it before because I figured she could do the cleaning on her day off."

"She's real pissed about it now." Gavin gave it some thought. "Or maybe she's really just jealous about what you and me are doing together while she's working at the Club."

"We didn't do anything. I just sucked you off, that's all."

"That's what I mean. She could be real jealous even about little shit like that."

I had to think about it for awhile to understand why a

blow job could have any particular importance for anyone. It seemed like the small change of sexuality.

Gavin put three taco chips into his mouth, chewed, swallowed. "Women are like that. That's how my mom was sometimes."

I started thinking about Gavin and his mother. What exactly *did* they use to do? It wasn't any use guessing, though, and I think even Gavin would have resented a direct question on the subject.

"Really, man, I think we ought to get going on cleaning up the kitchen. Mom's gonna be mad as hell if she gets home after all that work she does for us at the Club and finds the kitchen still looks like crap."

I went to the kitchen. Gavin shouted one last instruction. "Hey! Get me a whiskey while you're at it!" I couldn't tell him he was drinking too much, even if that's what I thought. He would get the idea I was turning into a nagging bitch.

When I got to the sink area, I could see what you were talking about, mom. I don't know how I could have let things go like that. It looked like somebody had a gigantic food war six weeks ago with open cans of soup as the main weapon. I grabbed a dish towel and went to work. It took me about an hour to make any headway. I'm not really good at that kind of stuff. I think I'm a people oriented sort of person, not a kitchen cleaner.

Gav was deep into some sort of adventure movie when I got back to the living room. On the screen some people in pith helmets and khaki clothes were walking around in a jungle. "I guess I better take a bath," he told me. "Mom's gonna be home in a few hours and I don't want to smell like a whiskey factory." He drained his glass. About an ounce or two had been stuck at the bottom.

Two minutes later I could hear the water filling the bathtub. Gavin was singing. "Zippity-doo dah, zippity-ay!" He really loved to take baths. This was number two or three just for the day.

I followed to the bathroom. Gavin was stretched out in the tub when he saw me. "Don't just stand there, come on in. What are buddies for?"

You couldn't bring customers to our apartment now, mom. Gavin made that definite. He was going to straighten us both out, as far as the prostitution thing, whatever it took. Even though he sometimes understood the economic need, he couldn't keep his jealousy under control, at least in your case. You still made some extra cash from the "big tippers" in their hotel rooms, but Gavin's rule cut off a substantial portion of the clientele, the ones who were staying in hotels with their wives or somebody else. Cash was getting scarce. Gavin's tips for "tutoring" gradually got reduced to five dollars a "lesson".

"Five bucks, man! What the fuck am I gonna do with five bucks?"

We switched to wine, but even that was in short supply. Gavin didn't really like wine. He said it tasted like old grape juice or something. No kick. You might as well swallow a bunch of water. Finally, Gavin found what looked like a practical solution. Normally he would have been totally opposed on principle, but these were desperate times. "Marsha, looks like you gotta go back to Polk and let Trilla find you some work. We're livin' like a bunch of peons here. I'd go to the city and work my ass, but it's too hot right now. Those drug guys passed my name on to the police."

I was willing, but I wasn't able. The truth was that neither of us even had the cash for a one way train ticket to the city. I clued Gavin in to this situation. "And I can't borrow anything from mom. She wouldn't lend me a quarter if my life depended on it. She says I'm an 'incorrigible wastrel'. Yeah, that's how she puts it, 'incorrigible wastrel'." I wasn't going to mention my little bank account. That had to be saved for ultimate necessity.

"Fuck everything!" Gavin slouched down in the living room armchair and just watched the screen like it was the day after doomsday.

Around eleven o'clock I served the evening soup. "'S'not bad stuff," Gavin said between gulps. "But I'm getting fuckin' tired of nothing but soup, man. I mean, I'm not in kindergarten anymore."

I slept alone in the closet that night, as usual now. In addition to our afternoon activities, Gavin and me typically had a roll at it when he took his bath before you came home, mom. Then he slept in your bedroom.

The next afternoon you woke me up early. "What happened to the money in my purse?" You were standing inside the closet.

I sat up on the mattress. "I don't know. I don't got it."

"Stand up!"

Fortunately, I'd had enough sense of decency to sleep in my panties. I think maybe I inherited the habit of trying for decorum from my father, whoever he was.

Slap! You hit me in the face. "You're a liar. And you've always been a thief. I want that money back now!"

I started to cry. "I did-unt!"

"Where's Gavin?"

SON OF A WHORE

I looked around the little closet. "I don't know. He was sleeping with you."

"He took the money, that cheap little operator! Don't you ever bring a boy like that to this house again!"

Gavin was gone again. I went into this depression mood. Gavin was, he used to be, the only friend and real lover I ever had. When you don't go to school beyond eighth grade, and you look mainly like an underdeveloped boy and think you're a girl, you're not likely to collect a big fan club. I mean, Robarb used to say he was my friend, but that was so much cheap crap that even he probably realized he was a phony, which in his dictionary was by far the best thing to be. (Con men are the ideal for a certain portion of the sales community). Gavin was gone. I loved him like he was Superman and I was Lois Lane. Now there was nothing left. I hardly got out of bed for three days. I didn't want to go back to the living room where me and Gavin spent all that time happily watching TV and drinking whiskey, with the occasional head job thrown in. It would have been too lonely. I amused myself alone on the mattress between bouts of depression.

Money was coming in again, because you brought a new boyfriend home almost every night. Maybe in some psychological way you were getting even with Gavin for cutting out. You introduced me to some of them.

"This is my son, Marcus."

"Does he always wear skirts?"

"He's in therapy. The doctors say his psychotic father drove him into a state of 'gender uncertainty'. Sometimes he imagines he's a girl."

I was a girl. I knew it, despite what they all said. That

was the way I was arranged inside my head. Anyway, I was now in what the psycho doctors called "denial" about Gavin. I avoided emotional collapse by telling myself that Gavin would be back in a day or two. He came back before, didn't he? So he had to come back now.

Days were passing. Finally I got some money out of your purse when you were fast asleep with some palooka guy. I decided to go back to Polk. There was nothing else to do. I mean, the only thing that can make daytime TV bearable is drinking whiskey and having someone fantastically sexy and loveable like Gavin by your side. That was over. It was reality TV now.

I put on a pair of jeans and a yellow t-shirt. For some reason, like I repeated for the therapy effect a few times before, I looked more girlish dressed in jeans than I did in a skirt. Maybe it was the femmy lines of my body in pants, while in a dress it was just baggy cloth above knobby knees. I borrowed your short chartreuse jacket, mom. I didn't think you'd ever find out, since there wouldn't be any of those stains on it, probably.

I stood on the sidewalk of Polk across the street from Tramp's. I could see Trilla sitting at a table inside. She was too big to miss. I think she could see me, too, but she wasn't about to let on. She wasn't going to wave me on in. She was too smart for that. She wanted to make it clear that everything was up to me and that she couldn't care less after the shit I pulled. I sauntered into the bar.

"Hey, hey, look who finally turn up! Just like a bad penny." Trilla raised her glass in a salute. "I guess you got tired of sittin' on your ass all day, right?"

I sat down on a chair opposite Trilla. "Um, yeah.

SON OF A WHORE

That's sort of it. The truth is, my mom kicked me out of the house. She said she wasn't going to have a whore for a son." This was another lie, obviously.

"Huh. Sounds like the kettle callin' the pot black."

I nodded. "Yeah. You should see all the guys she keeps bringing home. At night our apartment looks like Grand Central station."

"Okay." Her voice was serious now. "What you got to do now is get back to work." Trilla signaled the bartender to bring two triples.

I sipped.

"Yeah. So tell me. You still hangin' out with Gavin?"

"No. He took all the money out of my mom's purse and hit the road. That's really why she got pissed." It felt weird telling the truth for once.

"Uh-huh. Just what you mighta expected. That little dude ripped me off for three hundred dollars once. I shoulda know better than fall asleep with him in the room."

Gavin was a thief. That was clear enough by now. It was strange, but that only made him more lovable in my eyes. If only Gavin would take me away with him, anywhere, I'd take the flight. But it was pretty obviously over for me.

We were finishing our whiskies. That is, Trilla was finishing her whiskey, probably her eleventh for the day. I had drained my glass in two sips.

"Okay, Marsha Marsha Bo-barsha, I'm gonna get you some sex interest for hire. Hold on." She went to the phone. Trilla might seem to be a low class, laid back alcoholic black woman, but in reality she was a first class business lady. She always knew what she had to do next.

144

I sat watching the people who were walking by on the sidewalk, like last time. You were getting a lot more weird people on Polk now. There was this new fad for everybody to shave their heads and dress in rags or leather jackets and wear rings in their noses. Then someone I knew came into view. Harv! He looked into Tramp's. I'm sure he recognized me. He was dressed like an ancient Roman soldier, with a helmet, breast plate, metal greaves, kilt and all. In his hand he held a little statue. I waved. He only sneered back. I don't think he ever got over that little burglary episode. He flipped out psychologically. I mean, that ancient statue meant everything to him. And he never complained to the police because when I ripped the status off, it was after a prostitution gig, which is illegal. I doubt it ever crossed his mind that, otherwise, I'd never of got paid for that lousy ass-up trip.

Trilla was back in only a few minutes. This time she didn't waste a lot of quarters. "Okay, Marsha, for once you really luck out. I got you a dude who gonna make St. Francis look like Attila the Hun. I mean, he ain't no double wimp or anything like that, but he treat the boys nice, like they was royal princesses or something."

I nodded. That was great, but was it really true? She said the same thing about most of the customers and some of them turned out to be guys who made Attila look like St. Francis.

Trilla handed me an address written on a little piece of paper. "Wow! Swanky neighborhood." It was on Nob Hill, some high rise apartment building with at least eleven floors.

"Yeah, see, I give you the best. All you gotta do is your part. That's just lyin' flat out, right? Nothin' more easy."

It wasn't as easy as it might seem. You had to play a certain role the whole time, and the fuckers could do some real damage if you didn't watch them. Anyway, I had to go with it. There was no Plan B. "Trill'? There's something else. I had to leave home with nothing but one-way train fare to the city. How about throwing in a few bucks for a cab? I can't walk all the way up those hills. I'd get there looking like Sir Hillary on top of Mount Everest, all covered with crap." A lie. Another one. I needed to lie for psychological reasons (a shrink told me it was because of an "absent father" and "unresponsive mother". They usually say stuff like that.) I had a ten I got out of your purse, mom, since you were making it again after Gavin left. Minus the train fare, that left me with almost seven. You were back in the trade, although probably you were only doing it out of "feelings of abandonment". That's the way Freud would have put it.

"Okay." Trilla came across with a five.

I looked sadly at the bill. "I won't be able to leave a tip for the cabby, so I'll probably have to walk back, even with the money St. Francis gives me."

"Don't worry, exercise do you good. A lot of these guys like the athletic type." Trilla gave me a contemptuous look-over. "Ain't you never done no runnin' in school or anything like that?"

"I didn't go to school."

"Mmm. The school I went to, even the girls gotta run half a mile every day." Trilla saw that this comment was having a negative effect on my morale. In our trade morale is half the game. You have to *feel* the part too. "Don't you worry. Don't matter none. You look real cute, just about like a girl. And that's what this one go for.

Hey, just hold on a minute." Trilla opened her purse and took out an eyebrow pencil. She sketched in a few lines above my eyes. "Now you look real romantic, kinda like Liz Taylor."

This was only flattery, I knew it, but it felt good anyway.

Mr. Sonorian lived in an apartment that looked like a museum. Not a museum of old Greek and Roman junk like Harv, but a modern art museum. Everything in his place was made out of glass or metal and was twisted around in a fantastic style. That showed he had money. And for once, Trilla was right, he *was* nice. He talked to me for some time. He showed me pictures of his family in some other country. I forget which one it was. Maybe Aramia or something. He told me he went to Harvard and had all kinds of degrees, but he didn't need them because he had tons of money that he inherited from his father who started by selling these little sandwiches. Anyway, I didn't understand all of it, but that was what he said, and he was friendly and gentle. He wasn't all that bad looking either, if you like them like that. I mean old and a bit short and a bit too much around the waist. I guess the physical side isn't everything after all.

The bedroom. He had this gigantic bed that could seat ten at a time (I found that this is common with the "sleep-around" class), although there was only him and me in it now. He wasn't short at all as far as his little thing. It was about three times my size, which seemed to turn him on.

He gave it to me four and a half times during the next few hours on his enormous bed.

SON OF A WHORE

I can tell you, it was an experience. I had never felt so completely feminine before. I did now. I lay there and groaned in satisfaction, which excited him to plug away on me even more. He used a condom. In fact, he had to change out six times, since one of them broke in mid-action. Naturally he didn't want to risk contracting some loathsome sexual disease from a prostitute.

After we were through, after he was through, we sat in bed talking for awhile. I told Mr. Sonorian that my father was a real creep, that he always made fun of me, with reference to the fact that I took it in the ass. Mr. Sonorian sympathized. He didn't know all whores are liars. Around three o'clock it was bye-bye time. He offered me a glass of milk. Maybe he thought I was younger than I really was. I gratefully accepted, for the sake of appearances. I poured it down the kitchen sink when he wasn't looking. At the door of his plush apartment he shook my hand and gave me an envelope. I opened it in the corridor while I waited for the elevator. He put in a forty dollar tip!

When I got back home to Cerrito you were already asleep, mom. So was this guy you had with you. I peeked into the bedroom. Wow! You could really pick them. This one must have weighed three hundred pounds! He didn't have much hair on his head, but he was pretty shaggy around the shoulders. The blanket had slipped off his huge bulk while he was sleeping. His dick looked about two feet long even resting. For a minute I thought about checking his pants out for a wallet, then retrieving a few bills, but I rejected this. You had taught me to have more sense. If he woke up, or checked his cash in the morning, he might have sat on me.

SON OF A WHORE

In the kitchen I found a quart bottle of whiskey that was still half full. I filled a glass and drank it. It washed away the milk taste I picked up in Mr. Sonorian's kitchen.

I went to bed right away. With Gavin gone, TV didn't have much appeal for me.

Anyway, since Gavin's stay with us I had figured out that it was a lot safer if I stuffed my money deep into a little hole in the underside of the mattress, instead of in that old coffee can. I hadn't counted it up, but there had to be more than two hundred dollars inside my mattress by now. About half of it came from the guys I met via Trilla, and the rest I rescued from your purse or even got as a tip from your boyfriends, who felt sorry for your pansy son. They weren't a bad group of guys at all, even if, like I mentioned, most of them might have made a hit in Hollywood doing the Godzilla role, not for the romance lead.

It was around two in the afternoon the next day when the big guy left. I could hear talking and some laughing, then the front door shutting. I came out of my closet and went into the living room. I wanted to say hello, to see if everything was friendly. You were there, dressed in that very expensive bathrobe, the silk or satin one with dragon designs and all kinds of furbelows. "Hi mom! Good morning!"

You looked at me and an expression of disgust changed your face in an instant. I followed your annoyed stare. Sure I was wearing panties. I always did. What was wrong with that? Then I saw that there was this gooey stain front and center. I must have come when I was with Mr. Sonorian without even knowing it! This was probably some drip out after I got dressed in his high class apartment. "Put on some pants! You are revolting!"

149

I went to the closet and put on some jeans. They didn't look all that much better. Then I went to the kitchen and started to heat up some soup. That's all there was, just soup and whiskey.

Half an hour later you came out of the bathroom fully dressed and made up for work. You came into the kitchen.

"Mom, you want some soup? It's good. Gavin always said I made great soup." I drank right out of the bowl, just like Gavin did, although he had the knack of doing it that way and I let quite a bit slop down the front of my yellow t-shirt.

"I want you to clean this kitchen and this apartment before I return from work! I am paying the rent and the food. You will have to contribute something or you will be out on the street with your low class friends!" Repeat stuff. You were gone. But now you thought that Gavin was a "low class friend". Not like before. I missed Gavin, and when I thought about him I felt I had a hole in me. I don't mean in the rear.

I gave the cleaning a try, although it was not the sort of thing I took to naturally. I got all the empty soup cans together and dumped them in the trash bin behind our building. Then I took a wet towel and scrubbed the stains off the kitchen counter and the kitchen floor as well as I could. I didn't vacuum the apartment. We didn't have a vacuum cleaner anymore. One of your customers, mom, who used it in his sex gig, took it with him when he left. The bathroom was too far gone to do much without special protective equipment, but I sloshed out the tub and the sink and sprayed the toilet with a disinfectant that made me cough for ten minutes. I left your bedroom as it was, not too bad. My closet was too small to be a problem.

SON OF A WHORE

When I finished cleaning the apartment, I stood back and admired it. It wasn't perfect. The place still looked pretty much like a slum. But I think it showed that I was not too bad at all as an ingénue housekeeper. I daydreamed about me keeping house for Gavin, while granny left to live in a home. Granny was you, mom, even though you were just under forty at the time.

Housework was fine, but I had to make a living, too. To get ready for Trilla's choice for the night, I went to the bathroom and let the tub fill. Taking a bath without Gavin just reinforced the feeling of what I had lost. There was no one to provide those twelve (actually eight) inches of relief that made me feel so much what I was inside, and that's completely leaving aside the emotional part. I stroked my own much smaller version for a few moments, but without much effect. At least I was following the advice the deodorant commercials gave you on TV. "It's a terrible thing to offend with body odor!"

I was walking up Polk Street from the station and pretending that I didn't care at all if Gavin showed up on some corner or other. I tried to convince myself that I was over all that. I looked around anyway. There were a lot of guys who looked a bit like Gavin, at least from a distance. Dressed in leather, blond, whether real or dyed, tough, aggressive, masculine. But when you caught up to them and looked at them close, they turned out to be totally different. They had twisted noses, wide mouths, low foreheads. They were fat or short or bent forward like a Neanderthal. All of this was not at all like Gavin. Gavin was pretty much perfect in the looks department. I admit that, ideally, he might have been a few inches taller.

It was embarrassing that I was taller than my onetime boyfriend. Basically, though, that didn't matter. Besides being tops on the physical side, Gavin was a problem solver, a protector, a manager, someone who liked you and who knew how to show it. He was a flatterer, but you got the feeling that he really felt it and meant it at the same time. The problem was that he wasn't anywhere. He had disappeared. Maybe he was working out some drug deal arrangement in the Fillmore or South of Market. What if I never saw him again? I felt that huge hole open up in my middle. I'd be alone, with no chance for anything except with some guy with a twisted mouth or a low forehead. I'd be stuck forever fucking Trilla's sad leftover customers and vacuuming the apartment with an imaginary vacuum cleaner!

While I was sorting these possibilities in my head, a "normal family" was coming toward me along the sidewalk. They were all there, together: dad, mom, and the kids. They were impressive, all dressed up, not really in the latest fashion, but "just right". Of course, that sort of thing wasn't for everybody. It obviously wasn't for me, even though I thought that the mom/dad/kids group was sort of an ideal that even I, in some way difficult to understand, was helping to promote.

I don't know if you, mom, were ever actually married to my father in any sort of way (or even knew his name?) You told me a lot of different stories about who he was. I'd seen a whole bunch of your boyfriends and, judging by them, I guess I lucked out by not having the bastard around.

The normal family was coming closer. They were so bright in their clothes and grooming that I thought they must be from some upper middle class suburb like Novata or Casa Ramblas. I looked at them, at each of them, all perfect in their way, mom, dad, the adorable kids. They shot me a smirk as they passed on the sidewalk. It was not, though, the worst I'd ever had. Then I looked at my reflection in a store window. Again, too much make-up. Way too much. No wonder mom and dad and the kids were smirking! Even though I always told myself to go easy when I was applying, because I knew that I tended to overdo it, it came out the same every time. Too much cover-up. Obvious.

I was on my way to work and I wasn't too thrilled about it. I might get lucky and end up again with someone like the Professor or, even better, with someone like the rich and generous Mr. Sonorian, but I might just as well find myself with some ass-buster deep into s/m. I dropped into a little street corner grocery store. I bought a cigarette. Just one cigarette. They sold them that way in some of the Arab groceries. I got a light from the counterman.

I was walking down Polk and I took a look at myself in every store window. The cigarette was dangling from my lips. I had wiped a lot of the make-up off my face with a shirt sleeve. I was wearing a green blouse again and my orange pants. Kind of chic. It certainly made me stick out. Maybe I could whore myself off to someone before I got to Tramp's. That way I'd save Trilla's sixty percent commission.

Then I saw it. I wasn't sure if it wasn't a hallucination or not, but what it looked like was a shiny red nineteen fifties Cadillac convertible, piloted by Gavin, and with an outrageous bouffant-haired, sequin dressed drag queen in the passenger seat! It shot across Polk, burning a red light, and sped toward Van Ness. I shouted after the Cad, "Gavin, you fucking bastard! Fuck you!"

If it was Gavin playing chauffeur to a drag empress, that was the end. I could see no more reason to go on living and whoring. If it was Gavin. He'd played loose with me before. This would be the limit, though, showboating with a freaky transvestite with terrible taste! (N.B.: It is important to emphasize that transvestites and transsexuals are not the same thing at all. They are almost opposites.) I sucked the last smoke out of my cigarette and sent the butt end flying after the car. I'd get even if it was Gavin playing around like that. Taking up with what looked like a Broadway floor show star when he was supposed to be saving our family!

Tramp's. I didn't bother to stop outside and take a look into the bar in order to brace myself. I walked right in and sat down at Trilla's table. She wasn't alone. She had this short, thin guy sitting next to her. He looked about eighteen, if not a couple of years younger. A small, boyish face, very slight trace of moustache and beard hair. Dark hair, but pale complexion, regular features. Cute effect. He probably wasn't wearing make-up at all, or only a little.

"So how's everything out there in, what was it? San Remainder?" Trilla almost laughed her head off. She was in a comic mood. I think she had drunk more than usual and maybe ingested some drugs, too. Her face was shiny, smiling, not focusing.

"San Cerrito," I corrected.

"Oh oh oh, yeah, that's right. Cerrito. Not that there ain't that much of a difference. This here's Alberto." She pointed to her table companion. "I think he got the 'o' from VO5." Trilla broke out laughing again. "See, he, he used to be just Albert, but that's kinda too plain. Alberto, this here's Marsha. She don't come in too often, but when she does, she's all business." I was "she" to Trilla a lot of the time and I liked this, but everyone knew that Trilla didn't mean it to be taken in the conventional sense. Not even Trilla fully accepted my claim to be a girl. This was sad.

Alberto offered to shake hands with me. I took his hand and, rather than shake in the ordinary way, we just held hands and looked at each other. It was clear that we liked each other, in the physical sense at least. "Hi!"

Trilla snapped her fingers in the direction of the bar. This meant whiskey. Soon we each had a triple in front of us. "Good to see you two guys are friendly. Just don't get too friendly, not on my time." Trilla laughed on. She was just cracking herself up. Alberto gave me a wink, as if to say, "she's pretty far gone, isn't she?"

"You already had one on my tab, 'Berto, so I'm takin' this one out of your pay." She had seen the wink. Trilla didn't miss a clue, no matter how stoned she got. That's how great she was. She was a really impressive black lady. We didn't use the word "Colored" anymore. "Okay, listen up, men. How'd the sissified two of you like to do a duet?" That meant that we'd share a client, but each would get the regular prostitute's cut, or pretty close. It was always the customer who asked for two, or even three, in order to supply a particular psychological need. Anyway, it was safer with two in case you met up with some psycho armed with a razor blade, although that was rare.

I looked at Alberto, who was actually very good looking. I nodded to Trilla. "Sure. Why not?"

"I thought you'd go for it. And I don't even have to ask 'Berto. With him, it's the more the merrier." Trilla laughed again, but not as much as before. Despite her persistent hilarity, there was a sad teariness pooling around Trilla's lower eyelids. "I got this customer who like to see two young guys doing it together, then he sort of join in when he feel like it. But wait on. Marsha, you need a makeover for this dude. C'mon." She towed me to the ladies' room again. As usual, she took a wet paper towel and rubbed my face. "Damn, you do go at it with your momma's paint!" When my face was clean she opened her purse, took out a bottle of light cream basic, and applied a few dots to my face. "Okay. That's way better. Go easy on it. You ain't Marine Antoinette. Stay put now." She took out her eyebrow pencil and gave me a few light strokes. I mean above the eyes.

We went back to the barroom. From a distance I saw Alberto's hair shining under the electric lights. He used something to slick it back. It didn't look bad. Sort of exotic.

"Okay, if you guys are ready, it's time to go." Trilla wrote out an address on the notepad she always kept nearby. She was paying off the police anyway, so she didn't mind leaving this little bit of evidence. "I know I can count on you. Only, just you behave. Once I sent two guys out on a gig and they rob the customer, left him tied up nude. Even took his clothes. But I know you two'd never do nothin' like that. If you did, I'd shut you down flat and hand you over to the polices."

The address was close enough to walk. "Jees," Aberto commented as soon as we were half a block from Tramp's, "she didn't have to say that stuff about robbing a customer.

I'm not that type and I'm sure you're not like that either."
He looked at me. He seemed to appreciate the effect of
Trilla's make-up on my face. I knew I looked pretty and
some guys like that.

"Yeah. I think it must have been all the booze she
downed. She's drinking more and more. I can tell the
effect, because my father died from alcohol." I was
talking about Robarb, who was my step-father, I *think,*
and he didn't actually die of drinking, but really from
the side effects of something. That is, if he really was
dead.

"I'm sorry about your father. I don't even like whiskey.
I only drank some just now because Trilla thinks it's the
best thing since penicillin." I laughed at this description,
so sadly accurate.

Alberto told me that he was actually thirty years old!
It was hard to believe, because he looked like someone in
his teens. If you looked really close, though, you could
see a lot of small wrinkles under his eyes and around
his mouth. His hairline was just starting to recede.
He probably admitted his real age because he wanted
to impress me with his youthful looks. Where Alberto
fell short was in his height. He was about five feet four,
maybe five five. That's part of what made him look like a
teenager. I'm close to six feet.

We walked along Polk, heading toward the bay, then
turned up a street in the direction of Nob Hill. "I only
engage in this sort of activity for the excitement. It's a new
thrill every time," Alberto told me. "I could get a regular
job anytime, perhaps enter a profession. I graduated from
Berkeley." I could now tell from his speech and from his
facial expressions that Alberto was educated and that he

was much older than the teenage years. He was still very good looking.

"My mom's a teacher," I said. "She's really smart and she likes to help people low down in the ignorance department." Obviously I was lying, and I think Alberto knew it, but he signaled his approval with a nod.

We were walking uphill now. It was an effort. I didn't like exercise. It reminded me too much of school.

"So how did you get connected with Trilla and her rent-a-whore business?" Alberto.

"Oh. It's because my mom won't give me any spending money. She says we have to save everything for my college education. She wants me to go to Harvard. That's where she went to school." The truth, of course, is that you went to City College for two years.

"Your mom seems to be a good sort of person, but I think she's too hard on you."

"She is, all right. She slaps me for a bad word. But I guess it's because she wants me to grow up right." It was really too late for me to grow up, but I put that in anyway.

Alberto gave me a hug around the shoulders and a kiss low on the cheek. He looked at the street where we were walking, at the houses and cars parked nearby. If it had been the right place, I think he would have done a lot more.

Now that we were going uphill, it was really clear how short Alberto was. Not that it mattered, especially lying down.

We were almost at the address Trilla had given us. I felt that I liked Alberto. He was good looking, nice, and he cared about other people. Where he fell short, in a way that *was* important, was that he wasn't Gavin. He lacked the special way Gavin had of taking hold of people, of invading them and making them part of himself. Gavin was over, though, and I had to try to accept it.

We were right in front of the building now, the address Trilla wrote down. Wow! It was like twenty or thirty floors and it was new. This guy had to have cash. So far, it looked like a normal prostitution assignment, and in fact one of the better ones. Little did we know, Alberto and me, that we were about to meet "The Ringmaster"!

Alberto pushed the intercom button for the apartment.

"Hello?" Suspicious, nasal voice.

"We were sent here by a friend." Of course Alberto did not mention Trilla by name. Prostitution was illegal, even if the police were getting their take.

"Come up." The buzzer sounded and I pushed the lobby door open.

Then we were in the elevator. "Okay," Alberto said. "This customer is obviously in the upper ten percent. Let's be nice to him and do whatever he wants. That way we'll get a good tip. I mean, within the realm of reason. I met one customer who wanted me to cut his nuts off. That sort of thing is to be avoided entirely." Alberto was a very well educated guy.

"Yeah. I know what you mean. You always have to be polite. Trilla taught me that from the start."

The hallway on the eighteenth floor had a lot of big flower pots on the floor and mirrors fixed to the walls. There was a framed painting opposite the apartment that we were looking for. It showed a lot of fat, nude children dawdling in front of their fat, naked mothers.

"Rubens. At least a copy." Alberto identified the painting immediately. "He was one of the greatest renaissance painters." He knocked on the apartment door. Two minutes later it opened.

"Hello. Come in." It was a guy around fifty-something dressed in red trousers, a blue shirt and a gold colored jacket. I noticed his carefully marcelled graying hair. He looked us over. He seemed to approve.

"In here." Marcel wasn't wasting time with light conversation, which made sense, because this was obviously going to be a fantasy thing for him. He led the way to a bedroom. The whole apartment was decorated with expensive furniture and all kinds of artistic things, like paintings of people with three noses or whole canvasses of splattered paint and other junk like that. Then we were in the bedroom. It was like a small living room. In the center was a huge bed with the naked bottom sheet exposed. Marcel lit a cigarette. It wasn't tobacco and it wasn't just marijuana. He inhaled deep, then offered it to Alberto. Alberto took a couple of long pulls. He seemed to like it. Then he handed what was left of the little cigarette to me. I took two small puffs, just to be sociable. I don't really like things you have to inhale. I have no problem with swallowing.

"All right." Marcel quickly got down to business. "I like to see young guys like you two getting it on together. I'll just watch, and maybe I'll touch you a bit."

This seemed reasonable. It made sense that an old guy in his fifties wouldn't want to take his clothes off or actually get involved in sex directly. Alberto took off his shirt and t-shirt. He had a nice build and quite a bit of hair on his chest. He turned me on already. It would be okay that Marcel would be watching.

When we were both naked Alberto began to rub

my chest. He seemed to like the fact that I had no hair there and very little elsewhere, except on top of my head, where I had enough to make up a bouffant if I wanted to. Meanwhile Marcel had put a funny little cap with a black visor on his head. He motioned us onto the bed.

Alberto began to fondle me but when he saw that it didn't produce much of an effect, he twigged. He turned me onto my stomach and started to get himself ready to penetrate. Marcel was smoking another cigarette and the room had a definite druggy odor. Soon Alberto was inside me and it felt really good. He started to pump hard and I felt that feminine sensation that turned me on so much. I wasn't paying much attention to anything else when the first whip crack sounded.

Marcel was holding a circus type whip and he snapped it in the air. Then he snapped it just above Alberto's head. "Screw the boy," he commanded, as if that wasn't exactly what Al had been doing. The whip cracked in the air. Now we both understood the gig. It wasn't exactly ideal, but you had to play along. Professional honor was involved.

Alberto was moving fairly good, despite the constant whip snaps. I think he was more than halfway there when the leather landed across his back. I felt the recoil when his body winced. Then I got one on the legs. It didn't hurt too much really.

"Screw him harder!" the marcelled ringmaster commanded. "The idea" was that we were circus performers or even circus animals, and he was The Ringmaster. It was sort of nuts, and I think he must have been short on personal romantic interest for one reason or another.

Okay. It was part of the deal. We both tried to

cooperate as much as possible, even though the scene was bizarre and obnoxious. I wanted to go through with it and I think Alberto did too, if only for the money. "On with the show!" was our motto.

Soon Alberto seemed almost there, in spite of the whip snaps and actual blows now raining down on his back. At a certain point, though, he went limp. He pulled out and fell onto the bed, on his back. You couldn't blame him. I mean, there may be nothing wrong with that sort of thing from a theoretical point of view, the whipping and all, but it takes a certain type. He sat up on the bed. Alberto's back had several deep red stripes. Angry, almost in tears, he said, "that' it. That's all I can take."

I was rubbing my legs where some whip blows had landed.

Marcel offered him another little cigarette. "This will make you forget the pain." Alberto refused.

Alberto and I sat naked on the bed while the Ringmaster stood there in his show time finery.

"I told Trilla what I wanted and she said she'd send two boys who were willing. Now you both drop out before the show has hardly started!" Marcel was angry. He wanted value for the money that he paid for things, like the paintings of people with three noses and the same number of breasts.

"It's just," Alberto began, "I can't take too much of that kind of thing. It was very uncomfortable." He reached an arm behind his back and rubbed the red stripes. "If it was just symbolic or very light, that would be okay, but it went too far for me. It was too painful." He was whimpering.

I was putting my clothes on already. Marcel noticed that I was wearing girls' underwear. He shot me a look of disgust. Alberto seemed to think it was only natural, considering what he knew about me.

"You would have received appropriate compensation," Marcel argued, directing his words to Alberto. He appeared to accept the fact that the scene had collapsed, that the gig was over, but he wanted to justify his *conception* of the event. "I think you would have found that after a certain level, pain is its own reward." I was impressed with his educated speech. He must have gone to Harvard.

Al was slowly pulling on his jockey shorts, but they were still below his knees. "I just can't take it. Sorry." I focused on his crotch. His genitals were large and well furnished with dark hair. It turned me on so much that I just might have been willing to try the Ring business again. For Alberto, though, it was definitely out. He had taken the worst of it, after all.

When I was dressed I just stood next to the bed. I didn't know how Marcel planned to handle the money aspect and I was afraid that he might refuse to pay, since his little gig barely got off the ground. At least that's probably how he saw it. Alberto was now in his shorts and sitting on the bed. He couldn't see where his trousers had landed. He looked up at the Ringmaster, wondering what came next. I think Al too was worried about the guy defaulting on payment.

"Well," I said, "I have to get home. My mom'll be worried about what the hell I've been up to." This was not true. I'd be home long before you, mom, would "in all probability". I think that's how Marcel would have put it. Anyway, it was not the sort of thing you would have been surprised at, not from me, anyway. I stood there. Was he going to hand over the cash, or what?

Soon Al was dressed and standing too, but we made no move to exit. We were waiting and hoping.

Marcel came forward and took something out of his Ringmaster coat pocket. He pressed it into my hand. It was a twenty dollar bill, the tip part for me. Fucking cheap skate! "I'll let the other boy settle payment matters with your friend on Polk Street." He moved me toward the apartment exit. Alberto followed.

We were at the door when Al turned to the Master and made a suggestion. (I think he had seen my miserable tip). "Why don't we try something more regular? Just to see how it goes?"

It was clear that Marcel was far more attracted to Alberto. He just didn't like effeminates, probably, and it wouldn't have improved matters if I explained that I was really a transsexual and that I was psychologically a girl, etc, etc.

"Stick around a few minutes," he told Al. Then he opened the door. "Bye." He pushed me the rest of the way out and closed the door.

I stood listening in the hallway for some time. I was curious about what would happen between Ringie and Alberto. Would they tee up? Or would Al be exiting soon with the rest of the cash? After about five minutes I heard talking, then laughing, then the sounds of footsteps inside the apartment on Marcel's marble floors. Most likely they were heading back to the bedroom. I trudged to the elevator. I still felt the stinging on my legs. The fucking freak had maimed me, then cheaped out on the tip!

Now I had to trek back to the train station and try to catch the last cars headed to east bay north. There was some hope that I could collect forty or at least thirty dollars from Trilla after Alberto settled our gig with Marcel, but I was walking away with only twenty, not that much more than train fare and other expenses for the evening. I cooled off as I walked the blocks to Market Street. I felt that it would have been a real neat experience just between me and Alberto, but I didn't resent the fact that he went on alone with the customer. It was the trade, after all. Marcel didn't like pansies (effeminate persons who are less masculine than the average Joe), but that wasn't going to be the case with everybody. For me the problem was that not too many of them were willing to pay for the experience.

I stayed in bed late the next afternoon. I heard you leave the apartment at the usual time, around two thirty p.m., but I didn't get out of bed until four. I spent part of that time thinking about Alberto. He was a really handsome guy and very, or at least considerably, masculine. The rest of the time I jerked it around, just imagining how last night's event might have gone without *el senor* Ringmaster.

When I finally got to the kitchen I found that there was only one can of soup left. I lucked out. It was potato vegetable beef, my favorite. It had all that salt that filled you up again after a night of whiskey drinking.

The television was on. Probably I forgot to turn it off last night when I was having a few bedtime drinks after the painful and disappointing circus routine. Now they were showing the end of a program about sheep in Australia. There was a long commercial break, then a discussion show started about the cost of doing or was it not doing something? Education or highways, I think.

The telephone rang. For a moment I was scared that it might be the school attendance officer, but I remembered that I was about six months over eighteen now, and I already told them off about it, so they couldn't bug me anymore. Probably it was a wrong number or maybe you were calling to remind me to clean the place up and wash my ass after my night away. I answered. "Hello. My mom's not here."

"Marsha, man, you gotta help me! Pick me up dude, I'm stuck here!" It was Gavin's voice.

Gavin was back! I was thrilled. My hand went unconsciously to my heart. "I'll be right there. Where did you go? You never came back after you were here the last time."

"I'll explain later, dude. Come and get me out of this dump before the cops or somebody worse murders the fuck out of me!"

"Gav! Okay. Yes. I'm going now." I stood up, looked around for my shoes, then the question hit me. "Where are you?"

"I'm right down here in Cerrito, at the station. I can't go anywhere because the police have about ten warrants out on me and those motherfucking burn artists from the Fillmore really got pissed this time and took everything I had and said they'd kill me wherever I hid out!"

"Oh! Okay. I get it completely. I'm going down now. Don't move anywhere, Gav'. You got to come home to help me and mom. You wouldn't believe how fucked up we've been since you took off!"

"Maybe I would. Bring a raincoat with you. I gotta go in disguise. And a hat. Not one of your old lady's."

I hung up, then I rushed around the apartment. I

didn't have a raincoat. I took yours, mom. In raincoats, there's not too much difference between men and women, right? I didn't have a hat, either. I found one of uncle Robarb's old hats (he liked to wear hats. He wasn't bald, only he just looked better covering up most of his head). But it was so old and filthy and beat up that I just couldn't let Gavin wear it. Then I had an important question to decide. What should I wear for face make-up? It had to be fast, so I just took a large dab of basic and applied it to my face as far as it would spread. Despite the urgency of the situation, I thought that my physical impression on Gavin after a long absence was important. Obviously I wasn't going to "dress up". I mean in drag. There wasn't time and, anyway, I knew that Gavin didn't really like that sort of thing. I pulled on my orange pants and that green shirt that used to be yours. I was out the door.

Gavin was back! Whatever the problem was, whatever arguments he had with the police and drug dealers, the main point was that he had come back! Life could begin again. With all his faults, and he had them, Gavin was a real person, somebody stuffed with actual physical humanity. That's more than you can say about a lot of the ringmasters.

The San Cerrito train station was a ten minute walk. I think I made it in six. I had a way of walking that a lot of people laughed at, but it could put out the m.p.h.

I checked out the station as I got closer. I didn't see anybody yet who looked like Gavin. I should have remembered his unconventional "disguises" from before. There were a few old ladies who probably just came back from cleaning offices in San Francisco, waiting for a bus. There were the usual bums and panhandlers. A taco truck was the main attraction for most of the crowd. Close to the sidewalk was a long bike rack and at the end of it somebody had left a large bundle of old clothes. I rushed past the bicycles and headed toward the ticket gate. Suddenly the large bundle spoke.

"Here, man! Over here. It's me."

I looked again. Under layers of what might be soot and dirt or camouflage paint, I made out the attractive features and bright blue eyes of Gavin. This had happened before about three times, the discovery of Gavin as a pile of old clothes. It was part of his lifestyle, his version of the "eternal return". That's from Nietzsche, a kind of German guy from a thousand years ago, who I read about later in jail. "What happened? What did they *do* to you?" My voice was tearful and unsteady.

"I'll tell you later. I had to hide out for days in a dump spot behind Polk. I was on the run again and I didn't have a dime. Only today I got lucky and ran into a guy I knew before and he lent me some bucks for the train ride to Cerrito. Otherwise I might be dead right now."

I gasped at the horror of this thought. Even in disguise and covered with what looked like some sort of camouflage grease, Gavin was still far out handsome. His sexy body was clearly outlined despite the squatting position he had taken to avoid attention. "No!"

"Let me have that raincoat, dude." He put on your raincoat, mom. He looked good in it. It gave his body an elegant finish on top of the well made limbs and torso. "Did you bring a hat?"

"Uh-uh. We didn't have one. Turn the raincoat collar up and keep your head down. That'll be almost as good."

"I don't know." He tried it. "Okay, let's go."

We walked out of the station area at a moderate gait. We didn't want to look like criminals fleeing the scene. "Shit, dude," Gavin groaned as we got nearer to home. "I haven't eaten in about two weeks. When you got police and dealers working together to do you in, all you can do is run. I hope your old lady's got some stuff in the fridge."

I doubted it. I had finished the last soup can about an hour ago.

When we reached the foot of the stairs to our apartment we stopped and looked back, to see if anybody was following us. Then we took the steps three at a time, and we were inside. Gavin locked the door behind him. He took me in his arms and gave me a hug. "Thanks man. You saved my life one more time. I mean, the bastards I been dealing with wouldn't kill you just for a quarter. They'd do it just for fun." Gavin shed the elegant raincoat and started to take his clothes off. They hadn't seen a laundry room in weeks. He took his pants and underpants off first. His member was already half erect. It was probably the excitement of escape. He stood waiting. Well? It took me half a second to twig. I got down on my knees in front of him. I could tell by the way he reacted to my efforts that Gavin must have had a large number of head jobs in the last few weeks. Probably he was paying me off now for my help so far. He was fully erect within seconds. I could see his hairy, muscular legs and his large, dark scrotum as I worked my mouth around his dick. Only about half of it would fit in. It was a thrill for me and I'm sure he enjoyed it too. When he shot out he moaned in a way that was unmistakably genuine.

"Awh! Thanks, man. It really relieves the stress after all the shit I been through." He walked in that sort of cowboy gait he had over to the armchair and fell into it. His pants, shirt and shorts were on the ground near the door. He raised one foot and rested it on the seat of the chair. His central area looked fantastic, and he wasn't even thinking of it, just like several times before. I hadn't come yet. I would make a try for it later. Gavin tuned in to the television. He was totally oblivious (got this from Webster's. It means like forgetting something) to his naked glory. "Hey, man. You couldn't get me some kind of grub, could you? I mean, I don't want to die off from starvation and add another number to those U.N. statistics."

I laughed. Gavin, although completely uneducated, had picked up a lot of information just by watching TV. "I'll have to go to the grocery store. Mom forgot to do the shopping. She's been busy."

"Yeah." Gav' understood. He'd been pretty busy himself. The same was true for me.

I waited, looking alternately at Gavin in his glory and the TV screen. I thought he'd come through with some cash. He ought to have some left after all those deals (I didn't really believe his story about the train fare). Again, Gavin understood. His native intelligence had taken it in at a shot. "Sorry, man. I don't have a nickel left from that loan I got from a friend. Three weeks ago I could've given you a few hundred for the service you just did for me right now. I was carrying thousands on me. Those guys held me up at gun point and didn't leave me a plug cent."

"I understand. I can borrow a few bucks from mom." I left the living room, but I went unobtrusively (Webster's) to my closet. I knew you never kept money in your bedroom. You'd been in the business long enough to know better. I took the roll of bills from inside my mattress and peeled off a twenty. I never kept anything in the coffee can anymore.

At the store, that is the liquor store, I got things that you could eat without cooking. I knew Gavin wouldn't want to wait while I played Julia Child. I picked up a huge bag of barbecue taco chips, a package of cheese and one of salami, and two quarts of whiskey. When I had dumped all of this in front of the checker, he looked at me from behind his black mustache and thick glasses. "You don't look twenty-one. You look about fifteen. No I.D., no liquor."

"I'm buying it on orders from my mother! Mr. Sarcafarian knows both of us and he always let me pay for alcohol for my mother before." Mr. Sarcafarian was the owner of the store. The mustache and glasses was probably a relative of some kind. He nodded in deference at the name and took my twenty and handed me back eighteen cents in change.

I rushed back home. I knew Gavin was hurting. When I finally reached the living room I found him drinking out of our old whiskey bottle. Not much was left even before. He was sitting in the armchair with both feet on the ground and naked below the waist. His shirt (a sense of decorum obviously led him to put it back on) was open, displaying a fine arrangement of light chest hair.

He took one of the bottles. "I'm glad you thought of getting some more of this stuff. I'm still totally freaked out." He cracked the bottle top and took an impressive swig.

I handed him the taco chips. I planned to put the other whiskey bottle away in the kitchen. Gavin would pass out on too much generosity.

"Far fuckin' out, man! Thanks tons. You're the best girl friend I ever had. And you know what? It don't matter a bit that you got a little dick on you."

These words coming from Gavin gave me a thrill. I felt I had finally made it. I was a success. Almost. I handed over the cheese and salami.

"Whew! Party time. Dude, if I'd had this stuff a few days ago, I coulda avoided all that malnutrition junk."

I sat on the floor next to the armchair. I watched Gavin eat. He could really put those taco chips away! Well, it was a lot easier when you could wash it down with large swigs of whiskey. Soon he was rather full and ate more slowly, sometimes putting a bit of cheese or a slice of salami on top of a taco chip, then chewing at a leisurely rate. His eyes were generally stuck on the TV. "What's your old lady been up to?"

"Oh. The same routine. She's at Bombo's Club working right now, as usual."

"Yeah. I really admire your mom. Like I told you before, there's not a whole lot of 'em who'd slave away for their family like that."

I thought about this. I suppose it was true, at least in part. It wasn't entirely for "the family", though.

"How about you? What the hell sort of gigs you been up to? You haven't just been watching the boob tube all day, have you?"

"No." I looked at the floor. I wanted to be honest with Gavin. Also, I wanted him to know all about my life so that he could arrange the improvements he promised. "I've been working for Trilla some nights. Last night she sent me and another person to see this guy who lives in a high rise on Nob Hill. He used a whip on us!"

"You did a trick with a fucker who used a whip on you? I would've kicked his balls to L.A." Gavin ruffled my hair affectionately. "You don't have to take that shit even if you are a whore."

"It didn't get too far. We both sort of pulled out when this guy got really violent. I only got a few hits on the legs."

"Shit! You got into some crap like that? Now I know I have to take good care of you. Your mom said you liked to have guys spank you, but that's not the same thing at all."

The spankings. So you'd mentioned that to Gavin! This was highly embarrassing. It only happened a few times and it was generally light. It's hard to find a good looking guy who likes to show that kind of hard domination. "We did it to each other." This wasn't true. "Just sort of playing around."

"Ah. Yeah. I had a few customers who liked me to use a paddle on them. Well, okay, it's their money."

A movie was starting on TV, some kind of love romance flic where the female lead uses a lot of scarves. Gavin watched intently. He took small sips of whiskey from time to time. I had provided him with a glass. To me it seemed to make the whole experience more high class. I was drinking, too. It didn't bother me that there were small pieces of taco chip floating in the whiskey.

When a long commercial break came on, I had a question for Gavin, something that had been bugging me for some time. "Gav'? I was on Polk Street a few days ago and I saw something really odd." I had to approach the subject in a way that didn't make it seem like I was jealous or angry. I wanted to keep Gavin in a good mood, for obvious reasons. "I saw this huge red Cadillac convertible speed by and the driver looked a lot like you."

"Uh? Yeah. It was probably me alright. I had to work this job as a chauffeur for a while just to get a little cash so I could survive. It only lasted a few days. Fucking Cad couldn't stop in time to avoid hitting a dump truck in the rear end." He thought for a moment. "I was taking a toke when we hit, so I like couldn't concentrate too good on the driving. I guess I was going about fifty on the street, but the bitch was making me do it. She thought it looked real cool. Like everybody was watching her."

"You mean that drag queen that was in the car with you?"

"Yeah. La Empressa. She does a top drag act at a night club on Broadway and pulls in loads of cash. She wanted me to be her chauffeur, so everybody would see that she had a young dude at her service. She must be pushing forty and it ain't pretty when she's out of make-up."

I considered this. "How long did you work for her?"

"Well, it was like two days total, plus two nights. She kept me going twenty-four hours." Gavin took a full drink from his glass. "I had to take off on foot when we hit that trash truck. I don't have no license."

So that explained it. It was perfectly innocent on Gavin's part. I guess he had to give La Empressa a couple of romantic thrills, but that hardly mattered to me, seeing her age.

The evening was getting on. It had been dark out for a couple of hours. Gavin was relaxing in front of the screen, where the romance movie was still playing out (the trailer said it was "the original unedited version". Maybe this wasn't too good an idea.) He'd taken in a good deal of whiskey, considerably more than I had, but he still hadn't put his shorts back on. "Gav', maybe you better get dressed, don't you think, just in case mom comes in early again?"

"Uh. Yeah. I didn't think of that. Although, I don't see why it ought to bother her. I mean, she's seen it before, right?"

We both laughed. This wasn't meant to be a put-down at all. But why not be honest about it? I retrieved his shorts and pants and he slowly pulled them on during commercial breaks. I had seen "it" before too and it certainly didn't bother me. I took your raincoat back to the bedroom, mom, and I hung it up carefully in the closet, smoothing out some of the wrinkles. I knew how you could get about borrowing your good clothes.

I was back in the living room in time to see the final end of the love romance movie. Gavin was thrilled.

"Wow! That was really cool when he got married to her in the end, after beating off all those jerks. I mean, it showed he wasn't just a prick or something."

I sipped from my whiskey. It was only my fourth for the night, although it was getting sort of late. "We ought to think about something, though. What if my mom brings some guy home tonight? She doesn't know you came back. I mean, how are we gonna deal with that?"

"Oh, yeah. Well, I suppose she has to do it for now to help with expenses and all, but I don't know. Maybe we could tell the guy to flake off, so that we could all get adjusted together again after me being away. You know what I mean?"

I didn't know exactly, but I could try a good guess. I mean, he probably planned to sleep with you tonight, mom.

The telephone rang. It was on the table next to the armchair, so Gavin naturally picked up the receiver. "Hi!

Yeah … yeah. Gavin, that's right … I had to drop by to see how you and Marsha were doing … yeah … He said Trilla sent him to do a trick with some guy who beat him with a whip … Yeah … Terrible … Much worse than spanking … He's got marks on his legs … Yeah … I think that shows you both need me here to help you out … Yeah … Thanks, mom … What? … But … Why?"

Gavin hung up the phone and turned to me. He wasn't happy. "She wants me to sleep in your room tonight. And she told me not to get rough with the customer, or I was out for good."

"Mom can be real strict about the customers. It's her business, see, but she also has some personal involvement sometimes."

"What? With those slobs? You gotta be nuts."

"It's true most of them wouldn't look good even in a police line-up, but there's something psychological working in mom's head that makes her bring these guys home. I think she's like getting even for all the times some other guys dumped her when she was younger."

"Like your dad," Gavin suggested. It was an obvious probability.

"Maybe. I don't know too much about him, whoever he was. Mom's not totally sure herself."

"What time is it? When's she usually come back home with these dream boat guys?"

I went to the kitchen and read the hours and minutes on the little clock on the front of the stove, then came back. "It's about two o'clock," I told Gavin. "Mom usually gets back before three, so I guess we better get out of the way." I tried to sweep up some of the mess on the living room floor, the crumbs from the taco chips, the pieces of cheese.

"Shit!" Gavin stood up and stretched his arms. "I hate crowding into that dinky little cubbyhole when there's a huge bedroom waiting almost empty." He filled his whiskey glass before walking off to the bathroom. I could hear the sounds of a huge urination when he yelled back, "what's worse is knowing your mom has to do a stunt with those fucking creeps! That's what really pisses me off."

Before three o'clock we were both in the little closet. "Fuck, though, man, if I hear any sounds of some guy getting like brutal with your mom, I'll clean kill the fucker off."

Some time later a key sounded in the apartment door lock. We could hear talking and laughter. The man's voice was a base, maybe a base baritone. The closet door was open. It gave onto a little hallway that connected to the living room. We could tell when the living room lights were turned off. Then there were sounds from the direction of the bedroom.

I could see that Gavin was getting upset. "I can get to the kitchen even in the dark," I told him, "in case you want another whiskey or something to eat."

"Fuck you, man." Gavin rolled onto his side and pulled the blanket over his head.

I turned the closet light bulb off. It must have been close to four o'clock. There were definite noises coming from the bedroom, but they weren't sounds of anger or fighting. More the opposite, kind of a fun time, fully paid.

In the dark, Gavin threw the blanket off. We were both sleeping nude, so there was no need for preparation. He rolled me onto my stomach. He started to smack my butt with the palm of his hand. "This is what you like, isn't it?" He began hitting hard. I think he wanted to make sounds that would annoy the two of you in the bedroom, and at the same time to take his jealousy out on me. Anyway, it wasn't so bad at all. After ten minutes or so—my ass would have shown fire engine red if the light was on—he entered me. He began to pump inside me, inside my butt. Soon he was close to arrival time. He started moaning. "Marsh ... Marsh ... 'Salka!"

The next day I hit out to the store as soon as you left the apartment. Once more I caught sight of your "friend" on my way out, mom. He was heading down the street. Ugh. Bad taste. He looked like a washing machine on short stilts. A lot of your customers looked like that. Either that or they were the thin, dried up, mean kind, which is almost worse.

Gavin was sleeping late. When I got up he seemed close to being in a coma. It was pretty clear that he was depressed. I knew this from what the shrink told me that time when the school creeps made me go to therapy. You get depressed and you don't want to do anything, say anything, fuck anything. I think the reason was that he really liked you, mom, and he was blasted away when you came back with some asshole on the first night of his return. For him, you were mom and girlfriend rolled into one.

I got some more supplies. I wanted to have Gavin's favorite soup on hand when he woke up. It usually calmed him down a lot. Good old canned soup. Maybe they put some kind of tranquillizer in it.

When I got back to the apartment, Gavin was up. He was sitting in the armchair in the living room. The TV was on, some kind of political talk thing where these guys sit around agreeing with themselves. Gav' was still pissed off. You could tell from his expression.

"Man! Here I am tryin' to get this family back to a normal, decent way of doing stuff and your mom brings home some fucker that looks like he just got turned loose from some psycho fat farm." I think Gavin was thinking about the one before, because he hadn't actually seen the last psycho fat farm guy.

"Yeah. I don't like it either, and I've seen it about a million times. It's the trade she's in, though. Maybe we can work on her slowly and get her away from it, like you were planning."

"And you, too. One of these days some guy with a whip is gonna like take a razor to your you-know-whats. Not that it'd bother you all that much."

I laughed. "My mom likes you, Gav'. I think you picked up on that. It's plain as day." I ought to have said night. "Only, she's still stuck in her old 'behavior pattern', like they say on TV. The therapy hasn't started on her yet."

"Maybe she does like me, but she sure has a shitty way of showing it."

"It's because of her complexes. She has this thing about men. See, she never even met her own father. I think he died in the Franco-Russian War. Grandma said something like that."

"Okay. I'm gonna really start to work on her. In a psychological way, that is." Gavin was completely naked as he sat in the chair. He was playing with himself in an absent-minded way.

"I'll heat up some soup for you." I walked toward the kitchen.

"Naw, I don't want any of that shit. I'm not even hungry."

After ten minutes I came back with a bowl of nice hot soup. I handed it to Gavin. He drank directly from the bowl, as usual. He wasn't happy, but he looked considerably more content as he finished the soup. A loud burp followed.

We were about half an hour into some old war movie about enemy spies sneaking around London when Gavin decided that he definitely could use some more head. Since I was sitting on the floor next to the armchair, like before, I was the obvious candidate.

Fully erect, Gav' had to push it halfway down my throat to get real satisfaction. I almost choked a couple of times, but on the whole it was a terrific experience. I think it showed that he really thought of me as Marsha and not as Marcus, and he was almost the only other person who thought that, besides me. I think you weren't sure about it, mom, which is understandable. After all, you made out my birth certificate.

Gavin was taking it easy that day. He wasn't drinking whiskey at all, only a few beers, then a couple of glasses of wine. A new mood of seriousness had taken hold of him, as if he had finally decided what he had to do after a considerable period of just fucking around. When the news came on at six o'clock, Gavin watched intently. It seemed he wanted to know what was happening in the world in order to take it into consideration for the strategy he was thinking up. All of that bang-up business in Vietnam was mostly over now. They were just figuring out the last details. Stock markets were weaving in and out, predictions betting on boom or bust. Striptease artists with huge breasts were attracting bigger crowds than ever on Broadway. They were doing a report on it. The last part of the "special segment" grabbed Gavin's attention. He pointed at the screen. "Look. That's Empressa they're showing now. Yeah. She can really put on a performance. I watched it from backstage a couple of times. Her big problem, see, is she can't do topless. Even with all the hormones she takes, her boobs aren't really huge. So she has to keep that phony bra on."

I sympathized with this problem. It must have been a real drag to get yourself castrated and then take all those pills and still only have relatively medium breasts. "What does she do in her act, then?"

"Oh, she does a sort of comedy routine and bumps and bustles around dressed in a low neckline dress with all these sequins and a lot of padding around her ass and tits. She tells jokes about drag while the drummer puts in hits. All the tourists from Kansas think it's funny as hell, they can't stop laughing." Gavin took a hit from his wine glass. I had taught him to drink from a glass whenever possible. This might have been my biggest achievement so far.

For dinner, Gav' wanted something besides the old soup. This was understandable. I went to the avenue and brought back a burger and fries.

"Far out!" Gavin always appreciated everything you did for him. That was one of his best virtues. He took a large bite from the burger, then began stuffing fries into his mouth.

When dinner was over, we both started to think about what would happen when you got back from work, mom. (Maybe I should say "back to work"?) We knew how important it was for you to be happy about Gavin's return. The main question was whether you'd bring home another guy with a poor love life and extra cash. I thought you wouldn't, because otherwise you would have called to make sure we were out of the way. Gavin wasn't so sure. "Maybe she'd forget to think about that until she walked in the door. Anyway, this time I'm going to put my foot down. No more fucking prostitution in this house! I made that rule before, but I let up on it after I got lost around SF for a week or so, but that's over. We have to start putting all this shit on an even keel!"

I nodded. I had been in agreement from the start, from the first time Gavin announced his project to save us from vice and make us into a normal, decent family. I had an afterthought, though. "If she does bring some overloaded slob back with her, you might wait ten minutes or so before you try a bust up. The reason is, she always collects before, since you can't count on getting anything afterward. If you time it right, we get the money *and* the palooka goes out the door."

"I don't know, man. You can do a hell of a lot of shit in ten minutes."

Gavin was still relaxing with a glass of wine when the Johnny Carson Show came on the screen. It was his favorite. Gavin didn't get all of the jokes, but he appreciated the high class tone of the entertainment.

"Okay," Gavin stood up when the Show ended. It was one o'clock. "I gotta get ready." He was still naked. He'd been naked all day. It seemed almost his natural state. Soon there was the sound of bath water running. I came into the bathroom and began taking my clothes off. Gavin was already in the tub.

"Not tonight, Marsh. You already had a go earlier and

we got it on last night. At least I did. I have to save my energy, if you know what I mean."

I did. I was disappointed, but I knew I had to play along. I thought about what Gavin should wear for your benefit. Just his jeans and a t-shirt seemed too common. That wouldn't have especially impressed you, mom. I got a fresh pair of jockey shorts for him from the supply you once bought me and that I never wore. I added a knee length blue silk bathrobe with running horse motifs that I retrieved from your closet. I think it used to belong to one of your boy friends who lasted longer than most of the others. All of this I brought to the bathroom and hung on the towel rack. "Use this stuff, Gav'. I think you'll make a bigger hit with mom." His fine blond chest hair would look great through the low cut bathrobe.

Gavin scrubbed up as he lay in the tub. His member was already showing significant activity. He picked up on my expression of disappointed longing. "Don't get upset about it, Marsha. You always get your turn. And remember that your mom really loves you. She told me that again over the phone. She thinks you're gonna be a doctor or a lawyer some day."

I'd have to start high school first. This was a disagreeable prospect. I nodded. "I guess she does, in her way."

"Sure she does. Hell, if she didn't love you 'cause you were her own son, she'd probably want to go for a roll in the hay with you." We both laughed at this. It wasn't meant as a put-down. It was just giving things their due consideration.

When the key turned in the apartment door lock, Gavin was still in the bathroom, where he was putting a few last finishing touches to his hair. He had combed his big blond mop partly over his forehead, with just a wisp over one eye. I admired his hair. My hair was light colored too, but lank and sort of reddish.

You came into the living room at the same time Gavin entered stage left from the bathroom in his jockey short/bathrobe combination. No palooka: Gavin had talked to you about the palooka business before he cut out for Polk Street last time, sort of announced the general rule, and now it seemed finally to be working, probably since he talked to you in a general way over the phone earlier when you called to rant at me about the cleaning thing, only he answered instead. He tried to give you a hug. You pushed him away.

"None of that, Gavin. If you want to live in this apartment you'll have to behave properly and contribute your share of work. Otherwise, I don't care how many gangsters and police detectives are looking for you."

"I will, mom. Don't you worry about a little thing." Gavin gave you a kiss on one cheek. I could see that you enjoyed it as much as he did. You walked to the bathroom to start your late night routine of make-up removal and clothes changing.

"And you can start by cleaning the damn bathroom after you use it!" you shouted from the other room. "It's like a swamp in here."

"You oughta taken care of that," Gavin told me in a low voice.

"There wasn't any time. I think she got back too early because of what you told her before about leaving out the slob element." I looked at my feet. "It just took a while to set in."

"Anyway, go get me an' her a couple of whiskies. It'll help relax her and put her in a better mood."

When you came out of the bathroom, you didn't look happy. "I don't want any high jinks from you two. I had a bad stretch at work and I'm not feeling well." This was generally the case, judging from your late night moods.

"What's wrong, babe?" Gavin put his arm around your shoulder.

"I'm extremely tired and my stomach is upset. I'd appreciate it if you two would clear out of the living room and go to bed."

"Oh man. Take a little sip of this." Gavin handed you a glass of whiskey. "This stuff always helps me out with a little tummy ache."

You followed the doctor's orders. It seemed to work right away.

"I'm sorry you feel tired, mom. Maybe there's something I can do," Gavin said. "My mom used to do massage like for a profession and she taught me a lot of the moves. It'll like relax you and give you back some energy."

"No. Not tonight." You went into the bedroom. Gavin, dressed in his blue silk running horse bathrobe, followed.

I stayed outside. I mean, I understood that the gig would work better that way.

"No, mom, c'mon, let me give you a few rubs, just to relax the muscles."

Gavin closed the bedroom door. I stood listening just outside. I was curious about how things would work out between the two of you. I could hear movements, some sounds of relief and satisfaction. "Better?" "Oh, ah, oh, uh."

There were sounds of a low volume conversation that I couldn't make out. Then some louder words. "I'm glad you called me when Marsha was out at the store and explained again. Now I understand why you have to stay away from the city." Your voice.

"Yeah. And Marsha's been a real help. She like saved my life again, almost. She's a real pal. Those drug guys don't play games."

"Exactly." Your voice changed to sarcastic. It was jealousy, I think. I recognized the tone right off. Now I was "the other woman". "For you, he's almost like a girlfriend for a boyfriend in need." There was a pause. I imagined a few sips disappearing from a whiskey glass. "You told me about his experience with that man with the whip. You're doing nothing to discourage him. He's going to get himself killed one of these days. I think I should have had him castrated by a doctor years ago. That way he wouldn't want to do all those revolting things."

It hurt to hear you talk about me like that. I still wasn't sure that you liked me, despite what Gavin said. I think you put in that part about castration because you were jealous over Gavin, although the idea itself didn't really bother me. Many transsexuals have it done themselves. It's not a huge loss.

I listened outside the bedroom door for a long time. When I was fairly sure that I was hearing sounds of sex contact, I went back to the living room. I sat down in the chair. The screen was moving, but I'm not sure if it was an old movie or a cooking show. I picked up a half full glass of wine and drained it at a gulp. Gavin had left it there when he changed out for whiskey. Problems. How many guys—I really want to say girls—have a boyfriend for a stepfather? It seemed to be turning out that way. Gavin and you had done it before. I might as well be frank out and say you two had fucked a lot before. At first it didn't bother me. I felt proud that the guy who was my boyfriend first was also making the scene with my mom. It showed you approved of my taste. It was a tribute to my maturity. Now I was looking at it differently, especially after I twigged that you were getting jealous feelings about our co-boyfriend.

I was up early the next afternoon. I hoped I would be able to serve Gavin some soup when he woke up. In a way, it seemed to be the key to his heart. You came into the kitchen fully dressed and made-up. You looked terrific, as usual, only tired. Maybe Gavin had given you too much of a run last night?

"I don't know how much longer I can keep working to support you two boys." Complaint time. I was used to it. At least you could have said "one and a half boys and half a girl".

"I'm wearing myself out every day while you lie around the apartment drinking and watching television. That is going to change. I want you, and I want Gavin, to find jobs, real jobs, so you can contribute to expenses. Do you understand?"

"Yeah." We'd gone through this routine, except for including Gavin, a few dozen times before, and it didn't seem to mean much.

"Find a newspaper and look at the jobs offered section. You ought to be able to find something. The hamburger restaurants are always hiring."

"Yeah."

"Yeah," you mimicked. "I'm serious this time. If you don't make a real effort you'll find yourself out in the street, even if you are my son. And I'm not completely sure you are. Just after you were born I was rooming with a blond girl who had a son the same age and the same size. You could have been switched." Then you were gone.

I opened a can of soup. It was tomato clam rice. Not my favorite. I was in a daze. I put it down on the counter. Rusalka not my mom? That seemed crazy. You had always been my mom. Otherwise you wouldn't boss me around like that. I thought that you were just getting back at me for not being an aspiring doctor or constipationist or whatever, or maybe it was more of the jealousy thing. I went to the bedroom, trying on the way not to think, "what if she isn't my real mom?" I needed some insurance.

Gavin was still asleep, turned on his stomach. He had the blanket pulled up around his ears but half of it had dropped to the floor on one side of the bed. The part of his body beneath his waist was totally uncovered. I stood admiring the smallish, well rounded, hairless buttocks and the lithe, hairy legs for as long as I dared.

"Gavin! Wake up!" I shook him by a hairy leg. "Mom just told me maybe she's not my real mom after all!"

Gavin stirred slowly. Finally he was able to focus partially. He cast a blurred gaze in my direction. "What the fuck you talkin' about?" He sat up in bed and rubbed his eyes.

My voice sounded teary even to me. "Mom. She just told me that maybe she's not my real mom after all, that maybe I got changed out when I was little for some other kid with transsexual tendencies."

Gavin dismissed this with a wave of his arm. "Aw hell,

of course she's your mom. She only wants to get at you because she's pissed at you for a couple of dozen reasons. She talked about it."

This was a shock. I knew you had complaints against me, but *that* many? "Like what, for example."

"Oh, I guess it's mainly typical shit. For one thing, she was always hoping you'd be the man around the house and here you end up going drag."

This part I knew from long back. It was sort of the main background of our relationship between you and me, mom. You couldn't accept me as Marsha, even if I did make a poor Marcus. "What else?"

Gavin scratched his chin. He had noticeable beard growth after only twenty-four hours. I shaved once every two weeks, but just the upper lip. "The usual. My own mom used to hit me with that crap all the time. Not working at a regular job. Not keeping the apartment clean, fucking guys for money, that kind of shit. And she's mad about you using up her make-up again. She says she spends half her income on cosmetics and you drench your face in it whenever she's out."

"I use a little too much, but only when I have to go to work for Trilla."

"That's one thing you gotta stop." Now Gavin was pissed on his own account. "I said no more prostitution in this fucking house, and that includes outside it! Some guy's gonna beat you cold shit dead some day if you keep going to see Trilla."

I nodded. I knew this was part of Gavin's plan to save us. "I won't go back to see her. I didn't even get paid right for the last one."

Gavin was talking, and at the same time he was gently

scratching his genitals. He added laziness, slovenliness
and lack of education to your complaint list. I started to
whimper. I took the family history story up again.

"Mom says she found me under a rose bush or
something. Now I don't even know for sure who my
mother was." I was on a full crying jag, with tears rolling
down my cheeks, although it was at least half because I
had to conclude once again that Gavin preferred fucking
you and not me (this was confirmed and emphasized by
the massive stains I could see on the sheets).

Gavin put out an arm and dragged me toward him
as he lay on the bed. He kissed me on a wet cheek and
hugged me around the shoulders. "Of course she's your
mom. Don't even think any other kind of shit. You look
exactly like her, or pretty close. Same shoulders, same
waist, face almost exact and all kinds of other things.
Besides, she even told me that your father was this guy
she used to go with, and he was a fag, too."

I wasn't a fag. I was a transsexual, which is completely
different, but I didn't want to contradict Gavin since
he was being so sympathetic to me. I'm not sure he
understood the difference, anyway. For him I was Marsha,
that's what mattered.

Gavin stood up and put on his blue silk running
horse design bathrobe. He did it for the sake of fashion,
not modesty. He went to the living room. I followed. He
dropped into the armchair.

"Man! I'm tired as piss. Your old lady put me through
a hoop last night."

I went to the kitchen. Ten minutes later I came back
with a bowl of soup for Gavin. I liked doing things for
Gavin. I guess I had the homemaker's instinct. He took it

and began drinking. After several minutes he looked up. "You don't want any of this, dude? It's some kinda clam rice tomato crap."

"No. I'm not hungry. Thanks." I couldn't stand the little bits of clam they put in the soup. They were tough and tasteless.

After breakfast, we both started to think seriously about things. Gavin was focusing on the TV, but he had something to say. "Marsh. Mom's not feeling too good and she's on short pay because she's not bringing guys home, you know, because I told her not to. You couldn't go down to San Pablo Avenue and cut a gig, could you? The money's running out. I'd do it myself, but the cops got ten warrants out for me. I'd be headin' for the slammer in two minutes. Meantime, I'll do what mom told us to do. I'll try calling for some jobs on the phone."

There wasn't much action on San Pablo Ave, not in Cerrito. Maybe if you went down the avenue three or four miles to Oakland you would have seen a good deal of the trade, but that was a different scene altogether. In Cerrito, you might get an offer if you hung out in front of the pornographic bookstore, but it usually wasn't worth the effort. "Okay. I'll try. Last time this guy wanted to pay me with a bunch of bananas and an old transistor radio. He even tried to stuff one of the bananas up my butt!"

Gavin laughed. He slapped me on the back. "No, man. Don't get mixed up in any of that shit. Check the bastards out real good before you go with them. And don't get into any car with two guys. Especially, don't go inside a house unless you know it's no set up."

I went down to the avenue. I stood and walked around in front of the porno bookstore for a couple of hours. One old creep (I think he must have been at least ninety) who came out of the store invited me to his place for a "cup of tea". That's not my drink. And I doubt he could have come up with twenty bucks even if his social security check just arrived in the mail. Then another guy, a big fellow if I ever saw one, came right out with an offer of ten dollars to bugger me. No way. Twenty, minimum. You take a lot of risks, especially with a three hundred pounder. This guy could have sat on me and reduced me to a ribbon for life.

Hours later, when I got back to the apartment, I hadn't made a dime. In fact, I was poorer by a dollar and sixty-seven cents, the price of a fish sandwich at a fast food palace.

Gavin was still plunked in front of the set, but he was talking on the phone and he had a newspaper in his hand. "Hi! I'm calling about the job for Executive Trainee. Education? Shit, yes. I got tons of the stuff … You want me to bring my old diplomas? Well, see, the dog ate them … Then fuck you!"

Gav' caught sight of me. He hung up the receiver. "Man, what a fucking drag with all those jerks! I hope you did a lot better than I done."

I shook my head. "No dice. I got two offers, but one of them wanted to pay me in wet tea bags and the other one was like one of those guys in the newspapers who weigh six hundred pounds."

Gavin shook his head. "Fuck, man. This is a bad scene. We're almost out of money and there's all these bills to pay. Rusalka gave me a run down on our finances. There's the phone bill, the electricity, gas, all that crap, plus the rent and food, and mom only makes four hundred a month at Bombo's." Gav' didn't mention your "tips", but most of that came from "extras" that you couldn't do now.

I stood mute. I never guessed that our economic situation was that bad. Finally, I had an idea. "I suppose I'll have to go back to Polk Street. I'll tell Trilla that I need work but I definitely won't take any more whips or chains or branding irons. And if I want to get castrated, I'll have a doctor do it."

Gavin was not happy with this suggestion. "No, Marsh, not that pimp woman, not yet. If it comes to that, I got a few other risky ideas we can try first. Why'd you want to get castrated anyway? I mean, your two aren't having any special effect on you right now." We laughed at this. It was basically true. I felt flattered.

It was night outside. There was no point in flogging a dead horse about getting a job. Gavin said, "at least we gave it a fucking good try. I think mom would be proud of us." He looked in the direction of the kitchen. "By the way, man, we're totally running on empty as far as whiskey. Could you go down to the liquor store and get a bottle on credit? Tell 'em there's a big payment coming in tomorrow. I gotta get relaxed after this fuck hole of a day I been through, so I can put mom in a good mood tonight."

"I'll borrow some money from mom's room," I said, although, again, I knew you didn't leave money lying around in your bedroom. "It's legitimate business expenses, after all."

Instead, I went to the closet and took another twenty out of my secret stash of bills. I was almost out the door when Gavin called out, "and get some more of those taco chips, if you can. You know, the ones with the red stuff on 'em."

"Okay." The barbecue chips. They were Gavin's favorite, along with tomato clam rice soup. I couldn't refuse Gavin anything, even though he often found an excuse to refuse *it* to me.

When I got back to the apartment about twenty-five minutes later, Gavin had a variety of empty whiskey and wine bottles lying on the floor around the armchair. He had got them out of the kitchen cupboards and drained each for the few remaining drops in an early attempt to relax. Gavin wasn't an alcoholic, I was sure of that. He could go days without drinking if he had to. It's just that he liked to party.

"Hallelujah!" Gavin shouted when he saw me come in carrying a large paper bag from the liquor store. Obviously he wasn't religious, although he told me once he had an uncle who used to be some kind of Baptist or Episcopal minister but got kicked out for fucking women members of his flock and going too heavy on the altar wine. Gavin got the whiskey bottle out of the bag before I was halfway into the living room. He snapped off the cap and took a heavy one direct from the bottle.

I fetched a glass from the kitchen for Gavin. I put it on the little table next to the armchair. Then I began to collect the whiskey and wine empties. Obviously I had to get them out of the way before you got back, mom. Although that probably wouldn't be for another six or seven hours, it was easy to forget that sort of thing.

Back in the armchair, Gavin took another swig out of the whiskey bottle. He held the filled glass in his other hand. "Okay, dude. You know we're in pretty rough weather from here on out. I been through this kind of thing before and you just gotta keep going and trying one thing after another till you find the magic pill. When I was fourteen I had to get my mom off Quaaludes by tying her to the bed for a week. Nothing else would work. It was lucky she had a customer who liked that sort of thing. So the deal is, we might gotta try something kinda extreme."

I nodded to show I understood. When Gavin finally put the bottle down I poured one for myself. For the next twenty minutes he didn't say a word. There was a reality crime show on the screen and it was showing some gruesome scenes with battered and bloodied bodies. Gav' tore the large package of barbecue taco chips open with his teeth and helped himself freely. Drama gave him an appetite.

"Man, some dude really went the limit on that one," Gavin commented, pointing with a chip toward the TV image of a decapitated body. "Now that kind of crap I'd never do, no matter how bad the problem was."

"Yeah. I don't blame you. It would be nauseating." I took a small sip of whiskey, slightly turning the glass in my mouth as I drank in order to avoid a large swallow at once.

Soon the whiskey bottle was nearly at half mast. It was time for dinner. I headed to the kitchen. From inside I called out, "chicken noodle or pea?" No answer came from the living room, so I went back in. Gavin was mildly playing with himself as he sat watching the tube.

He looked up at me. "Oh, the pea, I guess. Why the hell not?"

I had to go back to see Trilla after all. Gavin never came up with another suggestion after he laid out the situation the night before. Since you weren't working, mom, except for your official job as salesgirl at Bombo's gift shop, there was no other choice. Gavin had been formal about it. No more fucking prostitution in our house! But, given our economic condition, he was now more flexible about my activities. Gavin was mainly jealous about your customers, and I was too, but in a different way (you could call it envy). Also, I wanted to avoid pulling more money out of my secret stash. You always taught me to keep as much cash hidden away as possible, "just in case".

I left for the train station. Gavin knew where I was going but he didn't say anything. This was a reform that would have to wait.

The train bumped and jangled along for forty minutes. From the looks of them, most of the other passengers were probably going to their restaurant kitchen jobs in the city. Finally it was arrival. I scudded up Polk, stood on the corner for a few minutes to catch my breath, then walked delicately into Tramp's and sat down at Trilla's table. She gave me a sly look and said, "hmm."

I had to order my own whiskey. A triple. Then I gave Trilla a complete report on the whip incident. "He really knew how to use that fucker, too."

She laughed. "I heard all about that. You got it a bit on the legs, but Alberto, he got welts all over his back. And you know what happen anyway? He come off with a two hundred dollar tip!"

"Wow." But tip or no tip, the rough stuff was out for me. I said so.

"Okay, little man, I got a sweet little gig for you and you gonna get treated like it was your own momma doin' it."

SON OF A WHORE

That's how I got sent to see Mr. Tralanger. Trilla was actually very understanding about how I felt after the whip incident. She even gave me cab fare to get to the place, since Mr. Tralanger lived way out on the avenues, near the ocean, a real swank neighborhood. "This guy is so nice and gentle-like you probably gonna get your ass bored off," Trilla told me.

It was a top expensive house and all furnished with art antiques. It made Marcel the Ringmaster's (not to mention Mr. Simonian's) place look like a dump. I mean, this guy really had some loot. He showed me this antique statue that looked like it was made out of gold. He said it was from Athens or Italy, somewhere like that, and it was thousands of years old. I was impressed. He had a lot of other Greek statues too, mainly of muscular young nude guys with their balls hanging out. Harv's collection, though heavy on the young athletes, had more different types of statues, including nude women with tits that didn't overdo it, like they did on Broadway. Mr. Tralanger's statues were nice to look at, I admitted. I felt bad that my own body was anything but athletic. I think a lot of rich guys collect stuff like statues. They have to do something with their money. You can only spend so much on trips to Italy and prostitutes. They like little cigarettes, too. The nicotine and drugs in the cigarettes pull them out of a kind of hereditary constipation.

Mr. Tralanger said that he was the director of some corporation. I don't know what they made. Maybe cock rings. He inherited the job from his father, he added. "It has grown hugely under my management." He was tall, pretty old (I'd say at least fifty), half bald and sort of inflated around the middle. Pretty much like the other johns, at least as far as appearance.

He showed me some pictures of his villa in a town in Italy. It wasn't too far from Greece, judging by the looks of the old buildings. He asked me if I had any brothers and sisters. "I have two sisters, but one of them's in the army right now and the other's a policeman." He laughed.

"My mom's really proud of them. She says she's glad they're carrying on the family tradition, because my father was in the Navy."

"What would you say to an aperitif?"

"Okay. Sounds all right." I didn't know exactly what that was, but I figured it had to be alcohol.

Mr. Tralanger took two small stem glasses out of a cabinet and filled them with a green liquid. He handed one to me. It tasted all right, maybe a bit too sweet.

He took a sip from his glass. "So, to be quite honest, you are a prostitute."

This was so obvious that I thought it must be part of his gig to talk about it. I had to play along. "Yeah. But I don't really think of it exactly like that. I like meeting guys for a little sex, and if they can help me out with some money, all the better."

"I see. You must have had some interesting experiences. How old are you? Twenty? Twenty-one?"

"I'm eighteen. I think I am, anyway. My birth certificate got smudged with some greasy junk and my mom doesn't remember the exact year."

Tralanger laughed again. "You are a quite an entertainment."

I laughed and smiled. This was flattering. The green stuff was going to my head. I started to tell him about

Marcel the Ringmaster, although laughing about it all the time.

Tralanger turned serious. "Then your friend, Alberto, was the winner. He came out of it with far more than you did."

"Yeah, I guess so. But it took him a long time to recover."

"Ah." Now Mr. Tralanger took a small, hand rolled cigarette out of the pocket of his "smoking jacket". He lit it with a golden lighter, inhaled, then passed it to me.

I didn't know what was in the little cigarette, but I was sure it couldn't be lethal or Tralanger wouldn't have dragged off it himself. I puffed on it and took the smoke down into my lungs. I held it there for about a minute. This is what you're supposed to do to get the maximum effect. Wow! Suddenly all of Mr. Tralanger's gold and silver statues in the large "reception space" started to change color and to glow. His nude statues were almost dancing, their balls flapping back and forth like they were doing The Frug. For a while I didn't know where I was and I must have stared at Mr. Tralanger like he was an exhibit in an aquarium.

He put his hand on my shoulder and steadied me until the initial high passed. "I think we can begin the business of the evening," he said. "I suppose you have no objection to being buggered?"

"Huh? No. It's, like, just my cup of tea." I was glad I could say something that sounded high class.

I don't remember how we got there, but soon we were in a bedroom that was smaller than Marcel's, although maybe furnished with better taste. There was a painting on the wall that showed what must have been a scene in

France about a hundred years ago, with green fields and cows and a guy in a top hat and a nude lady who ought to have been on a diet, both just lying on the grass looking like they were doing something artistic. Another painting, more modern and with really sharp detail, showed two young guys who didn't bother to wear clothes positioned face to face and grabbing each other around the neck and the waist, while they tried tripping maneuvers on each other's legs. It was entitled, "Boy Wrestlers".

Okay. The gig was going to be really simple, or so it appeared. Mr. Tralanger told me he just wanted to fondle my nuts while he buggered me. It was the most natural thing in the world, at least with the crowd Trilla knew. I stripped and lay down on my side on top of the bed. It was a large waterbed and the wavelike motion of the water inside the mattress made me slightly nauseous while I moved to get myself into final position, probably because of the green stuff and the smoke.

Tralanger lay down behind me. Soon he had it stuffed in. He was pretty well developed. I noticed that when he was "disrobing".

"You've got a nice butt," he said. "It's your best point by far."

Well, I already knew this, but it was flattering anyway.

After he started to thrust away inside my flattering derriere, he reached a hand over me and took a grip on my balls. This actually felt good at first. I experienced that feminine sensation that I liked so much behind, and at the same time there was this feeling of dominance and control of me by a man on my front quarters, such as they were. After a couple of minutes Tral's grip on my front two increased. Soon it became uncomfortable, then actually painful. In synch with his plugging away behind me, and as his tension and energy developed, his grip on my testicles increased. It was like he wanted almost to pull them off, maybe so I'd be even more like a girl.

Tralanger twigged on my obvious discomfort, but he kept going. "Just a bit more, you little whore," he tried some poetry. He was going in and out faster and faster, but my pain in front from his hand grip was getting too much. He started to stretch my nuts, pulling them out four or five inches. This was more than I could take. I tried to tear his hand off of me, but that was even more painful. He had a good grip. He wouldn't let go. No doubt he had a lot of practice.

"Lay off, you fucking freak!" I grabbed his arm with both of my hands and tried to free my things. It didn't work. He was a lot stronger than I thought from the smoking jacket, Harvard, green liqueur impression. He kept on pumping in my rear. He was breathing harder and harder. My nuts were caught in a vice. Finally he let loose with a huge yelp and fell back on the mattress. His dick was dripping with the remains of his ejaculation. I lay whimpering and cradling my bruised and battered balls. Mom, you wouldn't believe how painful it is to have some lunky dope drag your nuts out half a foot and try to crush them! Don't ever let anyone try that stuff that on you.

Gasping for breath, I tried to massage myself gently in order to lessen the pain. It was still at about seven on a scale from one to ten. "You monster! You fuckin' crippled me for life!" How could I possibly work as a young male prostitute when my balls would probably need some sort of prosthetic device just to keep them from dropping off?

I rubbed myself repeatedly in the scrotal area, trying to appease the half destroyed organs.

"There should be no permanent damage." Tralanger, not overly concerned, opened the drawer of a little *armoire* next to the bed and took out a carved glass *flacon* that looked like it contained cognac or something pretty similar. He also brought out a little glass that could hold about a thimble of the stuff. He filled the thimble and handed it to me. "This will help you."

I threw the little glass at the nude wrestlers. I grabbed the bottle from his hand and swigged deeply from it. "You damn bastard!" I croaked between large swallows.

Tralanger stretched himself toward the armoire and pulled out a box from deep inside. He opened it and retrieved two hundred dollar bills. He tossed them on the bed next to me.

"I don't want any fucking money! I'm going to call the police and have them throw you in jail for assault! You really fucked me royal!" I massaged myself. I drank some more of the cognac.

"You will soon feel better."

"I won't ever feel any better, you butcher!" I picked up the hundred dollar bills, just in case I had to run for it.

"My poor, dear, sweet boy. I'm sorry I was so rough. I was carried away simply because you are so sexy. You're almost as pretty as a girl. I could easily have thought you were a girl if it weren't for those little things in front."

"They're about to drop off!" I massaged. It was probably the cognac that made me feel better.

Tralie put his hand on my naked back and rubbed. "I know it hurt, but I think you will always remember this as a deeply erotic encounter."

"I'm gonna try to forget all about it!" I drank again from the cognac bottle. I had just about drained it clean out.

On the way to the train station the pain was still so bad that I had to stop every half block or so and cup my hands over my crotch. Quite a few people noticed this and stared. They probably thought I was some kind of pervert.

It wasn't any better on the train. As usual, the cars bumped and shook like they were doing the mambo in Rio. My injured parts felt every brusque lurch and jump.

I had a tip, anyway. Before I left the mansion, I made a lot of threats against the old creep, but it wasn't serious. How could I go to the police when what I was doing, prostitution, was illegal too? Besides, the police might find out that Gavin was at our house. I didn't want him to go to jail. I knew what they did to good looking young guys in the slammer. That stuff wasn't for a macho person like Gavin.

The train was clanking on from station to station. I thought that if I ever got to be the kind of old psycho who liked to pull guys' balls off for the fun of it, I hoped they would put me away in some place with locked corridors.

After limping from the Cerrito station, I came into the apartment walking with my hands cupped around my aching balls. Gavin was in the chair watching television, as usual. There was a nearly empty whiskey bottle on the floor in front of him. He started to laugh when he caught sight of my posture. "Aw, stop it dude, you're too much." He thought that, for a joke, I was impersonating someone, like a male prostitute, for example, who'd had too much of a workout.

"This fucking old bastard almost pulled my balls off!" I shouted. I took my pants down and showed him the injured part, although there was nothing in particular from the outside that would indicate damage. It was all on the inside.

"What the fuck?" Gavin leaned forward in the chair to look more closely. He drained the pathetic remains of his whiskey bottle.

"Yeah! Trilla sent me to see this old rich creep and he has this gig where he likes to butt fuck guys and pull their balls at the same time. Only he got carried away on the pulling part. He was on some kind of freaky drug."

I limped toward my bedroom, leaving my pants on the entry floor. Gavin rushed to my aid.

"I told you not to go to that damn Polk Street bitch! She's working for a crowd of psychos! You're damn lucky he didn't cut off your whole show." He propped me up at the shoulder and helped me to the closet.

I lay down, easing myself slowly onto the lumpy and stained mattress.

"Hold on, man. I'm gonna get something for you."

Ten minutes later Gavin came back with a cloth folded over and some ice cubes inside. He applied it to my crotch. "I hope you don't get frost bite down there on top of everything else," he joked. It wasn't completely a joke. "And here. Drink some of this." He handed me a freshly opened wine bottle. No glass. Gavin just didn't think about things like that.

"Maybe they'll have to do surgery on me," I whined at one point, when the pain from Tralanger's pulling and squeezing was particularly bad. "Do some kind of 'ectomy." The operation itself wouldn't bother me too much. I was only worried about the cost. I took a swig from the bottle. "It'll cost hundreds." Then I felt I had to explain how the whole fucking gig happened. "At first he didn't seem to be, you know, crazy off his nut, and he was rich as hell. You should see all the expensive junk he has in his house. It was like some kind of big museum." I drank again. "But when he started on the rough stuff I couldn't pull out. He had me wedged in front and behind."

"I see, man. Don't worry. I'll have you fixed in no time. I mean, I'll have you well in no time." He removed the ice pack and palpated my things. I winced a bit. "It's bad, but it's not all that bad," he said. He felt the outlines of my balls. "Yeah. Feels sort of swelled up. Anyway, if they have to operate, I know the county's gonna pay for the best damn whacker they can find."

This was comforting. "Yeah. Make sure they use plenty of anesthetic." I sucked probably a full glass out of the wine bottle.

Two hours later I felt better. I prodded my nuts and it wasn't as bad as before. "I think the ice packs are working," I told Gavin as I started my second bottle of wine.

Gavin came up with an idea. He said I ought to put on a jockstrap to support them and ease the discomfort. Then I'd be able to get around better, maybe sit in front of the TV.

No. I never wore those contraptions. I didn't like them in principle and I didn't have one. In junior high Boys' P.E. class I drew general contempt and ridicule as the only one—maybe there were a dozen others in the six county area—who wore panties under his (her) gym shorts, instead of a supporter. I shook my head violently.

Gavin accepted this. "Who'd a thought them bitty

things could cause so much pain? Don't you worry, baby, doctor knows best."

It is a fact that trauma to the testicles is an injury that no medical doctor and very few private individuals would have considered treatable by buggery. Gavin knew better. He rolled me over on my side and lay down behind me. Soon he had penetrated (Gavin had this special quality of being able to go from zero to full erection in seconds. He was greatly appreciated for it). He took his time getting to the goal. He would pump and pump, working himself up, then relax and withdraw. Then he would enter me again and start all over. All of this was part of the treatment. It took about twenty-five minutes.

Afterwards I felt much better. I sat up on the mattress. Then I was able, without too much discomfort, to raise myself to a standing position. There was still a lot of pain, but not close to the hell hole I felt before.

We were both sitting in the living room when you got home, mom. Gavin occupied the chair, of course, and I sat on the floor at his feet while I slowly finished the last of the wine. It must have looked odd, because I had the ice pack parked between the crotch of my jeans and my lower abdomen. It looked like I was hiding something really huge.

"What exactly are you two up to now?" You had noticed the padded area and naturally that was nothing like what you expected to see.

Gavin became the spokesman. "Marsha got sent on a gig by Trilla that went way off wrong. He met a dude who tried to wrench his balls off. That's Trilla for you." I thought for a minute that he might have used politer language with my mom. He might have said, "tried to wrench his manhood off", but this would have been confusing to everyone.

You were exasperated. It was clear that, once again, you had had a hard day at work, and now this on top of everything! You let go with your standard version. "If you're going to let that black woman influence you to do dangerous and disgusting things, don't expect any sympathy from me."

My things were still giving me a lot of pain, especially after the brushing down you just gave me. I clutched the area and moaned.

"It's too bad," you said, "but I'm not a nurse. Especially for that type of injury."

"Don't worry, mom," Gavin stuck in, "I'm keeping the problem under control by giving him ice packs."

You walked to the bathroom. You called over your shoulder, "you should put one on his head."

When you were out of the room Gavin said, "see, she's pissed because she wants what's best for you."

I nodded. I thought that might be true in some way, but I had a hard time figuring it out.

With your cosmetics removed, moisturizing cream in place, and dressed in your elegant bathrobe, you came back to the living room. You looked at Gavin, then went into the bedroom.

"Okay, I gotta go. Sayonara, buddy. Oh, wait. I'll help you back to the closet. I know you still got aching balls syndrome."

My nuts were still hurting so much that lying on the hard and lumpy closet mattress would make it worse. Or so I claimed. In fact, I was jealous of Gavin being alone with you, mom, especially since I was now sexually disabled, at least in part (front). I thought that by sleeping in the main bedroom I could keep a watch on my interests (Gavin). "It would be a lot better if I could sleep in the bedroom," I told Gavin. "That would help with the pain and stuff."

"No problem as far as I'm concerned, but I don't think mom's gonna like the idea too much." We trudged to the bedroom, with Gavin supporting me at shoulder level.

You said absolutely not! You said the three of us couldn't sleep comfortably in one bed and that you were certainly not going to sleep in my closet.

"Why not let him sleep on the bed, way over on one side," Gavin put in. "I have to give him these cold compresses every couple of hours anyway."

You still balked, mom. I admired your sense of morality. After all, a lot of people would have thought this was getting close to incest.

Gavin whispered to you, "we can knock him out with a couple of your sleeping pills and a shot or two of whiskey and he won't know a thing."

I whined and sniveled to be allowed to sleep in the main bedroom with you and Gavin. I was suffering, how could I be left alone in the closet? What if I needed something desperately? Whaa-a!

You shrugged and lay down on one side of the bed. That seemed to mean "okay, but don't cause any trouble".

"Here's some pain pills, bud." Gavin handed me a couple of pills. He didn't know I had been sneaking your sleeping pills for years and they didn't have much effect on me anymore. "And wash it down with this." Gavin gave me a quart bottle that had maybe an ounce of whiskey left in it.

SON OF A WHORE

I turned on my side, away from the two of you. I pretended to sleep. I even gave out a phony snore or two. Gavin switched the light out.

Gavin always slept naked, of course, and he had pulled his clothes off the minute we were in the bedroom. I didn't know what you were wearing under the expensive silk bathrobe, although I had taken inventory of your lingerie dozens of times, trying to figure out what would fit me best. Anyway, the room was dark, except for the dim light from a window that shone through the curtain.

Then it started. First some movements that gently shook the large mattress, then some hushed sounds, not exactly words, but almost like words. There were some oohings and ahhings. Soon I could see forms and shapes in the room. Gavin was on top. I mean, of you. Naturally there was nothing wrong with this. It was the "most natural thing in the world". The problem part was that I, your natural son, was stretched out on the same mattress and that your partner, Gavin, was supposed to be my lover too.

The motions came quicker and stronger. I saw Gavin's nicely shaped buttocks moving up and down. I couldn't resist the temptation to put a hand on them. He didn't seem to notice. Or maybe he expected this. You were underneath. I saw your breasts. They were pretty hot, too. It was all like a porno movie, only made at home.

Things were moving ahead fast on your side of the bed. I could tell it was about to happen, the main event. For a moment I wondered, I wished, that Gavin was my father, and maybe my lover too. Things were getting complicated.

SON OF A WHORE

The next afternoon I got out of bed just past noon, when everyone else was still dead asleep. I went to the closet and lay down on my old mattress. My balls weren't hurting so much anymore. My psyche was aching. I didn't understand exactly why, but I think Freud would have twigged right off.`

It must have been around four in the afternoon when Gavin shook me awake. "Hey, buddy. You can't sleep your whole life away. Here, have some breakfast." Gavin offered me an open whiskey bottle, but I waved it away.

"I'm not hungry."

"No wonder, after Trilla sent you on that piss out date last night. How are your balls? Any better?"

"A bit." I might have asked him the same question. I turned away and pulled the blanket over my head.

"C'mon, man. We got a lot of work to do. Mom said to get this place G.I. clean before she gets back from work." Gavin had known a lot of military guys, so he had picked up the language. He dragged the blanket off my head. He saw a grotesque expression of misery.

"Okay," he said. "I get the picture." He had figured out something that it would have taken a shrink ten years to do. "You're all bent out of shape because I screwed your mom last night and you were right there too. I can understand how you feel. Only, listen. I did it because I love your mom and I love you, too." Now he was expanding the boundaries of Freudian thought.

I sat up on the mattress. What Gavin said was reassuring in a way, but it was just as much a puzzle. "You love me, so you screwed her? How does that work out?"

Gavin was standing again. He put a hand under his chin, looking vaguely like Doctor Freud. "It's like this.

See, naturally I met you first and I thought you were really hot, so I fucked you a couple of times. When I saw your mom wanted to get it on with me, I was pulled in because to me she looked a whole lot like you. With the obvious differences. So I fucked both of you, just out of love."

"Oh." Gavin was ironing out the wrinkles. He was good at that. "Gav? Do you like me?" I asked this because it seemed that love had more to do with sex.

"Hell yes! You're my best friend and lover." He knelt down beside the mattress. He put his hand on my bare, hairless thigh. "You've got the stuff, Marsha baby. And besides that, you're a great girl friend, always doing stuff for me and things like that."

It made me happy to hear this. I forgot about the scene between you and Gavin, at least for a while. "Everyone always said I was just like my mom. The guy at the liquor store said that, and a couple of relatives who I don't know much about."

"They were right."

It was a thrill to be able to make soup for Gavin once again. I think it was a can of beef and rice, but I'm not sure. They all taste about the same.

"Hey, good stuff. Thanks, man." Gavin took the bowl out of my hands as he sat in front of the TV doing some kind of dance to a commercial jingle. He had had too much early whiskey. Soup was just what he needed.

I let myself down on the floor gently, just in front of Gavin. My nuts were still sensitive. The screen was showing a cartoon program with mice bouncing around and outsmarting a mean cat that got beat up every time.

I laughed. Gavin almost choked with humor as he tried to swallow soup and laugh at the same time.

Mainly, though, it was a slow day in front of the TV. We watched a few dull shows. Gavin dozed off a couple of times. Probably he didn't get much sleep last night. It must have been around five o'clock when he asked me to go get some groceries, that is, whiskey and maybe a large bag of taco chips and some dip.

I got up slowly, still feeling some pain, and headed toward the bedroom. "I'll borrow a bit more cash from mom," I said, just like before. "After all, she's supposed to be the one bringing home the bacon." The thing is, I was even more careful to make it a point to pretend that I was getting the money from your room because, in addition to wanting to keep my stash safe, I knew that If Gavin found it he'd grab the lot and go off on another dangerous and self-destructive drug spree. So just for the form of it, and hoping a miracle might happened, I went to the big bedroom and slipped my hand between the top and bottom mattresses. Nothing. I ransacked the drawers of the large chest. There was only the usual junk, no money. I would have to make another withdrawal from my privy fund.

Gavin saw me walking slowly toward the apartment door, leaving for my errand. I was easing myself with every step.

"Man, you sure you don't want to put on a jock or something, you know, keep it tight?"

I shook my head. I didn't want to go through the long process of explaining my rejection of those articles of dress, drawing on gender theory, public school practices and porno magazines. Besides, the fact was, as I mentioned before, I did not possess any such device. Gavin could have used a size extra-large.

Since I was sexually out of action for the moment, Gavin was forced to resort to self-abuse while you were out at work. Later that night, while we were watching TV, he pulled it out and began exercising it. I was fascinated and watched with vague expectations, but my attention was constantly distracted by the television. My head bobbed back and forth between box and reality until I had neck strain as well as the lower anatomical one. Gavin didn't actually get to the point.

We were both nicely in order, with pants on, when you finally came through the front door around three o'clock in the morning. It was a shock! You looked so worn out and crumbled that I was afraid you had been in a wrestling match with a customer.

"I'm very tired," you said. "I'm going directly to bed and I don't want any trouble from either of you." You dragged your purse on the floor as you walked to the bedroom.

"I gotta help mom out," Gavin told me. "Sorry, Marsh, you have to share the closet alone tonight." He took a last, large pull on the whiskey bottle. He stood up, then bent over and grabbed a handful of chips and put them in his mouth. "I'll give her some good massage therapy," he said as he chewed. "It ought to make her feel a hundred percent better."

"Mom can't get up at all! Something's real wrong." Gavin was in a panic. Except for last night, when I was "odd man out", he had been sharing your bed with both of us since he came back from the city. When you came in looking so tired the night before, he twigged to a problem. By morning he knew that something serious was wrong.

It was actually about two-thirty p.m. This is what the little travel clock on the floor beside my mattress showed. I always kept it wound up and it lost only about five or ten minutes of time a week. Gavin shook me back into consciousness. The night before I only got to sleep around dawn. I was too upset about getting booted from the bedroom while Gavin and you were cozying up together. I took about four trips to the bedroom, just to peek in, but nothing was happening as far as I could make out in the dark.

"She's probably just hung over. All those big tippers at the Club love to buy no end of rounds."

"No. It's worse than that. She's got a fever and she looks kinda yellow around the eyeballs."

I wasn't really worried. You weren't feeling well? That happened. A bad gig can do that to you, as I well knew. I went with Gavin to the bedroom so I could see for myself. He was nude. This was no longer a shock and, just by itself, not that much of a thrill anymore.

You were huddled under the blanket on one side of the bed, mom. Only part of your head was showing. I crept into the room and went over to where you were lying down. Your face looked dark and sort of puckered. I put my hand on your forehead. Fever. You groaned.

"Yeah. I think you're right. I guess we ought to take her to the doctor. I can't remember her ever not getting out of bed in the afternoon before."

"Right. Call an ambulance. The doctors at the hospital will fix her up, I'm sure. Just like on the TV programs." Gavin was worried, but now he seemed to see the solution.

"We ought to take her to old Dr. Shitaka first. Maybe it's not that bad. Dr. Shitaka's been our family doctor for years. He was the first one who recommended transgender surgery for me, but we couldn't afford it."

"Okay. I'll take her by the shoulders and you carry her legs, it's lighter on that end." Gavin moved toward the side of the bed where you lay, mom. "How far's this Shitaka?"

"Mmm. Not that far, but I think we better take a taxi. It'll be a lot easier trip for mom."

"Oh yeah, yeah, of course. I'm getting stupid. It's because I'm afraid mom's not all right."

Even though Gavin was your lover, I was your son, so I took the role of being adviser to you. I went over to the bed. I could tell you were awake because you were breathing through your nose real quietly with your eyes closed. "Mom? Gavin and me are going to take you to see Dr. Shitaka. Okay? He'll cure you right off. Remember when he fixed me up when I had gonorrhea front and back?"

"You get the fuck out of here!"

I retreated to the door. "She's mad at me for some reason," I told Gavin. "But I think it shows she's not all that sick."

Gavin stood in the living room and drank some whiskey out of a bottle. He was still very worried. I dialed the cab company and gave our address. "Let's get mom ready to go. The cab will be here in half an hour. You talk to her this time."

You were ready to go on time, mom. Gavin got you into your expensive bathrobe and put a scarf around your neck to protect you from the cold, although it was fairly warm outside. He got one of your best hats out of the closet and put it on your head, since you couldn't fix your hair, being too sick. You ordered him to grab your purse. You never went anywhere without it. Gavin picked it up and gave it to me to carry. It wouldn't look so odd on me. We were almost out the door when I noticed that Gavin was still without a stitch on.

"Gav'? Aren't you forgetting something?"

Gavin looked around. "Naw. I think we got everything. We can't bring the whiskey."

"Your clothes!"

"Oh yeah. Shit! Thanks man, I forgot all about it. This whole thing's just got me too knocked around." He dressed in seconds, putting his underwear on front to back. He left his trousers unzipped.

It took about five minutes for the taxi to take the three of us to the doctor's office. When we got there we discovered that both Gavin and me forgot to bring money to pay the cab fare. Gavin never had a cent anyway. To pay the driver, you had to open your purse and take the money out. Gavin paid close attention. He could see that you had a large pile of twenties in a hidden fold, which he found reassuring.

Dr. Shitaka. He was pretty old about that time, maybe at least sixty or seventy. He was your doctor even before I was born and that was when you were about as young as I was then. He wore a full length white lab coat. He was short and bent at the shoulders. His face was lined and grey. He looked like an actor in one of those Godzilla movies, one of the scientists trying to figure out what the hell was happening. "We will see what is wrong here." He helped you into the examination room. Gavin and me waited in the room with all the magazines and toys.

Gavin picked up a magazine, I think it was *TimesNews*. He held it upside down and only figured that out by looking at the pictures. Probably he was just too worried to pay attention, since he wasn't completely illiterate. After a few minutes he looked up from the magazine and said, "President Nixon's gonna pass a whole shitload of new laws and they're gonna be really terrific, it says."

We had something to look forward to.

You and Dr. Shitaka finally came out of the examination room. "Your mom is all right," the doctor told me. "Only she is a little sick with the flu. You must take care of her until she is better. Be sure she rests much and drinks many liquids. I am giving you this prescription for her." He handed me a piece of paper with funny writing on it. Then he looked me over from his lower height. "Now, do you still feel that you are really a girl?"

"Yeah. I mean, sure, because I know I am."

"We will talk of this at a later time." He went back to the inner part of the office.

The receptionist, who I think doubled as Dr. Shitaka's wife, called us a cab for the trip back.

Back home, we soon had you comfortably in bed, propped up on pillows. "Thank you," you said. "Marsha, I didn't think you would ever bother to take care of your mother. I suppose I've been too hard with you all this time." This showed that you weren't yourself at all. But I also thought a long statement proved that you were feeling a bit better. And maybe there was something to what you said, after all.

"We'll get you back in top shape real quick," Gavin said. He was convinced of it. "Marsh, you wanna go get that prescription old Takashita gave your mom? Probably it'll help her get better more fast. The lady at the desk in the doctor's office said he was a fuckin' great medical guy."

I went to the pharmacy to buy the prescription with cash borrowed from your purse, mom, from that secret inner fold. It turned out to be a codeine alcohol solution. I and Gavin must have ended up drinking at least half of it. It was lucky that the drugstore sold liquor and taco chips too. I loaded up on stuff like that, as much as forty dollars would buy, minus what the medicine cost. They didn't ask questions about my buying whiskey, maybe because they were selling me some of the same stuff as a prescription.

Gavin turned out to be a good nurse. I was surprised because before he would hardly get up out of the chair except to use the bathroom. He heated up some soup for you, but got distracted by the TV and let it boil over on the stove. He tried a second can and got it right. He brought it to you in a bowl, and actually with a spoon! He found it somewhere and cleaned it off under the sink faucet. I stayed outside the bedroom but eavesdropped efficiently, as usual.

"Just you try some of this, babe." Gavin handed the soup to you, mom. "It always gives me a lot of energy when I get hung over."

"Thank you. It surprises me that Marsha met a young man who is so nice and caring. All of his other friends have been bizarre perverts."

I'm not surprised that you appreciated Gavin's nursing talents. Dressed in his jeans and t-shirt, he showed that slim and athletic build that was a big turn on for both of us.

After listening outside the bedroom door, I went back to the kitchen. I didn't know how to deal with the mess.

The stove and the kitchen floor were covered with soup from the overflow of Gavin's first cooking attempt. We didn't have any dishrags or a mop and the only towel was hanging in the bathroom. I decided to leave it alone for now. That usually seemed to work for the short run.

Gavin brought back the empty soup bowl after a few minutes. "I think your mom's getting better. That codeine stuff gives her a good appetite."

Me (I?) and Gavin spent most of the evening in front of the TV. We made good headway on the whiskey and Gavin crunched constantly on his beloved taco chips. (He never put on weight. Probably he had a fast metabolism, as Dr. Shitaka would have put it). Every twenty or thirty minutes Gavin would get up and tiptoe to the bedroom and look in. He would report something like, "she's sleeping now", or, "I think she's resting okay." He gave you a spoonful of codeine every three or four hours. Meanwhile he and me took swallows out of the codeine bottle at much closer intervals.

Codeine and whiskey are a great combination for making you feel better when you're worried and all out of shape about something.

Since you were too sick to go to work, we didn't have to wait for you to get back from the Club that night. Just after one o'clock Gavin got up from the armchair. "Man, I'm tired. Playing doctor really sucks it out of you." In fact, he had swallowed enough whiskey to relax King Kong. "I'm headin' for the hay stack." He bent over and kissed me on the cheek. Then he went to your bedroom.

When the light got turned off in the big bedroom I was left alone with the TV and what remained of the whiskey. I wasn't sure what I ought to do. Gavin hadn't given me any final instructions. Maybe he assumed I would know that I had to sleep in the closet because of your illness, etc. When I say "etc." I mean Gavin nursing you and all that. But I didn't see why I couldn't help out too. Why I couldn't help Gavin out. In bed.

I turned the TV off and slunk toward the big bedroom. You both seemed asleep. I dropped my clothes on the floor and got in bed on the side opposite the patient, so that Gavin was between us.

When my eyes got adjusted to the light, the dim light from the bedroom window, I could see that there was something going on. Gavin had pushed the blanket off of himself. He had at least an eight inch erection that was vertical. He was fondling your breasts. I watched with absorbed interest, not in a pornographic sense, because it was like a family get-together, but out of curiosity. I still wasn't exactly sure how non-gays went about *it*. You moaned and turned away. You pushed Gavin as a way of letting him know you weren't in the mood. Not tonight.

Gavin turned on his other side and discovered that I was there. Maybe he expected me, had planned it as a kind of backup. He soon had me rolled onto my stomach. He entered me with a single direct plunge. I have to explain that, because of a good deal of previous experience, I was sort of "loose" by this time. He pumped. He plunged and backed and re-plunged. You didn't seem to notice anything. You could have been asleep. It was possible that you didn't care at all at that point. I mean, it was a pretty bad case of the flu. And anyway, wasn't I your daughter, after all?

I don't know when we finally got to sleep, but Gavin was snoring before I passed out.

The next day you weren't much better. It might have been because we were running out of codeine.

"Hey! I know what," Gavin said. "I'll make mom a hot toddy. That's what I always used to do for my own mom."

He went to the kitchen. I followed. I was curious, and also I wanted to keep an eye on things. Gav' took a pot out of the sink and partly filled it with water from the faucet. He took the pot to the stove. "What the fuck?" He looked at the stains and charred spots on the stove top from yesterday's overflowed can of soup. "Marsha, I told you you were a fuckin' good housekeeper, now you gotta prove it. Don't leave no mess like that lying around."

"We don't have any dishrags," I explained. "There's nothing to clean it with. Besides, I think it's baked on, now." I tried to scratch a burnt patch with a fingernail. No success.

Gavin put the pot on a burner and turned the gas on. "Place is like a fuckin' pig hole." He went back to the living room.

When the water started to boil I took it off the stove. I was learning. Sometimes you had to, the hard way. I went to the living room and stood watching the screen for a few minutes. It was a game show with a lot of comedy. Everybody was laughing their heads off. I couldn't tell exactly why. Gavin was laughing, too, but I doubt he could have explained it either.

"Your water's ready, Gav'."

"Oh, yeah. Thanks, man." Gavin stayed focused on the tube for another five minutes.

"The water's getting cold."

"Yeah. Hey man, I'm really diggin' this show. Could you go on back to the kitchen, pour some of that water junk into a tall glass, then put in a lot of whiskey? After that, add some sugar and some lime juice or something like that."

"I don't think we have any lime juice." I wasn't sure what lime juice was. Maybe it came from those green lemons they sold in the supermarket sometimes.

"Okay. Do the fuckin' best you can. It's for mom, after all." Gavin told me all this without looking away from the TV.

I grabbed a tall glass and filled it half full of whiskey. I thought it ought to be strong to have a good effect. Then I topped the glass off with hot water. I put in two teaspoons of sugar. Then I got the codeine bottle and let the last drops fall into the mix. It was ready, I thought. I took a taste. Not too good, but maybe it was supposed to be that way. I brought it out to the living room.

"Here's the stuff, the hot toady."

"Toddy. Thanks, man. If this don't fix your mom up, nothing ain't gonna do it."

Gavin brought the glass to the bedroom and I followed. "'Salka, I got something special for you. It's a old family cure for everything. Just try it. Swallow it down as much as you can. 'Salka?"

You didn't move. Gavin handed the glass to me and went to the head of the bed on your side. "Mom! You okay? Wake up some, I got some medicine for you." He took the glass from me.

When you turned over and faced us we were both shocked. You didn't look good at all. Your face was lined, dark, with bags under the eyes and sunken cheeks. You groaned as a response to Gavin's question. "Just try this, babe." Gavin helped you sit up and held the glass while you drank. "Drink all you can, but don't choke on it or nothing."

I admired the amount you were able to put away, even feeling pretty bad.

"Thank you." The glass was half empty. Your face took on a better tone. "I'm not actually feeling well, but I think I'm better."

"All right! Hey man, I'll keep feeding you these hot toddies. Best medicine you can buy for any money."

You were sitting up in bed and sipping the drink, but suddenly you weren't so happy. The toddy was probably having the reverse effect now. Gavin clued me later that that's the way alcohol works on some people, first you're real happy, then you're pissed as hell. Once you told me it hit my dad that way.

You turned a sharp glance toward Gavin. "You came here to teach Marcus and to make him into a normal boy, but so far there's been no change. You're not doing your job!"

"Sorry, mom, but, you see, I can't help on that part of it because Marsha's one of the kind that likes other guys. He can't change." Gavin forgot that he liked other guys too, at least in part.

Besides, I wasn't the kind who liked "other guys", because I wasn't a guy. Mentally and according to feelings and emotions, and that's what really counts, I was a girl. That wasn't going to change.

"You oughta just rest back and relax some more, mom. Here, I'll get you some soup again," Gavin said.

"Fuck your stupid soup!"

You always got in a bad mood when you were sick, but that didn't happen too often. I can only remember getting a soup bowl in the head once or twice. We both beat a fast retreat from the bedroom, but not before you pointed a finger at me. "You stay out of this room, you disgusting pervert!" I knew what you were talking about. You'd been awake last night after all.

In the living room Gavin threw himself into the armchair and tried to recoup his morale. "I hope your mom isn't even sicker than she looks. Maybe we ought to call that Doctor Hooshimoto again and get some more medicine."

"Dr. Shitaka. He's closed now. He doesn't stay open after five and it's nine-thirty already."

"Oh. Well, maybe we can get more of that codeine juice tomorrow."

We watched the TV for a few minutes. There was a demonstration somewhere and the police were taking people away in handcuffs. I was worried about something closer and more personal. "Gavin? Do you think my mom hates me because I'm a queer?"

"No. I don't think so. It's gotta be something else."

"Like what?" I was eager to get some kind of answer.

"Um, I'm not exactly sure, but maybe because she hates the guts out of your old man, whoever he was."

"Ah. That makes sense." I felt better already.

"No, see, it couldn't be that queer stuff, because in that case she'd hate everybody."

You never did understand the difference between queer and transsexual, mom. They're completely different things. Gavin didn't get it either and I already stopped trying to explain it to him. I was actually a bit vague on the subject myself.

The rioting stopped, at least on TV. Now the

announcer was telling everyone that today was Sigmund Freud Day. He was the genius who discovered that everybody was homosexual. That's what the announcer said. It was a San Francisco channel.

"Hey, wow! Too bad your old lady didn't hear that. Then she'd think there's nothing wrong with you."

I had another question coming up, actually a repetition. "She said my old man was queer too?" I wanted to get this confirmed.

"Close. She said one of the guys who could be your old man was queer, but not all that queer."

Now ambulances were taking the demonstration victims to the hospital. TV relayed the loud sirens. "Mom's not too well at all," I said. "What do you suppose we ought to do? They called from Bombo's Club this afternoon and asked about her. I said she got beat up by a customer so she had to rest for a few days."

"What! That's crazy. You're gonna get mom in a lot of trouble. What if she loses her job?"

"Why would they fire her just for something like that?" I thought about it for a minute. "Oh. Yeah. That's right. Sorry." Even at Bombo's they weren't all that thrilled about employees doing prostitution if everybody got to know about it.

Gavin held the whiskey bottle dangling at the end of his arm. "I guess we could try some more hot toddies. She went through a happy phase when I gave her the first one, even though the drink wasn't all that great, and then she got mad as hell at both of us. The next stage when you're drinking a lot and not too used to it is the maudlin one. She'll get real teary and start to whine a lot."

"Okay. Let's give it a try. It'd be an improvement on

the pissed off stage. I'll have to stay out of the bedroom. She doesn't want me there anymore." I thought, but I didn't say, she can't stand the competition.

Gavin was tuned in to the screen now. He got distracted easily. The cops were handcuffing more demonstrators and Gavin's eyes were fixed on the images. Probably he could imagine himself in the same situation. Getting handcuffed, that is. "Right. Gotch ya. I'll give her a refill in a few minutes. Get the hot water ready." He looked at the whiskey bottle as if assessing the possible damage. It was still close to half full.

We were through with a cop show when I remembered about heating up the water. It made you feel good that the police were arresting criminals and throwing them in jail. The show was about these drug dealers trying to hook young girls and make them into seller/user prostitutes.

"Fuck the bastards," Gavin said when the tube announced that the bad guys ended up with twenty years in the slammer. "They had it comin'." He took a good pull out of the bottle. "Hey, dude, go get your mom that hot water before there's nothing left." He held the bottle up to the light to make a more accurate estimate. The whiskey was evaporating like water in the Sahara.

Fifteen minutes later I brought back a glass half full of boiled water and with some sugar added. Gavin grabbed it and carefully measured in some whiskey. It must have been about a shot and a half. Not too generous, but not all that skimpy either. He stood up. "Here goes. Anyway, if this stuff doesn't make her happy, we'll have to try dope." He laughed.

"Gav'!" I called out as he was heading for the bedroom.

"Try to get her to have some soup. I'll heat up the best stuff we have, 'mushroom vegetable'."

"Sure, man, but you heard her. I don't think she's the soup drinking kind." It was true that you had most of your meals at Bombo's or on dates and you rarely went for one of the cans.

Gavin was gone for about half an hour. I went to peek into the bedroom, but the door was shut.

I used the TV remote control to switch the screen back and forth. Nothing on but the usual junk. I tried to listen at the bedroom door. I could hear what sounded like talking, although it might have been moaning and groaning. Mom! Didn't you have no (any?) sense of honor?

Finally Gavin came out of the bedroom. The zipper of his jeans was open. Inside the pants his thing appeared large and stiff. He was looking for the whiskey bottle. It was right where he left it. "Okay dude. I got to fold up for the night." He kissed me on the mouth. "You really do look almost exact like your mom," he said. He was smiling. He drank out of the bottle. "You act a lot like her, too."

"You can't go to bed yet," I pleaded. "It's only one o'clock." I could tell because the Carson Show had just ended. I wanted to delay "the inevitable" for as long as possible. Jealousy. Or maybe it was envy.

Gavin wanted to get back to your bedroom. But didn't you two just do it?

"That toddy drink gave your mom a big thrill. She wanted me to give her a massage, that kinda shit."

"She's better?" This part I was glad to hear about.

"I think so, but it's hard to tell after all those toddies.

I think they could do open heart surgery on you after you had enough of 'em."

Gavin was gone. I stood looking at his tracks for a few minutes. Lucky you, mom. If you got sick, you got Gavin as your personal 24 hour nurse. When I was sick I had to go the V.D. clinic.

I must have fallen asleep in the armchair. Gavin took the whiskey bottle with him when he disappeared into your room, so I probably got hit with boredom. I think it was about three o'clock when I woke up again, because they were playing *The Star Spangled Banner* on TV and showing a lot of cemeteries. After a dozen attempts at peeking through the key hole I still never managed to find out anything about what was happening in the bedroom. I finally moved to the closet and turned off the light bulb.

Gavin shook me awake around mid-afternoon. I wasn't really sleeping. I was only masturbating as I lay on my side.

"Marsh! Get the fuck up! Your mom's a lot worse now. She's got a bad fever and I can't hardly get a word out of her."

I stood up at once. I was naked and had an erection. Gavin didn't seem to attach any importance to this. No doubt he considered it was normal. It was just what he would have done if he had to sleep alone, although that didn't happen too often.

I followed him into the bedroom, after pulling on a pair of jeans. Your face was red, mom. I put my hand on your forehead and it was hot as hell! Your breathing was rapid and rough. "Mom! How do you feel? Are you any okay at all?"

You mumbled in response. This obviously meant no. I turned to Gavin. "We got to get her to the hospital this time. They can help her, I know, with all those miracle drugs and stuff."

"No, dude. We oughta keep her at home if we can. That way she won't feel lonely at night. Besides, only croakers go to the sick tank." That was what Gavin called hospitals. It was a word modeled on the pattern of "drunk tank". He had changed his first opinion on the sick tank idea. He was going to miss you more than I would.

We went into the living room. Gavin sat down in the armchair, but he didn't even look at the TV. He was looking at something beyond, at something even more distracting. After about ten minutes he picked up the remote control box and started to switch through the channels. Maybe he was trying to find a medical show that could give us some advice. Dr. Welby would know what to do, if anybody did. He went through the channel selections twice, two and a half times. There wasn't anything on with guys in white coats.

"I can try heating her up some more soup again," I said, even though this didn't sound like an Einstein idea even to me.

"Uh-uh, man. She can't eat anything. She's too fucking sick."

"Then I'll call Dr. Shitaka," I said. "I'm sure he can tell us something. He's a doctor. He even took my tonsils out once." Gavin's face registered agreement. I picked up the phone and dialed. "Hi! Mrs. Shitaka? Marsha. I got to talk to the doctor, right away. Yeah. It's my mom. She's in bad shape with a high fever and not talking. Maybe he can come by and give her a shot or something."

I looked at Gavin. "Mrs. Shitaka went to get the doctor. He's with a patient right now, but he'll get rid of him, that's what she said. Give him some pills or something."

"Good. Yeah. Ask him what the fuck we can do."

After about ten minutes a voice reappeared (?) on the phone. "Hi. Yeah. This is about my mom. Oh, oh, sorry. I'm Marsha. You know, the one who's really a girl." I listened. "Yeah. Yeah. Yeah. Okay. Yeah." I put the phone back on the hook.

"So what's he say we should do?" Gavin was nervous. He was trying to drink out of the whiskey bottle with the cap still on.

"He said she's got some infection illness and a high fever probably, so we should send for an ambulance and get her to the hospital."

"Oh, man. Dude's smart as hell. I could tell you all that stuff and I never even wasted four years in no medical school."

I called the emergency operator and told her that you were sick and had to get to some place where they could help you. She asked our address. She said to wait and to be ready to cooperate with the assistants. "Thanks. Bye." I told Gavin the plan. "They're sending an ambulance, but we have to watch for them and be ready to help." All of this was exciting, like something on television.

Gavin nodded unhappily. He accepted the inevitable. "Where the hell did I put my clothes?" Gavin looked around. "I guess I oughta wear clean underwear, just in case."

I brought him a new pair of jockey shorts from the closet. He put them on, then jumped into his trousers. He did it in one motion, jump and pull. It was impressive.

Gav' noticed that I had my jeans on, but no shirt. My chest was pretty much lacking in muscle development, and completely hairless, but it had a bright fresh pinkish tone. You could have called it feminine, except it was flat. He put his hand on my chest and rubbed. "You're really cute, in a kind of boy-like way."

I stood there. Gavin's attention always gave me a thrill, but this went even beyond the usual experience. Then he moved away. "Keep your shirt on for now, man. We gotta cooperate for your mom, remember?"

In the closet I collected my green shirt. I think it went well with my red hair. Soon there was a siren in the distance and it got closer every second. I rushed into the living room. Gavin was fortifying himself with a few short snorts from the whiskey bottle, the second of the four I had bought on credit. I told him, "Let's get mom ready. They'll be here soon!"

You were still in a sort of feverish doze as you lay on the bed under the blankets, mom. Gavin shook you and tried to talk to you. "Mom! We're taking you to the hospital so you'll get better. We wanna see you back on your own bed real quick."

You mumbled something. To me it sounded like, "not now". I got your bathrobe from the foot of the bed, where you usually left it. Then we tried to raise you to a sitting position. You were nude. I should have said you were unclothed. I could see why Gavin wanted to keep you at home. I hoped I would take after you a lot more than I did already when I got older. We searched for your nightgown under the blankets. I saw some recent stains on the sheet but ignored them.

"She had to take her nightgown off last night when she got too hot," Gavin explained. This made sense in a couple of ways.

Soon we had you ready, nightgown, bathrobe, the whole thing, even some lipstick and eyebrow pencil.

The siren was real loud now and it seemed to be right in front. I ran to the window and looked out. Two assistants were taking a stretcher out of the back of the ambulance. I opened the door. "She's up here! She's a little better now, but I don't think she can talk," I yelled out.

The ambulance guys ignored this. They probably heard the same thing all the time. They were super professional. They knew just what to do. I think they were both around thirty-five, not all that good looking, but muscular and masculine looking. One of them was thinner, younger, better looking than the other, like the guys who took Robarb away. After they reached the top of the stairs they came right into the living room. "Any violence?" the bigger guy asked. "Assault, rape?"

"Um. No. I don't think so. Not here, anyway." Me.

"Where is the patient?" the big guy looked toward the kitchen.

"She's in the bedroom. She's got a high fever and she won't eat any soup or nothing at all."

Soon they had you on the stretcher. They put a blanket over you, a thin white blanket. It didn't look like it could keep you warm, but maybe it was just supposed to tell everybody you were sick.

Gavin held your hand while they took you downstairs on the stretcher. This created a sort of bottleneck on the stairway, but the assistants went ahead anyway. "Don't you worry none, mom," Gavin said. "We love you and we're gonna be with you all the way. These hospital guys'll make you feel better real quick. They're like doctors, so don't worry."

The ambulance guys said we could ride along with you to the hospital. The problem was that they weren't taking you to the nearest hospital, close by, the one in Oakland. San Cerrito was in a different county, so they had to take you to a different hospital. The rule is, see, unless you have money or insurance, you have to go to the county hospital where you live. For some stupid reason they built *our* county hospital, the one for Cerrito, way out in the sticks (suburbs) about thirty miles away. The ambulance could take Gavin and me there, but there wasn't going to be any free return trip. We'd have to walk back through the mountains.

Gavin took all this in when the ambulance guy, the big one, explained it. I looked at the thinner one. I wondered if he was interested.

"No, man. That's a trip too fuckin' far. We'll get there later. I can call a friend in the city who's got a car. He'll give us a ride out there and back. He's got a BMW."

The ambulance guys put the stretcher with you still on it in back, then they got into the front of the car. They didn't seem to care much about what Gavin said. This was all probably routine stuff to them, although in San Cerrito and places like that, they had to deal mostly with overdose cases, rapes and assaults. The bigger guy gave Gavin a card with a phone number and an address printed on it. "Contra Costa Regional Hospital, Where Wellness is Our Problem".

As the ambulance drove away we both stood on the sidewalk looking at it until it turned the corner onto San Pablo Avenue, heading north to the freeway entrance. We could hardly move, we were so shocked and confused. This was the worst thing that could happen, what you thought never would happen, but it did. Dazed and silent, Gavin turned slowly and began to climb the stairs to the apartment. His expression showed the despair that had hit him. I followed. I wasn't as blown away, but I didn't know what to do either. By force of habit we dropped in front of the tube.

It was past eight o'clock at night, two cans of soup and most of a bottle of whiskey later, when Gavin said, "I suppose we ought to go visit mom in the hospital. Maybe she's a lot better now and she can come home." He swallowed the last tiny portion of soup that had sat in the bottom of the bowl for almost an hour. I took advantage of his distraction to seize the whiskey bottle and gulp a good two or three ounces. I didn't know when I might get another opportunity.

I had to explain again that it was a long trip by train and bus out to the middle of nowhere—that's where the hospital was, in a town called Rodriguez, the "county seat". If we went tonight, the trains would stop running before we started back to San Cerrito.

"Oh. Yeah. Okay, tomorrow then, first thing, we go out and see mom, even if it's halfway to hell."

"What about your friend with the BMW? Can't he give us a ride? It only takes half an hour by car, but the train and bus trip would take us half a day."

"See, that was sort of a story I told them. I don't have

no friend with a car, not since I cracked up La Empressa's Cadillac. I only said that to make those guys think we were rich, so they'd treat mom better."

The next afternoon we had finished breakfast and were sort of waiting around in front of the TV, trying to figure out exactly what to do, when the phone rang. We both knew it was probably something about you, mom. I grabbed the receiver. Gavin took it out of my hands.

"Hello? Yeah? She all right yet?" Gavin paused, seemed to listen for about ten minutes. "Okay, sure, sure, right, sure, right, yeah. Okay. Just what you say, doc." He hung up and reached for the whiskey.

"So, is she all right now and everything?" I was eager to get any good news. I managed to borrow the whiskey for a moment.

"Um, no, not too much better. That was this guy called Doctor Ramsey, some guy who concentrates on communication diseases. He said mom's got meningitis or encephalitis (that means your brain). They took some tests and that's what it came up. They're gonna try some antibiotics out on her and see if it works. He talked to her a little and he found out she works at Bombo's Club. There's been a lot of this meningitis stuff breaking out there. It's like a 'focal point of the epidemic', that's what he said. Probably she got it from some big spender." Gavin repossessed the whiskey bottle from me. He took a long pull. Talking on the phone, especially bad news, made him thirsty.

He looked at the TV, checked in on the program that we were watching. "She's in quarantine," Gavin whispered, almost whined. "It's sort of bad."

On the screen, the cops arrived just in time in front of this house where criminals were holding this young blond girl wearing a ponytail.

I managed a not too small swallow of whiskey while Gavin was still holding the bottle. He was that distracted by the show.

After the program ended, Gavin turned to me, finally ungluing from the screen. "Worse thing, though," he said after sniffling back some tears, "if we wanna go see her, we got to get all dressed up in gowns and masks and gloves like we were going to do heart surgery or something." He pulled the bottle in. "Just to see mom!"

It just didn't seem to work out for the trip to Rodriguez to see you, at least not that day. I had to make another trip to the liquor store to buy groceries. The money came from my private little cash set-up in the closet mattress again. My stash amounted to three hundred and forty dollars, including Mr. Tralanger's money, at least at first. Ten cans of soup, a large plastic bag of taco chips, three quart bottles of whiskey and some tubs of avocado dip took me back about twenty-five dollars! I consoled myself with the thought that if I continued to pray at night the way grandma taught me, asking for you to get well, you might be back to work at Bombo's and earning money in just a few days. I know this sounds mercenary and greedy, but you always told me to think of the practical things too.

Late that day the hospital called again. They didn't have anything new to report about you, mom, but they told Gavin that me (I?) and him had to go down to the hospital to have blood tests to see if we got any contagion from you. Gavin grunted "yeah", then put the receiver back.

He told me about the tests. "They wanna stick us with these big fuckin' needles so they can tell if we got the disease. Hell, I'm a hundred percent okay as far as physical. It's only mom being sick that's the pain. Besides, I can't stand needles, man. I had to get all that polio junk in the ass when I was a kid and it hurt like shit!"

Later that evening we were eating dinner. I heated up two cans of soup together. I combined a can of vegetable noodle with a can of clam chowder. I poured more than half of it into a bowl for Gavin. I ate mine directly from the pot, since there was only one bowl. I used the soup spoon Gavin found for you, mom. It seemed really elegant.

While we ate I couldn't help snivelling a bit myself. I felt like I was abandoned, although I knew it wasn't your fault you were in the sick tank. I understood that, well, to put it politely, you weren't exactly thrilled that your only son was a pansy, but still, blood is thicker than water and I thought that maybe you missed me, too. "I wish mom were here," I finally told Gavin. "Although I know she's not crazy about soup."

"Yeah. She's a fuckin' great lady." He reached for the whiskey. He took a good hit, then poured some in the bowl to mix with the rest of his soup.

I and Gavin (me?) were both sleeping in the big bed since you went to the hospital. There was no reason why not to. I would have been scared to sleep alone in the closet now that you were gone, sick, maybe for a week or more. And I knew Gavin hated sleeping alone. For one thing, he didn't like jerking off. He said it was immoral. Also, it took a long time for him to do it because of the length of his penis. He had to have direct stimulation.

SON OF A WHORE

Early in the morning, after about two-thirty, Gavin took his usual bath. When he got out of the tub he was bright pink all over, he was almost vibrating. His cock was at a ninety degree angle. It swung through large swaths as he walked. "Let's hit the hay, Marsha," he told me. "We got a whole lot of work tomorrow thinking about what to do."

Gavin made me lie down on your side of the bed, mom, even though I was used to the other side on the few times I slept there.

We were both in bed, with the blankets drawn up to our waists. Gavin was smiling. "You sure are a lot like your mom," he said. "Especially from a certain point of view." He switched off the bedroom light.

About five minutes later he tapped me on the arm. I turned over on my stomach and lay there with my arms at my sides and my face against the pillow. I felt his eagerness, his energy. He went in me with a quick push.

The next afternoon I got up before Gavin. He must have been tired out by his nocturnal activities (three sex calls total. Obviously he felt a strong need to purge anxiety. The passive role is less enervating. See Webster for where I got this word). I was getting some soup ready in the kitchen when the phone rang. I ran to the living room and picked up the receiver. It was that doctor.

"This is Doctor Ramsey from County Hospital. It's about your mother. She's in a semi-coma and she's only conscious at times, but she has asked to see her son."

"That's me. When is she going to get better?"

"It may take several weeks. This is a serious case. Are you Gavin?"

"I'm Marsh … I'm Marcus."

"She wants a visit from her son." I could sense confusion at the other end of the line. The family situation was complex.

After I hung up the phone Gavin tumbled out of the bedroom, staggered across the living room and fell into the armchair. There was a noticeable stain on his penis. "Who the fuck was that?"

"The doctor. He says mom won't be well for a couple of weeks." My voice must have showed the fear and worry acting inside me. I slumped near the armchair in a sudden depression attack. Gavin knew just what to do. He reached behind the armchair and brought out the backpack where he kept his few personal items. He searched in the bottom of the pack and pulled out a tiny cigarette. "It's the last one I got, man. Top hash." After we shared it, he had the second stage of treatment ready. He let me suck it.

Finally we had to go. It wasn't that we didn't want to see you, mom. We were both longing for that contact, that maternal presence that we were used to, although in different ways. It was just something about hospitals that was, as Gavin put it, "pure puke".

You weren't supposed to smoke on the trains. Gavin lit up anyway on the way to Rodriguez. The one yesterday wasn't the last after all. "It ain't tobacco, man. So the rule doesn't apply." Gavin puffed on the little cigarette for a while, then talked about the hospital. "I'm not gonna get no shots or have no blood sucked outa me. That's fuckin' rule number one."

At the end of the line we had to catch a bus to get to the hospital. It drove through suburban streets and along freeways. There were new houses and big shopping centers everywhere. Gavin looked around. "Why the fuck do people live in these dumps?" he asked rhetorically. He was probably wondering how anyone living in these well paved neighborhoods could manage to get a good supply of dope.

Finally, the hospital. We were both nervous, afraid that we were going to get a bad shock. Across the street from the medical complex there was a taco stand called "La Casa del Hospital".

"Maybe we oughta get a snack first," Gavin suggested.

I paid two dollars and sixty-eight cents for two burritos. They weren't bad, but the meat was like these tiny dried up little pellets that you had to drown with hot sauce to swallow.

Inside the hospital we asked a nurse or someone like that who was sitting at a desk to tell us where you were.

She looked at a list and checked for the name. "Room 554. You can take the elevator on your left to the fifth floor."

"Thank you, ma'm." Gavin beamed. He evidently thought the nurse had been admiring him. He was probably right.

We got off the elevator at floor five and walked around for about ten minutes, checking room numbers. Gavin felt the need to comment. "Man, they got a lot of real sick people here, dude. Makes you feel kind of creepy. Maybe they could give us some sort of tranquillizers for it."

Then we ran into this guy in a white coat. He stopped and turned toward us. "Are you here to visit Rusalka? Which of you is her son?"

"I am," Gavin shot out. Then he glanced over at me. "Well, I guess we both are, in a way."

"I'm Doctor Ramsey." You could read that on his little name tag. "I'm afraid your mother is seriously ill, but I think I can say that her chances of recovery are significant. It will take time. She's not over the worst of it yet." He surveyed us closely. "You look like brothers. Well, we'll do our best for your mother. She's just across the hall." He pointed to the door of a nearby room. "Since you were living with her when she became ill, you'll have to have blood tests and antibiotic injections before you leave the hospital. See the nurse for contagion ward protective covering before you enter your mother's room." He wrote something on a piece of paper and handed it to Gavin. "It's a very infectious illness." He walked away.

"Ramsey," Gavin mused. "There's a brand of rubbers with that name."

I was flattered that the doctor thought me and Gavin were twins or something. Gavin stared at me, as if he could tell what I was thinking. "Guy must need glasses. We don't look like brothers at all. Not that I don't think you're a super cute dude, because that's gotta be totally clear by now." He was obviously referring to our night (and day) time escapades.

We had to put on these green gowns, like we were surgeons on our way to take out somebody's guts, also paper masks over our mouths and noses that were held in place by little straps that went behind our ears, and rubber gloves. "Shit!" Gavin told the nurse. "I'm sure glad I never decided to be a doctor."

You were lying in a hospital bed, mom. You were sleeping. Your face was totally white, like someone who had been sleeping for eons. There were little networks of wrinkles at the corners of your eyes and mouth. You looked much older, but at the same time, sort of younger too. An I.V. bottle was dripping a clear liquid into your arm. There was a transparent plastic mask around your mouth and nose. It was connected by a tube to an oxygen bottle. We were both shocked. It seemed like almost the end of it all, and just a few days ago everything was normal and you were happy, at least as much as usual. At first, we were too terrified to say anything. Suddenly you opened your eyes. You saw Gavin and you smiled. You made a motion with your hand, a sort of greeting.

"Hi mom," Gavin said. "We came to see you. We really miss you. The doctor says you'll be okay real soon, then everything will be fine again." Gavin's voice was teary. I think he didn't exactly believe what he was saying. He had hardly finished his little speech when you dozed off again.

I wanted to say something. I thought of mentioning that I was keeping the kitchen clean and vacuuming the apartment and taking down the garbage (none of this was true), but I couldn't find the right moment to start. A hospital attendant came into the room and checked a few things on a sort of electronic monitor. She told us that we had to leave, that we shouldn't tire you out, or risk getting the illness ourselves by "too long an exposure".

Soon we were in the elevator and going down. While we were crossing the lobby to the outside exit, I said "aren't we supposed to get shots and tests like that doctor said?"

"Fuck that stuff," Gavin declared in a blank voice. "I told you I can't stand that kinda junk."

When we were in the train, destination San Cerrito,

Gavin gave out his first phrase longer than a few syllables since we left the sick tank. "I hope that doctor knows what the fuck he's doin'. He didn't look like he overdosed in the brain department." Gavin's eyes were red and moist. I could understand that he was disturbed and angry. I wasn't in seventh heaven myself. I thought I knew just what he needed. I'd make a trip to the liquor store as soon as we detrained in Cerrito.

On the trip back, Gavin began to masturbate while the train was passing through a long tunnel. The inside train lights were still on.

"Psst!" I pointed to other passengers who were looking at us with expressions of alarm and disgust.

"What the fuck difference does it make now?" Gavin said without looking up from his area of interest. He desisted when the train entered a well lighted station. "I don't give a shit about anything anymore!"

An expensively dressed, late middle-aged lady got off at Rockdale Station. "I shall inform the authorities about your degenerate and revolting antics!" she told Gavin before stepping out onto the station platform. On the front of her coat there was like a campaign button with the message, "Stop the War Now!"

"Fuck you, lady," Gavin shouted. "But get someone else to do it."

The train pulled out of the station. A lot of passengers were staring at us. A bunch of old men about forty or fifty years old watched us cautiously. I think at least one of them gave me the eye. But that was only one. "Let's get off the train before it gets to Cerrito," I told Gavin. "That old lady and these other creeps are gonna have the cops on our ass."

"For fuckin' what? Jacking off on the train? The cops do that all night in their squad cars."

Then we were in San Cerrito. I looked around the station after we got off the train. I was surprised there wasn't a mob of policemen and arrest vans waiting. On the way to the apartment, Gavin was in a daze. He mumbled with his head down, things like "fuckin' hospital'll kill every fuckin' bastard alive", and "that Doctor Ramsypansy there couldn't cure a mouse".

When he was seated in the living room armchair, Gavin almost came back to normal. The TV was still playing and he tuned in. It was sports now. These Latin American guys were running up and down a field kicking a ball sort of like what they use in volley ball, only they used their feet instead of their hands.

"Wow. Look at them little guys go! They sure know what they're doing."

I watched for a moment. "Yeah." I couldn't make out what was going on. The players ran one way, then another, they kicked, switched, turned. I think Gavin had an instinctive feeling for sports. At one point he yelled, "goal, goal, goaall!"

In the kitchen I checked on the supplies. We would be needing soup, chips, whiskey. Now that Gavin was less than dangerously depressed, I could safely leave him at home alone. "I'm going to the store," I announced. "Do you want anything?"

"Yeah. Get me some whiskey, some chips and some soup. Pronto. Going to the sick tank really pumps you dry."

All night Gavin seemed to concentrate on the TV. I think he was instinctively trying to distract himself from his anxiety feelings about you, mom. He kept his eyes glued to the screen for even the most mediocre shows. During some crappy old film about spies in Istanbul or Argentina, his mouth fell open in amazement half a dozen times. Of course, that made it all the easier for him to keep sipping from his glass of whiskey. He was giving the stuff all due honors. "Clan Glenfiddin" I think was the brand name. I bought him some really good booze in order to cheer him up a bit.

During the late night news we both lost interest in the tube. They were always talking about the same thing, some sort of scandal in politics and the last drag out reports about the war in Vietnam. Now Gavin had to focus more on reality. "Mom's really sick, and she's not in any good shape at all, but I guess that doctor must be right. They're gonna get her cured with all their modern medicine and tubes and machines. He said it was pretty likely, right?"

"He said it might take three or four weeks, though."

"Hm. Three or four weeks. That's a fuckin' long time. Well, I suppose we got to do the best we can." Gavin drank from his whiskey glass. He didn't notice it was empty. I rushed to give him a refill. I helped myself at the same time. That Scottish stuff was much better than the cheap bottles we usually got.

Gavin threw a few taco chips into his mouth and crunched slowly. "Your mom sure took good care of us when she was here. We oughta be real grateful for that. Now we gotta shift for our own selfs."

During the late night movie Gavin fell asleep. It was probably the workout from the hospital visit, not to mention the train ride home. Suddenly he woke up with a start. "Man! It's like I fell into a coma. Do my eyes look okay?" He pulled his lower eyelids down with fingers from each hand and looked straight at me.

"Yeah. They're okay. I don't see anything wrong." Gavin actually looked attractive even making faces like that. It gave him an exotic look. But this showed that he was worried about contagion.

"Okay. I'm going to take a bath, sort of wash all that hospital crap off me."

While Gavin was running the water in the tub, then splashing around, I tried to masturbate, like he did in the train. It didn't work. Probably the fact that Gavin's thing was three times longer than mine gave him an advantage.

Then Gavin was out of the water. He walked naked into the living room, steaming in his pink glory. "C'mon dude. We can't stay up all night. Time to fuckin' hit the pad."

As I told you before, we were both sleeping in the bedroom now. There was no reason we shouldn't make ourselves at home. I didn't even think it strange when Gavin insisted that I wear one of your night gowns from the chest of drawers. After I put it on, he reminded me to use cleansing cream in the bathroom to take off all that makeup (I never got over my tendency to overdo it).

In a few minutes I was back in the bedroom. I lay down on my (your) side of the bed. I was dressed in your nightgown.

Gavin looked over at me. "Dude. You never knew who your old man was, but did anyone ever tell you who your granddad was?"

I thought about this. It was an odd question. Maybe that Scottish whiskey gave Gavin an interest in genealogy, like the old clans and who murdered who on the bonny,

bonny moor, that kind of stuff. "No. Mom never mentioned it. I don't even know how she could know, since she wasn't sure who my old man was."

"Makes sense. Anyway, they say all kinds of things skip a generation and show up every third generation, something like that. He wasn't some kind of drag queen dude, was he?"

"Might have been. I wouldn't be surprised." Now I was sure Gavin had drunk too much. He could get mean when he went over a certain limit. I thought it was better just to play along.

Gavin reminisced a bit about his own family tree. "My granddad went to jail when he was kind of old already. That's what my old lady said. She told me he was so old he was dead before he got out of prison. He stole a whole bunch of money from a company he worked at and tried to double it in Las Vegas, only it came up black instead of red."

"Crap. I always bet on 'double O'."

"Okay, I can see you're not too fascinated." Gavin reached for the light switch on the little table. "I just hope that doesn't happen to me someday or other." Dark.

In one way it seems plain that Gavin was trying to make me into a substitute for you, but in another way what he was doing just seemed natural and normal and that he was treating me like he always did, as a girl, like I really am. This may be confusing, but the real thing is the physical, not a lot of psychological mumbo-jumbo.

After a few minutes of shifting around and tugging me this way and that, Gavin had my nightgown off. Then he was on top of me and I was facing the mattress. It went on for some time, a pretty good work out. Gav' sniveled and cried a few times as he pushed into me. He called me "Rusalka" again another few times. That was okay, because, what the hell? Then he started to pump full force into me. With each in and out he made a sound like "uh", "uh", "ah", "oh", which was kind of normal, at least for him. As for me, I felt very much that feminine feeling that I usually did—I mean, it would be hard not to, right? It was some time, maybe fifteen minutes—I was looking occasionally at the digital clock radio on the chest of drawers—before the big bang. "Ah! Damn! Damn! Fuck! Aaahhh!" He ended in real tears. He rolled off of me. A minute later I heard him snoring.

I turned over onto my back. I tried jerking it a bit, but nothing much happened. It didn't seem to matter, anyway. Before turning on my side and trying to sleep I wondered whether I should say those prayers grandma taught me. It just didn't seem the right moment.

Gavin was watching this show about training dogs when I brought out the afternoon soup. "Wait," he told me. He shifted position in the armchair. Then he changed TV channels with the remote control. "Okay. Hand it over." I obeyed.

I was sitting at his feet while I spooned my portion of soup out of the pot. I looked up at him from time to time to see what mood he was in. Maybe I would get lucky. Last night he seemed to be kind of pissed about something, but probably he was just upset about your illness and being in the hospital.

"Hey Marsha, did you used to get along pretty well with Rusalka? I mean before I got here."

"Not too bad. When she got pissed at me, and that

wasn't all that often because she was at work most of the time, I mean at work even when she was home, she used to call me a bastard and a son of a bitch, but it didn't bother me. I knew it was just a mood."

"I get the point. At least she never really held it against you that you didn't know who your father was, right?"

"That, no. Not that I can remember."

"Wha'd she get mad at you for?"

"Different things. Usually it was general principles."

"Like the fag stuff?"

"Yeah, it was that a lot. How was I supposed to be John Wayne, if that's what she wanted? I just didn't get the genes."

"Naw. I definitely can't see you being John Wayne. Maybe Peewee Herman." Gavin laughed. It wasn't exactly the nicest comment. Anyway, I had no need to be well-developed in that area, and that's probably what he was referring to.

A few minutes later a pack of commercials came on the screen. Gavin lost it. He started crying and shrieking. "Mom's never gonna come back from that place! That fuckin' doctor's just a big quack! She's gonna die there. Then what are we gonna do? We'll both be fuckin' alone!"

I had to give Gavin one of your tranquillizers. It had him calmed down in a minute. Then he dozed off.

About ten minutes later he woke up. "Shit, dude. I fuckin' crashed out right in the afternoon. It's because I didn't sleep too good last night. I was all worried about mom. You got any coffee back there?" Gavin motioned with his shoulder toward the kitchen.

I looked around for coffee. I checked all the kitchen

shelves and drawers. Finally I found a bag of tea. I boiled some water and poured it into a cup, then dunked the bag.

Gavin took the cup and brought it to his mouth. "This ain't no fuckin' coffee! What the hell d'you put in it?"

"It's tea. It's all we had left."

Suddenly contrite, Gavin reached over and tousled my hair. "That's okay, man. Hey, I'm sorry I been on your ass so much." It was clear that he did not mean this in the literal sense. "You know you're my best girl friend and I hardly ever loved anyone as much as you before."

I almost swooned after hearing this. It was what I had been hoping for, waiting for. Gavin said he loved me after all!

Later in the afternoon, actually it was almost evening, Gavin had some more practical thoughts. "Marsh? How come you don't go down to Bombo's Club and apply for a job for yourself? Just temporary, as a replacement. Then, after mom comes back, you can get ready to go on to college."

"You mean work in the gift shop?" I would have preferred a spot in the chorus line. With a little padding I think it would have worked out pretty well for me in those skimpy outfits, and I wouldn't even have had to shave my legs, much less my chest. "They don't hire boys at Bombo's. Mom told me that a long time ago."

"But you're not really a boy, right? You wear all that make-up stuff anyway, and we could get you dressed up in some of mom's clothes when you go down there. Worth a try, don't you think?" Gavin was considering our "long term financial future", like they said all the time on TV.

"I'd do it, except that when those businessmen wanted

to start some after hours entertainment, they'd find out in two seconds I wasn't a regulation girl."

"Yeah, that's true. Then you'd really be fucked."

Or not, most likely.

Soon the early evening news was transmitting on the television. Our troops were fighting a rear guard action against the enemy in Vietnam while the diplomats negotiated. There was actual film of the soldiers in action. They looked so brave in their camouflage outfits and helmets. They fired back with their M-16s against invisible opponents hiding somewhere deep in the jungle. A few were handsome, and at least two were sort of cute.

Gavin was excited by this scene from real combat. "Way to go, guys! Shoot their fuckin' guts out, those bastards!" He had met a lot of soldiers on leave in the bars and he said they were all nice guys, and real hot in bed. Gavin held his hands in a way that showed he was pretending to use a rifle. He made firing noises with his lips. "Rat-tat-tat-tat! Drop those dumb creeps dead!"

"I'd of joined up by now, but I'm too young," he explained. It was true that Gavin was still a month short of his seventeenth birthday and recruits had to be at least eighteen.

When the news program switched to some political guys talking, Gavin switched it off. But he was still turned on. He took his cock out. It was half-erect. Now it was my turn to go into action.

"Ah ah ah ah ah." After seven or eight minutes, Gavin fired right into the target. I got a full discharge of viscous, salty fluid in the mouth.

Gavin was so tired of soup that I volunteered to go

down to San Pablo Avenue and bring back a hot pizza. It was almost midnight, but the pizza place was open until two. They had to accommodate the post-bar crowd.

When I got back with an extra-large pepperoni, cheese and salami, Gavin was famished. It's probably true that man does not live by soup alone. You need other kinds of minerals. He tore into the pizza. At one point he held a slice of pizza in each hand and took bites alternately from one, then the other.

I tried to eat in such a way that the cheese didn't drip on my chin in long sticky threads. That would have been very unbecoming. I doubted Gav's army friends would have eaten in a sloppy way.

That night Gavin passed into dream time as soon as he lay down on the bed. I covered his nudity with a blanket. His organ was in fact quite clean, probably as a result of the activities that I described above.

It must have been just before dawn when he shook me awake. "Hey, Marsh. Call that fuckin' hospital and ask them how your old lady is. I had a dream where I saw her almost dying!"

I didn't know the number, so I had the operator connect me to Contra Costa Regional Hospital. "Hello? Yes. Could you tell me how Rusalka Zancsek is? Fifth floor. Is she any better at all yet? I'm her son. Yeah. Marsha Zancsek. Daughter. No, son, yeah. It's a long story."

I put the receiver back on the hook. "They say 'she is responding adequately to treatment at this time'."

"Fuck. That's great to hear. Man, I was worried. Dreams tell you what's happening in real life. My old lady told me that."

In a few minutes we were both back sleeping again. I dreamt I could hear Gavin snoring.

I woke up alone on the bed. At first I thought Gavin had just gone to take a piss, since he almost never got out of bed until I told him breakfast was ready. When I didn't hear a flushing sound for ten minutes I got up and searched the apartment. No Gavin. I panicked. For a moment I thought of calling the police and reporting him missing, but I remembered that Gavin and the police just didn't mix. I looked out the living room window. Nothing. I got dressed and went to the corner. There was no one anywhere even vaguely like Gavin. I was terrified that he had abandoned me again and gone back to some sort of risky drug activity in S.F. I walked back to the apartment.

The television was still lit up, but that meant nothing. We almost always left it on, as a matter of principle. An hour later I decided to take a train to the city and to trawl for Gavin on Polk Street, and if I found him to plead with him to come home and resume our happy family life. Then he walked into the apartment.

"Hi, Marsh." Gav' ambled over to the armchair and fell into it. He was not happy. "I couldn't stand worrying about it anymore, so I went to visit mom in that hospital dump."

I jumped at this. "How is she? Any better? She's got to be better by now."

Gavin took a slow drink from a pint bottle that he pulled from his back pocket. "I don't know if she's much better. I talked to her a little. She wants me and her to get married."

"What?" This sounded totally crazy. Gavin was younger than her son, me.

"S'what she said. I'd be all for it, cause I love your mother like she was my own mom, but I think maybe she just got deliriums or something."

When I thought about it more, it didn't seem to be such a bad idea at all. Gavin would be my very own stepfather, even if he was a year or so younger and not even legally an adult. He'd sure have Uncle Robarb beat on quality. "Well, if that's what she wants, if it would make her happy, I think it's okay." I thought maybe I could be maid of honor at the wedding.

"Yeah. It'd work out okay, but she's gotta get well first. She's like, in and out of being in consciousness now. It's as worse as them medical shows on TV."

Later I began to doubt Gavin's story about visiting you, mom. For one thing, I don't think he had been gone long enough to go to Rodriguez and back on the train. For another, I wondered where he would have got the money for a two way trip *and* a bottle of whiskey. Later that night, when Gavin was about to take a bath, I noticed brown stains on his cock. I thought now that maybe he just went down to the park and found some guy to bugger. Maybe that guy paid him for it. That would explain where the pint came from.

A bunch of letters came in the mail. There was one from the electricity company, one from the phone company, and another from the landlord. I opened them. They were all asking for a lot of money. The bill from landlord was the biggest. The bastard wanted a hundred and forty dollars! A hundred and forty dollars just for living one month in a slum dump! He ought to have paid us to live there. Right then I and Gavin were living on the money from my mattress stash, since the cash we saw in your purse when we took you to see Dr. Shitaka, all those twenties, had gone fast on pizzas and Scottish whiskey. My stash couldn't last forever, though. I figured we had enough money for maybe five and a quarter days of food expenses and then maybe a last bottle. Even cheap whiskey costs a ton when you put it away like Gavin (and me).

"Lemme see that." Gavin grabbed the bills. "Uh. Yeah, what a load of crap. Call these guys up, Marsh, and tell them that mom's in the hospital and she can't work right now. We'll get caught up on the bills as soon as she gets out."

I knew it wouldn't work, but I made the telephone calls anyway, because that's what Gavin said to do. They all said the same thing. They were very sorry to hear you were sick, but they had to have their filthy money anyway and damn soon.

Gavin stretched back in the armchair. He drank a good swallow of whiskey right from the bottle. "There's only one thing left to do." He paused for dramatic effect.

"What's that?"

"You gotta go down to the county offices and apply for Welfare. Apply for both of us."

"Why me?" I didn't like dealing with officials. They all reminded me of those junior high P.E. teachers who tried to make me wear a jock strap.

"Well, it's plain. I'm not actually eighteen yet, so I can't apply alone. I tried it once in San Francisco and they almost sent me to Juvenile Hall."

I searched my brain for some sort of alternative. Welfare offices were the worst kind of place. Uncle Robarb told me about them, and he should know if anyone did. They were exactly like the morgue, only for people still alive. You just sat there with all these other poor creeps and waited for them to call your number, if they ever did. It could take all day. Then you had to talk to some lady who majored in sociology and who acted like she was your parole officer. Something twigged in my mind. "Mom's got a bank account somewhere," I said. "I think it's in the Bank of San Cerrito. I saw a letter from them a few weeks ago and she had about three hundred dollars in the account."

"Okay! Go down there and get that money out. That'll keep us floating until mom gets out." Gavin thought of the hospital as a kind of prison. He wasn't far wrong. "We don't have to pay the rent right away. You can always keep that on hold for three months or so. My mom spent half her time fighting off evictions. What we gotta do is get something for the groceries and the electric."

I knew something about banks, because you told me about them. You once worked in one, remember? Only they cheaped out on salaries, so you had to quit. I remembered they had to keep all their money in a vault. Getting money out of your account seemed like a good idea at first, but now I realized it wouldn't work out too well. "I can't because mom's name is the only one on the account. She has to sign all the withdrawal slips and be there, too."

Gavin snapped his fingers. "No problem. We just dress you up as mom—you're almost there already—and you sign after you practice making her signature so it looks right." Gavin had had a short career as a check forger. He spent two months in the Hall when he was fifteen as a result. I didn't think it would work, but because Gavin was in favor of the plan, I agreed to go ahead with it.

First, we had to find a bank statement, so we'd know the account number and where the bank was, that sort of stuff. We searched the drawers in the bedroom dresser. There was all kinds of junk in there. Lots of women's underwear. I recognized most of the individual items. I had worn them at one time or another. Also, half a dozen scarves, heavy on pastel pink and lavender shades (my favorites too). Some jewelry, the cheap stuff. Your expensive pieces were hidden somewhere else. Gavin pulled out a dozen prophylactics. He looked at them closely, then at me. Suspicion.

"You been using these, man?" I think he suspected I might have been doing it with men when he wasn't around and then pocketing the cash. Gavin had firmly and definitely forbidden us to do any more prostitution, when at all possible.

"No. It wasn't me. Mom kept these to use in her work when she brought customers home."

"Don't you say nothin' bad about your mom, man, or you'll get a fuckin' hit in the mouth!"

How was I supposed to know there was anything wrong with your mother being a prostitute? To me it seemed as natural as rain. "Sorry."

There were a couple of tubes of sexual lubricant. Gavin tossed them on the bed. "I think we can use these later."

I caught sight of a piece of paper and I grabbed it, brought it close to my face. It wasn't a bank statement, though. It was some kind of letter, handwritten. I read it out loud because I knew Gavin was curious and it would have taken him an hour to read it phonetically on his own, if he could do it at all. "Rusalka Honey, You are the hottest fucking bitch I ever know. Them nights we had together make me think about it all the time. I know it wasn't just love that you did it for me and there was the money thing, but I want you to know that me fucking you was like the fucking end of everything. I can't wait to get back in there. Love, Joey."

"What the hell's that about?" Gavin asked. He sounded sort of pissed.

"Must be from one of mom's customers, from one of her whore stunts."

Slap! Gavin gave me a good one right in the face. I started to cry.

"Sorry, man." He put his hand on my back and rubbed it. "But I told you, you can't say that stuff about your mom, even if it's true. She's your mom, after all."

We went through everything in the drawers. Hidden away, as if to prevent unauthorized use, there were some nice pairs of new underwear that I stuffed in my pockets to wear later. I dropped the bras on the floor with the other stuff. I didn't need those. Not yet anyway. There was no bank statement. Gavin looked around the room.

"Where the hell she put the old bank statements?"

"Maybe she threw it all away so it wouldn't be stolen."

This sounded plausible to Gavin. "Then I guess we'll have to wait for the next letter to come in the mail before we make a move on the bank money."

I was glad to hear this. I wouldn't be embarrassed to dress up like my mother, but I was sure it wouldn't work.

I looked about twenty years younger than you, which I was. The cashiers would twig on that right away, then it would be jail time for me.

I woke up to find Gavin butt fucking me. It felt good, and I didn't object one bit, but after a minute or two I realized that I was lying on my back and that Gavin was actually underneath me! He was really pumping away, super-passionate, raising my whole body with his every thrust. That went on for about ten minutes, I think. Gav' was a really strong guy! Then came the sex explosion, the ohs and ahs and even a "shit, man, fuck" or two. Then he collapsed back onto the mattress. He eased himself out from under me and fell asleep. I looked at Gavin's face in the weak light from the bedroom window. He was so handsome, and his face showed a deep expression of satisfaction and content. This made me very happy. I raised the blanket and looked at his cock. I'd have to ask him to take a shower in the morning.

The next afternoon, which was when we usually woke up, since we were both used to waiting until you got back from the Club in the early morning before going to bed, Gavin was calculating the situation seriously. The bank was out, at least for now. That left only the Welfare Office. "We gotta do the county cash bit, man. No other way out."

Welfare. Even at eighteen years old I was legally eligible to receive the small monthly payments that the state provides to the indigent (this means when you don't have any money left). I knew, though, that the welfare officials didn't like to put teenagers, especially boys, on the rolls. They usually just told you to find a job or move in with a relative. When you answered that there were no jobs, that no one would hire you, and that you didn't have any relatives (maybe back in Romania, but they probably hadn't seen a kopeck in years), they shot back that you can always find a job if you look hard enough. If you really stuck it out at the Welfare Office, though, if you really insisted, you could force them to give you checks. You had the law on your side. I learned this from talking to some of the younger Welfare artists on Polk Street. Okay. I'd try it. Gavin promised he'd come with me to the Office. He couldn't apply himself because he was still a month or so short even of seventeen, but he was a hundred percent in favor of trying this angle. He said I could tell them he was my underage cousin who was living with us when you got sick. He said he could teach me how to act, what to say, how to give the best answers to the questions the Welfare jerks asked, and all that. We got ready early in the afternoon. Gavin put on his other pair of jeans, the cleaner ones, and even wore some underwear, which, except for medical stuff, he didn't usually like to do when he went out. He said it spoiled the impression. I wore a white shirt and a pair of slacks (not yours, which I would have preferred, but my own pair, which gave me a dressed-up boy look).

Even though Gavin had a lot of nerve, to say the least, he was still worried about the whole deal. For one thing, he was scared that if the Welfare people found out he was under age, they'd try to throw him in Juvenile Hall, like before. For another, he was afraid that our application would be rejected and we'd be left with nothing for groceries (liquor). Anyway, it seemed like the only chance. Before going into the office, we went into a little corner market so Gavin could buy some cigarettes. Normally he didn't smoke, unless it was something better than tobacco, but he said ordinary cigarettes helped him through nervous moods. He said he'd quit totally soon, without a doubt.

Then we walked into the County Office of Public Welfare. It was a huge dingy office, painted inside with a really bad taste shade of green about thirty years ago. It was on San Pablo Avenue, only about a mile away from where we lived. We hit it lucky in one sense, because at three-thirty p.m. there were only about twenty beggars waiting to talk to the specialists. They were mainly black people. Naturally, since black people have less of a chance of finding work and supporting themselves because of all the discrimination (they talked about this constantly on TV). There were some white people too, old broken down boozers, for the most part, and a few mothers with children who got stranded after daddy hit the road. Gavin walked right up to the reception desk.

"Marcus Zancsek and me want to see a worker about getting help, because our mom's in the hospital and she's real sick and can't work."

The Welfare worker gave us a long glance. She looked like a nice black lady, about fifty years old, with grey hair, a lot overweight (she had to stay mainly behind the desk). "How old are you?"

"Marcus is eighteen."

"Let him talk. Eighteen?" She gave me a close look over. She was unimpressed. She talked to me directly. "A boy like you should be able to support himself. Have you looked for work?"

"Yes ma'am. I filled out about a hundred applications,

but they all said that since I don't have any previous work experience and not much education, they can't use me."

"Hmm. Many young people without qualifications find jobs that have few requirements."

"They just said no, ma'am."

"You don't have to call me ma'am. This isn't Arkansas."

"Yes ... Mrs."

"And who are you?" She was looking directly at Gavin.

"My name's Gavin Zancsek. We're cousins, but we had different fathers."

"Then why do you have the same last name?"

"Wull, it's sorta because Marcus doesn't know which one was his father," Gavin explained. "See, I'm his younger cousin and I'm part of the family, but I used to live with someone else."

"Who?"

"Some guy."

The receptionist shook her head. She wasn't interested enough to ask any more questions. "I suggest you both go to the county casual labor exchange. Anyone can work a shovel or a broom."

"But see," Gavin went ahead, "we got all these bills now about the electricity and the garbage and the rent and they want to throw us out on the street."

The dignified lady was not smiling. "I think young men like you could easily provide for yourselves if you tried."

To me it seemed like I had two alternatives. I could start crying right away, or I could shout and make an uproar so that it wouldn't be worth it for her to keep saying no. "But we did and we can't," I whined. I started to turn on the water works.

The lady gave us a little ticket with a number on it. Number G57. "You will be called by an Application Examiner." Dismissed.

We sidled along to the nearest gray, form-fitting plastic chairs. There were about three hundred of them in the office, all worn and scratched and smelly. We eased into two of them. Gavin lit a cigarette right away. Smoking was still legal then, and even though Gavin was under the age for legally buying cigarettes, he looked older.

"Fuck!" he said, but not in a loud voice. "This ain't gonna be so easy. That old black lady's one tough mother."

"Maybe we just should call the doctor and find out if mom'll be getting out soon." I was getting cold feet. I felt like we were planning a bank robbery or something.

"Naw. We gotta tough it out, man. There ain't no other way. If they give you checks, then we can keep the place real nice for when mom comes back from the hospital. What the hell would she think if she got out and we were living on the street?"

"Yeah." I nodded. "She'd be like super upset." I looked at the clock. It was after four o'clock already. Since the Office closed at five, and the Welfare workers didn't work overtime, the interview couldn't last too long. "Give me a cigarette, Gav'. I feel nervous and kind of queasy."

Gavin handed me one of the white paper cylinders with a phony cork tip. He offered me a light from his plastic lighter. Although he had his faults, Gavin was always a real gentleman.

"Hough! Hough! Hough!" The cigarette smoke went down the wrong way!

Gavin slapped me on the back. He took the cigarette

away from me and lodged it between his lips next to the other one.

"Hough! Hough!"

"Breath slow, man." Gavin guided my head to an inclined position. "You took it in wrong."

It took me about ten minutes to recover completely from my coughing spell. The whole Office was staring at us. "Try to look normal," Gavin whispered sorta pissed. "So they don't call the fuckin' sheriffs on us."

When G57 was called, Gavin reminded me, "tell 'em we're both cousins but we had different fathers."

G57 was called to desk 9. We located desk 9 and zipped over. We didn't want to miss our chance. Behind the desk was our Application Examiner, a woman about forty-eight or fifty-six years old. This one had her hair done up in blond curls. She had a pale, pinky tone and "superior" features, like she was British (straight, thin nose, mouth a bit too wide, large cheek bones). We stood looking at her. The sign on her desk said she was Ms. Browley, although I'm not sure that's how you pronounce it.

"Yes," she said. "Sit down." Gavin made an attempt to sit on the floor before he realized that she meant the chairs in front of her desk. She smiled slightly, showing that she was rather amused at this contretemps (this means a faux pas). Maybe she didn't twig that I was wearing too much makeup and some of your clothes (the white blouse. I felt I had to change out from my own shirt at the last minute, contrary to Gavin's orders. Psychology stuff), or maybe she didn't give a damn at that point.

"We had to come down here, ma'am, 'cause the bill collectors are tryin' to close down our house." I felt Gavin didn't have to make it sound like it was a brothel.

Ms. Browley reached out her hand to take my application paper. I hadn't filled in anything except my name and the address. The other questions seemed too hard. The case examiner used a pencil to scratch behind her head. "You have not filled in the spaces inquiring about your income and assets."

"Don't got none," I said.

"Don't got any," Gavin, my former tutor, corrected.

Ms. Browley looked at the application and asked, "Which of you is Marcus Zancsek?"

I raised my hand. It was like being back in grade school.

"And you are?" she looked at Gavin.

"Gavin Zancsek. We're cousins but we had different fathers." Gavin couldn't mention his real last name because of the arrest warrants.

"If you had different fathers, but the same mother, then you are half-brothers," Browley said.

"Uh-uh, ma'am. We're both completely guys." Gavin hated to have his sexuality confused.

"All right." It was the end of the day and Ms. Browley was losing patience. "What is this about?"

"Um, see," Gavin began. "This is what it is. Our mom's in the hospital and she's been there for about three weeks and we don't know when she's gonna get out."

"She used to pay the bills because she works at this place called Bombo's Club, where they have nude dancing, but now she can't work," I put in, just to show that I could talk.

Gavin jabbed me in the ribs and took over again. "And now our whole family doesn't got no income."

"Any income," I corrected.

Gavin shot me a look that seemed to say, "shut up, stupid, or you'll wreck everything!"

"What are your ages?"

"Marcus is eighteen and I'm practically seventeen."

"Why do you have to do the talking," Browley asked Gavin, "if your cousin is the applicant?"

"See, he's older, but he never had no chance to have a lot of education and stuff."

"You have the same mother?"

"Yes, ma'am. She brought us up right and was always super kind and everything. That's why we're doing this for her." Gavin was spinning it out too much. I was afraid Browley would twig that we were operators. Although, I don't think we really were.

"You're doing this for *her*?"

"For when she gets out of the hospital, so she'll have a home to come back to," Gavin explained.

Ms. Browley wrote something on a notepad. Then she asked me questions while she finished filling out the application form. "Average annual family income for the past five years?" "Last place of employment?" "Years of education?" That kind of thing. I only guessed at the answers. I didn't know how much you actually made, mom. Obviously the biggest part would be from tips, but I couldn't say that because they might think you were a you-know-what. I think my education would be about eight years, which is not too bad, all things considered. I'd never had a job. I mean, any employment. "My mom worked in the gift shop," I told Ms. Browley.

"Are you employed at this establishment?"

"No. They don't hire guys. That's not what the customers come for." I hated to keep talking about myself as a "guy", because I knew that I was really a girl (see Sigmund Freud for a full explanation). Anything else would have sounded too complicated to explain and then we'd both be screwed.

"This is not one of our usual case file situations," she said. "We will review your application and you will receive a response in the mail." Dismissed.

"You really blew it, man," Gavin shouted once we were outside the Welfare Office. "She's gonna think you're some kind of nutcase from what you said."

"I only said the truth. To get the money out of them, that's all."

"Yeah, but when you mentioned that strip joint, she probably thought mom's a whore."

"She is a whore," I said. It was a family tradition, at least downstream.

Whap! Gavin gave me another hard slap on the cheek. I started to cry and to shriek in misery and outrage.

"Now, babe." Gavin looked around, checking out to see if the Welfare people or other cops had seen this. He kissed me on the other cheek. "I'm sorry, man, but I can't let nobody talk that way about mom after all the shit she went through for you and me."

I was still crying, but silently. Gavin had roughed me up a few times before. It wasn't so bad. I liked physically dominant guys anyway. As a sort of restitution he put his hand on my butt and rubbed it to produce anal stimulation. He knew just how to do it.

"You're just as pretty as your mom, Marsha. Everyone says you are. Maybe even prettier, at least from behind."

I knew Gavin was trying to keep me quiet, telling me that stuff again, but I had a feeling that it was real, too.

After all, you can't bugger anyone *that much* if you don't like him (her) a lot, can you?

When we got back to the apartment we both tried to relax and to forget about our ordeal at the Welfare office. Gavin slid into the armchair and zeroed in on the TV screen. He took a long, cool suck out of the fast draining whiskey bottle. "Man, I hope we don't have to switch to wine again. That stuff makes me piss a lot."

Gavin took the remote control device and switched off a detective program where the police were trying to dig up some real rotten operators who were stealing money from old ladies. It seemed too much like reality. "That Ms. Browley," he said, "I'm a hundred percent sure she ain't no whore. Too fuckin' ugly." After a minute's reflection he added, "She got real smart in college, but she forgot to work on her ass and tits."

I nodded. I was working on both since Dr. Shitaka had started giving me these pills that he said would delay "sexual differentiation" and "produce gradual feminization". That's one reason it was hard (I mean difficult) for me to get an erection, although I generally didn't need one.

Later I walked to the market and bought a small supply of soup and whiskey. I left off the taco chips and guacamole dip this time. Cash was getting low and we had to cut down to the essentials.

That night when we were in bed, Gavin was playing around with himself under the covers when he suddenly turned to me and asked, "Marsh? You ever try to fuck a guy? I mean, the way I do it to you?"

"Yeah. I did."

"What happened?"

"Nothing. It didn't work. My thing isn't long enough. I never got through."

Gavin laughed. He pulled the blanket down and felt my little member. "It's cute, anyway." He tried various ways of stimulating me with his hand, but nothing happened. Thank you, Dr. Shitaka.

The lights were out and Gavin was on top of me and pushing in all he could, which was a lot. Before he arrived at Point Z, though, I thought he called me "Graveline", like the Welfare lady's first name. It sounded like that, but I could have got it wrong.

We were working throught the money in my mattress fast. It was mainly in fives and tens, but there were a lot of them, so I thought they'd last a long time, but they didn't. Probably it was because of the new *stagflation* that the TV news guys were talking about now. This meant that prices went up, but there were no new jobs, because the economy was sort of stuck in neutral. I'd have to be even more careful about what I bought. Just the basics, like before, only less of it. When Gavin complained again about the monotony of our daily soup routine, I added a small bag of taco chips to the shopping list.

TV was getting dull. I mean, it is dull, because most of the shows just get played over and over, and it's all pretty much the same, but it gets worse when you just sit in front of the screen all day. Gavin couldn't go out much because of the arrest warrants that were out on him, and I didn't want to leave him home alone for longer than a few minutes. He might wear himself out and leave me celibate at night.

Then a letter came. It was from the Welfare Office. I ran up the stairs and showed it to Gavin.

"Okay, man. This is the clinch. It's here where we sink or we go broke." He took the envelope from my hands and tore it open. I looked over his shoulder and read it aloud to him.

"Your case cannot be decided without the submission of additional documentation. You must provide, for each member of the applicant family, the following documents:

1) Birth certificate or proof of naturalization.
2) Acceptable identification with photograph.
3) Evidence of income, expenses and savings.

Your initial interview has convinced me that you should both enroll immediately in speech courses. This will improve your prospects of finding gainful employment.

Sincerely,
Graveline Browley"

"What the hell's that all mean?" Gavin scratched his leg.

"We have to show photo I.D.s and a lot of other stuff to the Welfare guys before they'll think about giving us money."

Gavin got the idea quick. Photo I.D. He didn't have one. And if he had one, he couldn't show it. Problem about the arrest warrants.

"Fuck that." He sat down and turned back to the TV. It was a blow, a hard one, but there was always other crap to try.

"I don't even know where to get my birth certificates," I said. "I'm not even sure I was actually born. I mean with all the official papers and everything."

Gavin nodded. He knew the sort of problem it could be. "My mom said I was born in Novo Zapato or someplace like that in some weird state or maybe even a different country. She liked to have international boyfriends."

I saw that Gavin was thinking hard. The whiskey was draining fast. "Hey, let's check up on mom, see what's going on now."

We called the hospital. Gavin held the phone so I could hear, too.

"Mrs. Zancsek is in stable condition and appears to be adequately responding to treatment."

"When's she getting out?" Gavin.

"The doctor will make that decision. She is still very seriously ill."

We were down to our last thirty-three dollars or so. I wondered what Gavin would think about peanut butter sandwiches for dinner?

For a few days I took only the absolute minimum from my mattress stash, which was all the money that was left, to buy whiskey and a few other things. But I must have got careless again. I checked out the mattress hole the day after Tuesday, just after I got up, and it was empty! I put my hand in and searched around everywhere, like what happened to my butt when I did a trick with one of Trilla's customers who was into fisting. But my hand, unlike the customer's, got torn on the sharp end of a spring. I pulled it out bleeding. Trilla's customer just had to wash his. Then I looked around the apartment—it was mid-afternoon—and found out something else was wrong. *He* was missing. I looked through the whole apartment, the bathroom, under the bed, in the kitchen, on the back stairs. Gavin was gone!

You didn't have to be Perry Mason to put two things together. Gavin had taken the loot and hit the road, one time more. The truth is, I was not surprised. He had disappeared before, of course, then come back wagging his (tail?) behind him. This time he probably had over thirty dollars with him, almost as much as when he raided your purse that time. That would pay for a lot of wagging. Gavin had stolen all of my stash, and I can tell you it was a pain in the ass to earn it! The fucker just took my cash and split! For about two minutes I hated his guts. Then it sank in. I really wasn't mostly upset by the fact that I was left only with what I had in my pockets, that is, one dollar and sixty-eight cents. The main thing was that the emotional effect on me was like getting hit with the Great Wall of China. I'm not talking about that restaurant on San Pablo where you used to go with Uncle Robarb. I was hit hard. Knowing that Gavin was basically a street Arab didn't lessen the hurt. Gavin was everything to me. He was my first real boyfriend. He was the person who made me feel like … the girl I knew I was. (I made a mental note to mention this to Dr. Shitaka, if he was still alive when I saw him next time. He was getting pretty damn old.) Besides you, mom, Gav' was also my first real friend at all. And now he had plundered me down to my last two bucks and hit out!

I stared at the screen for a good thirty-seven minutes. I couldn't tell you what program was playing if you offered me a million. I told myself not to panic. Gav' would be back in a few hours, or at most a few days. Maybe he just took the money to buy drugs, like those little cigarettes. Then, supplied with drugs, he might just have gone up to Martin Luther King Park to meet some other guy who liked to get it in the ass, just to change out a little. Men liked variety, even when they were committed. You taught me that.

I rifled the kitchen and took an inventory of what was left. Half a bottle of whiskey. Four cans of soup. Some tea bags, one already damp. I found a good use for the whiskey right away.

Back in front of the visual transmitter, I drank from the bottle, like Gavin. Well, okay, he might be back at any time. I didn't dare tell myself that he might never be back. There was this program on about a bunch of rednecks who drove a hot rod car without any license plates and got chased by the sheriff every two minutes. I was glad when the commercials came back on.

That evening, and I don't even remember whether I bothered to heat up some soup, I went to the bathroom and started to experiment with your cosmetics. As you know, I always used too much. You told me a hundred times that I looked like a cheap whore. In fact, if you added up the money I got from the gigs arranged by Trilla, and subtracted her commissions and my expenses, cheap is really the word. But I wanted to see if I could create a whole new look for myself, one that, given a chance to work, would make Gavin more attracted to me. I gave my face a pale look with some "ivory tone" basic. Then I used a good deal of cover-up to make the pimple scars disappear, plus those lines on my forehead that I probably inherited from "dad", or so you used to tell me. I used eye shadow, eyebrow liner, lipstick and rouge. Then I stood back to admire myself in the mirror. Aaagh! I looked like the bride of Frankenstein! In the mirror I appeared fifteen years older and homely on top of that. I washed everything off in the sink. As you can see, I was starting to act a little crazy. Probably because I was "in denial" over Gavin's "flight". Freud used to talk like that.

I decided to try for a moderate effect. Now just some moisturizing cream and a bit of basic, well blended in. Some cover up just around the eyes, to hide those shadows caused by worry over Gavin's defection. A tiny bit of lipstick. Ah! It wasn't exciting, but it wouldn't shock most people this side of Nebraska. I wasn't Liz Taylor, but more like Liz than like Boris Karloff. All I had to do was to wait for Gavin to come back. If he ever did.

In the bedroom I lay down on your side of the bed. I didn't worry too much about the fact that you were still in the hospital. After all, you'd never been sick before, so I was sure you'd get better in a week or so. The "medical creeps", as Gavin put it, kept saying that you were "responding adequately to treatment".

The bedside light was still on. It must have been about two o'clock. The bars were just closing. I gazed at the ceiling. Gavin had to come back, since he couldn't risk getting picked up on one of those police warrants. I considered, again, the idea that he just went to pick up some hash—a few times he told me it gave you a real bang effect when you used it after drinking a lot of whiskey. I must have dozed off. When I woke up the digital clock on the dresser said four-thirty.

Now I was mistress of the apartment, but I was all

alone. No mom, no boyfriend/friend, no money, and only a few ounces of whiskey. That morning (afternoon), I went down to the liquor store on the corner, first leaving the telephone off the hook (this was a signal me and Gavin had arranged. If one of us left the apartment and the other wasn't there, we would leave the phone off and that would tell the other one that it was just a temporary thing. I don't know why we decided on this. Probably because it seemed secret and sort of exciting.

I managed a good con job on Mr. Ashatakian, the liquor store clerk—probably he was the owner's cousin or uncle. I gave him a line about you, mom, getting fired because you wouldn't do immoral things with the manager at Bombo's and how we were almost starving because of it but that we would soon be getting Welfare money to help us pay for expenses. I mean, I might have gone as far as giving him a blow job, but it turned out not to be necessary. The long story was worth two bottles of whiskey, ten cans of soup and a huge bag of barbecue taco chips. These Middle-East guys get emotional real easy. I bought a package of cigarettes with my own money ($.75). Not because I liked cigarettes, but because I wanted to help Gavin readapt when he came home. This had to happen soon, because earlier that afternoon I said half a rosary to make it come true.

It was midnight and I was watching the Carson Show, and still no Gavin. I was smoking a cigarette that I lit from the gas stove in the kitchen. There wasn't anyone to act the gentleman now. I was starting on the second half of a quart of whiskey. (I wasn't nearly as good at whiskey as Gavin was. I really just liked the taste). It was having an effect. Now I began to think of myself as tough, as a person alone, but who could go it alone. I told myself that I could live through the emotional castration caused by the loss of Gavin. Still, I was snuffling back tears and snot every few minutes. Back on the screen, I didn't get most of Carson's jokes again. They were too intellectual and, remember, I never graduated beyond junior high. I laughed anyway. On this point as well as the not understanding, I was starting to take after Gavin.

About two o'clock I was desperate enough to put through a call to Tramp's on Polk Street. I asked to talk to Trilla.

"Yeah, baby." She sounded tired. No surprise. Having to deal with customers and the male prostitutes she managed all day, plus her remarkable intake, would wear the balls off anyone.

"Hi, Trilla. This is Marsha."

"Marsha Marsha bo-barsha! How the hell you been doin'? And where the hell you been? I ain't seen you in donkey's years."

"I have been taking care of my mother. She has cancer."

"Yeah, yeah."

"I only called to know if, please, you could tell me if you have seen Gavin. I know you don't like him and I admit he has a lot of faults, but have you seen him around at all?"

"Get lost!" Trilla hung up the phone.

She hated Gavin more than you would believe. It was because he lived off her once, then dumped her for a better deal. I just hoped the same thing didn't work out for me.

I woke up feeling lightheaded. Probably I'd been drinking too much soup. That stuff has a lot of harmful ingredients inside it. I heard it on TV on one of those nutrition shows. For breakfast I ate a quarter glass of whiskey and a bunch of taco chips. I felt I was starting the day right.

Soon, though, my thoughts and feelings were dragged back to the loss (absence? gone?) of Gavin. There was this sense of hopelessness, like nothing was ever going to be right again. I'd had sex partners before, and I'd be able to have them again, but just finding someone to stick his dick up your ass is different from having a real lover, especially a whole personality, a power like Gavin, who could magnetize a family, a loveable boy who was half Bambi, half King Kong. I think that if you hadn't gone to the hospital, mom, Gavin might have been my step-father for a long time.

What to do now haunted me out of the living room, away from the tube screen. I went to the bathroom and took off my clothes. I wanted a good take of myself in the mirror, just to see once again what I was working with, as far as Gavin. My body was poorly muscled, but graciously curved. My buttocks seemed a frank provocation. Chest weak, but noticeably feminine around the nipples. My penis was rather small, and this is very widely considered repugnant and ridiculous, but profuse red pubic hair covered it almost entirely and could make you think that I didn't have one at all, but maybe something else down there. I stroked myself a few times, then checked again in the mirror. There was some enlargement, but when I did this sort of thing my testicles usually disappeared somewhere inside my abdomen. They hadn't fully dropped yet. Dr. Shitaka said I suffered from low testosterone levels, so that I hadn't actually completed puberty. Although, as far as most of my personal experiences, I wouldn't exactly have compared it to suffering.

Probably driven by a feeling of insecurity and loss, I decided to try to find a good aesthetic mean as far as cosmetics, so I could be sure about maximizing my attractiveness to Gavin. Not the disturbing excess that I had first indulged in, but not the weak moisturizer and a few dabs of basic that I tried after that, either. That look was okay for like, applying for one of those "management trainee" jobs that they advertized in the newspaper all the time, but were gone when you got to the place. But it didn't add anything dramatic to my looks. I wanted to try for a moderate but also noticeable effect. First, a covering of moisturizer (you taught me this years ago, that it was important in order to protect the complexion. You were explaining how women used cosmetics. You should have realized that I would follow enthusiastically in their—our—footsteps), then a bit of basic well blended in, as before, adapted to my natural complexion, and providing a thin cosmetic layer for my entire face. I used cover up only around the eyes in order to limit that sleep-late whiskey-consumption effect. It seemed to work. Then I used some powder on my cheeks, to prevent make-up glare and to highlight some of my best features. I didn't put on any eye make-up at all. No mascara, kohl, eye shadow or eyebrow liner. A tiny bit of rouge on the cheeks was the next step. Then lipstick, again, used in good taste. Moderation, the key. When I looked in the mirror, I was totally satisfied. I clearly appeared to be cosmetically enhanced, but not in the trashy drag queen style. I saw the young ingénue, the romantic female lead, the person who could play opposite a hot stud. I was almost as good looking as I'd always hoped I was. The effect was probably enhanced by my total nakedness. My little thing was showing a happy reaction.

Dresses. I've never really liked dresses. They seem cumbersome to me, and actually make me appear less feminine than plain old jeans. But this was a special occasion. I wanted to look special for ... when Gavin returned, because I knew he would, he had to, or if not, that was the end of everything, including me, and the soap operas were wrong. I went to your bedroom and took some of your best dresses out of the closet. Since you'd probably be in the sick joint a few more days at least, I didn't have to worry about imminent retaliation. There was a black lace thing that I dived into, dropping it from my head down to my feet. I looked at myself in the long closet mirror. Hubba! I was one very attractive feminine person.

I flounced into the living room, glanced at the view tube, went to the street door, opened it, and stepped out onto the landing. The world was out there. I raised my arms in greeting. No one saw it except a ninety-four year old lady who was passing on the sidewalk. She looked, shook her head, mumbled something. It was probably something like, "these young ladies today are no better than prostitutes", or "Rev. Harstelty was right. The perverts are taking over".

Back in the apartment, I rushed to the bedroom to try on another dress, another effect. Glamour! It was everything. I swallowed a run of whiskey, feeling even more right. I had to conquer the world, so that Gavin would come back.

I grabbed a white chiffon dress. I tore off the black lace, not damaging it excessively, and swooped into the cake dress. La, la! The mirror showed that I was right again. Good choice, dude. I had a definite resemblance to the kind of bride the newspaper society page usually showed in a large photo. In the living room I paused for two seconds to hear about some kind of landing near Da Nang. Military guys rushed the beach from a landing craft. Go, men! I liked our guys because, well, because they were our guys. I peeked out the door to see if the disapproving old lady was still there. No. She was gone, probably halfway to the nearest holy-roller convention by now. I stood on the landing between our door and our second floor neighbors' door (whoever they were now. They changed every two weeks). There was no one out there in the street. The world was gone. There was nobody to approve or disapprove. Shit! All star and no stage.

I know all this sounds like I was going nuts, but what would you do if you were a transsexual who might have lost his (her) only lover? A lot of the trans types I saw in bars in the city had to *pay* their lovers, who were really gigolos, most of them straight. That wasn't love. It wasn't Gavin.

Inside, I reoccupied the armchair. Gavin had sat in that chair. That made it kind of sacred. I lushed back in the seat. I was exhausted after all that running around and dressing up and undressing. Thank God there was some whiskey left! I drank. I kept on sipping, slowly, effectively, out of the bottle. I pulled my white chiffon dress up to a level above my waist. I spread my legs apart. Now, in search of emotional relief, I really tried to shake it into some action. After a few minutes I wasn't doing too bad. Four and a half inches? That's with the benefit of the doubt.

The phone rang. I froze like the Winter Queen in the fairy story. I picked up the receiver. Hesitating, scared like hell, I spoke to the phone. "Ye-es?"

I heard mumbling on the other end. If this was another one of those crank phone calls, I was ready to be pissed as shit! "Who is it, please?"

"H'lo. S'Gav. Um adda station. Come get me, man … I'm fuckin' dyin' alive!" He sounded two stages above drunk.

"Gavin! Don't move. I'll be there in two seconds. I knew you'd be back because I knew you were a good person!"

"I gotta get off the phone. There's all these cops around. I was fuckin' kidnapped!"

Phone disconnect. Gavin was back! Everything could still be saved. Happiness bloomed again in the distance. Now I had two seconds to make one of the most important decisions of my life: black lace or white chiffon? I went with the cake.

I ran to the door and went down the stairs in three step jumps. At each jump the dress flopped above my knees. I still don't know how I got to the station without being run over, because I didn't look right and I didn't look left. I had to pull the dress up so I could run. It was like the bridegroom hightailing it out of church, only in reverse.

When I got to San Cerrito Station I didn't see anyone who looked even halfway like Gavin. I looked around, peered into every corner spot. There were mainly just low class slobs, wasted bums and funeral bait. Then

SON OF A WHORE

I remembered the last time I did a station pick-up on Gavin. He could be transformed. I checked again and "sure enough" (I'd been watching too many "South" shows on TV. The next thing I would be saying "you all") there was an old kit bag lying near one of the gray, rain pissed concrete pillars that held the upper part of the station in place. The old kit bag was filthy and stained, it didn't move, but there was something so familiar about it. Once more I recognized the Gavin pattern. It happened again and again because, well, I don't know why it happened again and again. I touched the kit bag on the shoulder. What now appeared to be a head topped with a camouflage hat raised itself from the rest of the heap.

"Yeah?" A confused, bleary voice.

"It's me! Gav'! I came down to get you after you called." Although it was almost masked by an unwashed beard of several days' growth, like before, plus a covering of some sort of greasy stuff that might have been used for D-Day, I could now make out the face of what had once been Gavin. It focused on me as much as its inebriated state allowed. The kit bag had turned out to be Gavin at the station; this was déjà vu, like I said. The same thing happening over and over to the same person. For some, like Uncle Robarb, it was always localized in an armchair.

"Rusalka?" He must have been impressed by my dress and make-up. "How you been, man? Glad as hell you're out of that sick tank."

"It's me, Marsha."

"Ah, Marsh! Thank God you come down, dude. I been through the rinse and dry cycle about a million fucking times!"

"What happened?"

There was something in Gavin's eyes that told of intense suffering. "What happened? Just you try scuddin' down Market Street ahead of the police on Gay Day! Good thing they almost got lynched."

I rubbed Gavin's shoulder in sympathy. "Let's go home now. I'll get you fixed up."

"I mean, man, I feel like I just fought the whole fuckin' Wehrmacht and I almost didn't win." Gavin loved WW II movies. He could imitate "the Colonel" to a tee. "And it wasn't only like it was the police. All them drug guys were after me too, saying I robbed 'em fuckin' ass blind. Hell, a deal's a deal, you don't change it after you made it."

All of this was interesting and instructive and somewhat familiar, but I knew, mom, that first things had to come first. "Don't you think we ought to go? The police probably have reports out on you, even here in San Cerrito."

"Right, man. Let's blow. It'd be fuckin' hell if I got away from the frisco bouncers and got arrested in this hick town."

I helped Gavin to his feet. What was he *wearing*? It looked like a pair of pants and a shirt-jacket cut from a camouflage parachute. Anyway, he could walk, with a little help.

We were moving slowly away from the station platform, with lots of unwanted attention from curious bums. "Marsh? You got real dressed up for my homecoming." He was staring at my dress. "Thanks. You look great."

"Do you like chiffon?"

"Yeah. For women, it's like my favorite dress. My mom said she wore one at her wedding. I forget which one of 'em. There was about a million."

Chiffon! I had made the right choice!

When we got back to the apartment I helped Gavin take the stairs. He was shaky. He kept dropping his head onto his chest and making funny gurgling noises. Once we were inside I led him to the armchair, then went back to the door. I looked around for any sign of the rangers, then slammed the door and locked it.

Gavin was back! Now life could go on, it could get … I was going to say, "even better", but that's not accurate. It could bring back those really cool dreams. "Just you rest for now, Gav'. I'll get you some hot soup right away, then you can go to bed and start to recover all over again."

Gav' was watching the screen. He waved this suggestion away. "Naw. First things first. I gotta come down slow from getting all hyped-up with three different piles of bums chasing me. Get me a drink."

It wasn't exactly what Ann Landers would have recommended, but this sounded reasonable to me. I went to the kitchen and came back with a full beaker of whiskey. Gavin took the glass and swallowed the contents at a gulp. It must have contained four or five ounces. He handed the empty glass to me. Refill time. Okay, I guess you'd have to say Gavin was an alcoholic. There's worse things and Gavin was a sexy and loveable drunk. A lot of the soberest guys I've ever known have been absolute creeps and mayhem artists.

"Um, see," Gavin drank more slowly now, "what went on was all a puking mess that happened because some guys can't understand shit." He took a sip, smiled. "Canadian?" he asked.

"Yeah. It cost twenty bucks a bottle. I was saving It

for when you came back." In fact, the whiskey wasn't anything. It was the cheapest stuff they had.

"Thanks, dude. You and mom are about the only people I ever loved best in the whole world. You're both just the fuckin' end for me. Except for my mom, and I don't know where the hell she got to."

When I came back from the kitchen with some soup, Gavin was sleeping. I unzipped his pants and took it out. It had definitely seen a lot of wear over the past few days. I shook Gavin–not his thing–until he got back to consciousness.

"What? Fuck off, man, or you're dead wasted!" Then he focused. "Ah, Marsha. Sorry, I had this dream I was back in some alley off a Polk and those guys were point blank on my ass."

"Try this." I handed Gavin a bowl of hot soup. I had added a few shots of whiskey to make it more palatable to him.

"Ah, no, man. I'm not hungry." He tried a few spoonfuls. "Hey, not bad at all. You make it?"

"All fresh ingredients."

"Thanks, Marsha. I knew you'd save me if anyone could."

When Gavin finished the soup, he let the bowl fall to the floor.

"I'll help you get to bed, Gav'. When you're rested up you can tell me more about what happened."

"First I gotta take a bath. I been runnin' for days and I haven't had a chance to take a wash off."

I filled the bathtub with hot water, then I started to help Gavin to the bathroom. He fended me off. "I'm okay, man. Thanks, I can handle it now." The whiskey seemed to have steadied him. He couldn't do a straight line, but he could walk without falling against the walls or hitting the floor.

"S'great." Gavin pealed his clothes off in two seconds and dunked himself into the tub. "I had to trade my good clothes for this junk with a bum." He pointed at the camouflage pieces. "I was hiding out south of Market and I had to get into disguise."

Gavin lay back in the tub. I started to soap his well formed body. Then I noticed it. He now had a tattoo on his left shoulder. It read: Butt Fuck Stud/ Bend Over, Dude.

He took in that I was staring at this message. "Ha ha! Oh, that. I got way too far spaced out and this little guy I was with paid for the tattoo. He got a real thrill out of it."

I could imagine. I was jealous, but I said nothing. You always told me, mom, never let men know you're jealous. Then they'll just do it again.

"Hey, I hope mom doesn't mind me sleeping in her bed tonight. I'm too fuckin' tired to cram in that closet."

"Mom's not back from the hospital yet."

"Yeah, that's right. Shit! Some a them street drugs can really fuck up your memory. She's in the hospital. I remember. What the fuck are those bums down there doing? They oughta had her fixed up bright as new by now. I think these county places hire just the creepiest quacks and dopers. We gotta get her into a real hospital. Better yet, get her back here so we can take good care of her." That's what Gavin thought he had been doing before.

None of that would work, because we didn't have any money. I had already checked Gavin's trouser pockets.

The next afternoon, when we woke up, Gavin seemed to have recovered almost totally. I lent him some boy underwear and a pair of jeans. Gavin used his hands to shake up his hair and rub it close to his head.

"You know, dude, I think I overdid it a little on this last flight. I mean, it's great to party, but you gotta understand there's limits. I still got a fuckin' headache, but at least now I can see straight. Yesterday there was like two of everything." He was sitting in the armchair, drinking his soup directly from the bowl. He had lost weight. I could tell by the way the jeans kept dragging away from his waist.

"I was really upset when you left, Gav'. While you were gone I got so nervous I drank half a quart of booze just in one night."

"You ought to watch it, guy. That stuff can really wreck you up." Gavin seemed to be concerned about collateral damage to my areas of principle interest. He checked me out for wrinkles and bulges. "Anyway, Marsh, I'm sorry I just took off like that. It's … it's just that I was so worried about mom that I felt I had to get out and do something or I'd go fucking nuts. I missed you when I was off in the city. Those other fuckin' whores couldn't hold a candle to you, babe." He thought for a moment. "And I finally got a sure plan to get this family on the straight track, as soon as mom gets back. I'm going to start by bringing out all her inner nature as a mother and a lover." Gavin hadn't forgotten about the original idea after all. He was a steady guy in a lot of ways. I nodded, too emotional to speak.

The comparison with "whores", however accurate, wasn't exactly flattering, but I was happy that Gavin was finally back and that he was hardly at all worse for the wear. "You're right. I think we both ought to go easy on the drink for a while, too. My stepfather, Uncle Robarb, always used to tell me that there was nothing worse than a drunk. And he was like a Ph. D on the subject, so he ought to know."

"He was right. No more, that's it for me. Hey," Gavin turned toward me, cutting away from the TV, "did that Robarb guy, the one you told me a lot about, did he and mom every really … you know, in bed?"

"No. I doubt it. He was too old for that sort of thing. Besides, he was so fat he couldn't get it up even if he ever sobered up, and that wasn't too often."

"Man, sounds like some of the dudes my old lady used to hang out with."

We watched a soap opera on TV. It wasn't one of the better ones. It was about a woman who had a son who was always getting into trouble with the police and taking drugs and drinking too much. Her husband was this guy who looked like an accountant, or maybe a preacher, but he kept fucking around a lot with other women. She turned on the tear ducts every couple of minutes and shrieked at everybody. When it was over, I could see that Gavin had been emotionally affected. He used the remote control to change channels. "Enough of that stuff. Why the hell didn't she just dump the creep? And tell her no-good son to fuckin' get a job?"

I couldn't answer this. The program was way too confusing. They should have used it for educational TV.

Now we were on something reliable, an old movie. They had a lot of these old World War II combat and spy movies and they kept showing them over and over. It was emotionally reassuring.

"Marsha, man, could you like get me a short glass of whiskey? I mean, just for the thirst."

I filled a glass in the kitchen. Gavin took a first sip really slow, just savoring it. "Ahh! I really love this Canadian stuff."

The movie plowed on. At one point I lost track of who was helping the spy, but I didn't ask Gavin. He would have known the answer, being a past master at war/spy movies, but probably the question would make him think I was stupid.

With the next refill, I brought the whiskey bottle into the living room. That would save a lot of trips. Gavin's reading skills were so poor that he usually didn't try to read anything unless he had to, so there was hardly any chance he would discover from the bottle label that the rotgut he was drinking wasn't Canadian. We were both going to go on the wagon soon, so it didn't matter much anyway.

"You know that guy Harv, the old dude who used to get off on Roman statues?" Gavin came up with this during a commercial break while he poured another one. I think it must have been his fourth or sixth.

"Yeah. He was sort of okay."

"Dead. I heard that on Polk. Some pervert little twerp killed him by banging him on the head with a big bronze thing, then hit out with all of Harv's cash. They caught him, though. They identified him by the sperm samples."

"His or Harv's?"

"Harv's. Nobody'd be crazy or hard up enough to fuck Harv and leave sperm samples where they could find them. I feel sorry for Harv, though. He could be a real kick when he tried to act like an old Roman gladiator."

"He was my first trick out," I sniffled. Not true by a long shot.

Gavin rubbed my shoulder to comfort me. "It's tough, but that's the way life fucks out sometimes."

Gavin was still not completely recovered from his spree. That night in bed, instead of doing his usual highly athletic performance on my rear end, Gavin told me to just suck him off. This meant much less effort for him. I have to admit that I liked it almost as much as our normal routine. I knew, too, that his cock was clean. I did a thorough job on it with a bar of soap when he was in the bathtub, so much so that he had to grab my hand to avoid losing it in the bathwater.

Gavin's sperm had a special taste. It wasn't too salty or too much like over-boiled rice, which was often the case. Maybe it got that unusual flavor from all the Canadian he drank.

We both slept late the next afternoon. Gavin because he still had to rest up from his drug/booze jag in the city and me because I just usually felt like resting up. Dr. Shitaka said my low level of testosterone resulted in me being a trifle anemic. By four o'clock we were both in the living room, languidly tuning in to the screen, the autocrat of all passing time.

"I don't want no soup, man," Gavin declared. "I just ain't hungry today."

When I brought a bowl of warmed up chicken potato from the kitchen, he took it from my hands and started to sip. "Marsh'? I been thinking. This ain't too great a life for neither of us. I got some ideas to change all that out and get you and me and mom on a real better scale of living."

SON OF A WHORE

I was all ears. It seemed like a good idea, so far.

"When's mom getting out of the hospital, first off?" Gavin.

"They haven't said so yet. They always just say she's responding to treatment but she's got a long way to go."

"Bummer. Anyway, she's gotta get out sometime, and probably not too long from now. She's been in the sick tank for almost a month, isn't she?"

"About."

"So, this is my idea. When mom gets out of that phony med dump and goes back to work, there's gonna be a lot more money. I mean, me and you can't get jobs. We fuckin' tried. The only jobs we can fish up is selling our ass on the street, and that's fuckin' no! I decided that a long time ago."

I nodded. Gavin looked terrific as he laid down the law. Just slightly older looking now because of his drug holiday in Frisco, and with his naturally platinum hair close to white, he might have been an old prophet from the movie *The Ten Commandments,* or a TV preacher. I was impressed. "Thou shalt not commit adultery". But it wasn't adultery if it was with Gavin, who was showing us the way.

"What we do, see, as soon as Rusalka's out of that place, we buy a car—I seen some adds on TV, there's a 1964 Olds for seven hundred and forty-nine bucks. Plus ninety-nine cents. We buy a car like that and we go driving around the state. Maybe we'll end up in L.A. I got lots of friends there in the movie business."

It sounded okay to me. Maybe me and Gavin could play opposite leads in a remake of *Gone with the Wind*. I liked the way those old dresses with the hoops and falderals made you look. Maybe you, mom, with the right

291

make-up, could play the servant, the one from before *the war*. There was a problem, though. "I don't know if mom'll go for it," I said. "She likes to stay put. We've lived here ever since Robarb." I couldn't even remember how long ago that was. With that guy, it seemed like last lifetime. "And first she'll have to pay off the back rent on the apartment. It's two months since the blood suckers haven't got their money."

Gavin smiled. He was sure he could bring you around. "Forget about the rent money. Once we got the car, fuck, we're out of here, so goodbye rent."

I wondered how we could pack up the armchair. It was such an historic part of our lives that we couldn't just leave it. "Maybe we ought to start packing now." I looked around the living room. There wasn't all that much to pack, except the chair and the TV. Most of the other junk was in the bedroom. I thought the bed and the dresser would be the really hard part. "We have to think about the heavy stuff."

"Naw. We don't need any of that. Maybe we can off load it at a used furniture store. Anyway, how are we doing now?"

"I feel okay."

"No, man. How much do we got in money?" Gavin, although given to flights of fantasy, had a definite practical streak.

I thought for a moment. I didn't want to empty my pockets right there in front of Gavin. He would have panicked. "I think it's about twenty-two dollars and about fifty-four cents." In fact, it was closer to half that. I had scrounged most of it from the dresser and the closets while Gavin was recovering.

"Hardly fill the tank on the Olds."

"They might give us some cash for the dresser. It was my grandma's. She brought it with her all the way from Romania, so it's an antique." This part wasn't true. I don't think they had dressers in Romania, not from what grandma said. Usually they put everything in a big wood box.

"What the hell was she doing in a dump like that?"

"I don't know. I guess she was on vacation or something."

The phone rang. Gavin picked up the receiver. He was sitting in the chair. "Yeah? Yeah, this is her son. I'm Marcus Zancsek. When's she getting the hell out of there?" Gavin listened for a minute. "What? You're fucking lying like shit! Let me talk to that dumb asshole doctor!"

Gavin cupped his hand over the speaker and looked at me. "They say ... they say ..." He couldn't finish the sentence. His handsome face dissolved into tears and he started to shriek. He threw the phone on the floor and shot up to his full height. He grabbed me by the collar and pulled me off the floor. He shouted in my face. "They say mom's dead!"

I tore loose from Gavin's grip and retrieved the telephone. I put it next to my ear. The connection was over. I heard the dial tone. "I don't understand at all. A few days ago they told us she was getting better. How could she suddenly turn dead?"

"See what you did man! You killed your own fuckin' mom!" Gavin was in a rage, in violent grief. "If you'd been nicer to her when she was alive, she'd never have up and died!" Gavin grabbed me again and bounced me against the wall. He gave me something between a slap and a blow with his fist, right in the face. He repeated two or three times. I kicked him in the stomach and dropped to my knees. I tried to crawl out. He sent a foot flying to my rear, knocking me flat on the floor.

Later, after Gavin went through nearly an hour of crying and banging things, he collapsed on the floor, his head and back propped against the side of the armchair. His eyes were red and wet and his voice was choking. "I'm sorry, man. I'm real sorry now I laid into you like that. I just couldn't take it. Now mom's gone I love you even more than when it was just the two of you." He pulled me by the arm until I was sitting next to him. He put his arm around my shoulders and kissed me on the cheek three times.

"That's okay." I had taken about half a dozen knocks to the face and two or three to the butt. It didn't hurt all that much. I won't say I liked it, but it certainly showed Gavin as dominant male, which I rather appreciated when I thought about it later. I forgave everything when I heard Gavin say he loved me.

"I think them quacks at the hospital are just a pile of no good alcoholics." Gavin.

"What did she die from?"

"They didn't say. They said something about 'unexpected prognosis outcome'. The nurse said Dr. McMillan was the best in the industry and he exposed his sympathies and all to us."

"Nice of him." I wiped my eyes with the back of a hand.

"Like who gives a damn if he can't do his fuckin' job!"

SON OF A WHORE

I exhaled my repressed breath and let my head drop. I thought about the future. There were always practical things too. "When is the funeral? I suppose we'll have to dress up. You might fit into one of Uncle Robarb's old suits. They'd be way too loose around the waist, though." I could wear the black lace.

"They just asked if I … I mean you, wanted to view the body. County covers cremation."

"Mom was always real nice to us, more than any of us deserved, and she loved us like there was no tomorrow." Gavin sniffled as he drank directly from a bottle of "Canadian". "An' I think she loved me, I mean you, her own son, more than anyone, just like we loved her."

This wasn't entirely clear, but Gavin's explanation was emotionally understandable. In a way, we were both Marcus. I think.

"I don't know if I'll ever recover from it," I said, "but mom always told me death's the end, and there's nothing more to worry about."

"Didn't have to be fucking now," Gavin countered, the bottle neck still stuck in his mouth. "She weren't hardly that much older than both of us."

There was a sound at the door, not like someone knocking or trying to open it, but something else. Gavin switched to alert mode in half a second. Police? Gav' always had to think about things like that. After waiting in silence for ten minutes, he went to the door, opened it, looked around, then came back.

"Hey, some fucker taped this to the door." Gavin brought a piece of paper back to the armchair and handed it to me. "What's it say?"

SON OF A WHORE

I read aloud. "'Three Day Notice to Pay Rent or Quit'. It says we owe the landlord four hundred and fifty-eight dollars and we have to pay it or get out in three days."

"Four …! There ain't that much money. Fuck that bastard. If they want us to move, they'll have to make us do it!" Gav' held on to the arms of the chair and challenged the world.

"They'll send the Sheriff after they get a court judgment," I mused. "It got that far before, but mom came up with the money at the last minute and she went to see the landlord in person. I think he liked her a lot, because she went back three times and we didn't have to pay rent for two months. Then he sold this building to some corporation about a year ago."

"Sheriff? No way, man, we gotta get out and I mean now!"

"Where'll we go? What about all the bills and stuff? What are we going to dooo?" I started a sort of paranoid keening.

"Skip. Get out of this dump. I know a deal we can do in the city that'll bring in cash."

"And the armchair? The dresser?" These were like the memories of our family.

"Ditch it."

So that's what happened so far, mom. You weren't around for the rest, but me and Gavin took a change of underwear and headed for SF. It went pretty good, and for a while we were making loads of money selling substances to people who needed it psychologically to keep their heads on. Gavin skipped town just before the big bust, when the police arrested me and about eight other guys (most of them straight). I did sixteen months in jail. It wasn't a thrill, except that I met some men who didn't mind playing the active role at all. When they let me out, Trilla got a job for me as a waiter at Tramp's. She owns the place now. She always was their best customer. And she's practically like a grandmother to me and hands me free drinks about five times a day.

Gavin's not here, wherever he is.
Love, your son, Marsha.

Printed in the United States
By Bookmasters